Praise for Ryder

"WOW!!! What a Wild Ride!!! What a rush!!! The Sons of Sangue books are always backed with excitement, but Ryder was so much more and the teasers at the end with have you screaming in such colorful language and begging for MORE MORE MORE!!!!"

—*Trudy, GoodReads*

"Another thrilling ride in this series of vampire MC members."

— *Leanne, Tales from the Heart*

"OMG this book was AMAZING. Ryder Kelly and Gabriela "Gabby" Trevino Caballero are perfect for each other."

—*Cathy, Goodreads*

"The chemistry between Ryder and Gabby will blow you away. With the things that have happened in Ryder's past and with Gabby's uncle, this love story will have you on the edge of your seat."

— *LaWanna, Goodreads*

"Patricia A. Rasey has done it again!!! You literally feel the electricity between Ryder and Gabby from the moment they meet."

— *Lydia, Two Geeks and a Dame*

Other Books by Patricia A. Rasey:
Viper: Sons of Sangue (#1)
Hawk: Sons of Sangue (#2)
Gypsy: Sons of Sangue (#3)
Rogue: Sons of Sangue (#4)
Draven: Sons of Sangue (#4.5)
Preacher: Sons of Sangue (special edition)
Xander: Sons of Sangue (#5)
Love You to Pieces
Deadly Obsession
The Hour Before Dawn
Kiss of Deceit
Eyes of Betrayal
Façade

Novellas:
Spirit Me Away
Heat Wave
Fear the Dark
Sanitarium

Ryder
Sons of Sangue

Patricia A. Rasey

Copyright © 2018 by Patricia A. Rasey.

All rights reserved. No part of this publication may be reproduced, distributed or transmitted in any form or by any means, including photocopying, recording, or other electronic or mechanical methods, without the prior written permission of the publisher, except in the case of brief quotations embodied in critical reviews and certain other noncommercial uses permitted by copyright law. For permission requests, write to the publisher, addressed "Attention: Permissions Coordinator," at the address below.

Patricia A. Rasey
patricia@patriciarasey.com
www.PatriciaRasey.com

Publisher's Note: This is a work of fiction. Names, characters, places, and incidents are a product of the author's imagination. Locales and public names are sometimes used for atmospheric purposes. Any resemblance to actual people, living or dead, or to businesses, companies, events, institutions, or locales is completely coincidental.

Book Layout ©2013 BookDesignTemplates.com

Ordering Information:
Quantity sales. Special discounts are available on quantity purchases by corporations, associations, and others. For details, contact the email address above.

Ryder: Sons of Sangue / Patricia A. Rasey – 1st ed.
ISBN-13: 978-0-9903325-9-6

Dedication

To my readers!
You are my everything! Without you—
there would be no Sons of Sangue!

To my bestie, Lara Adrian—
Thank you for being in my corner and for all you do!

A special thank you to Carol Morales
for her help with my Spanish.
Any mistakes are my own and no fault of hers.

To my husband who understands my crazy.
I will love you an eternity!

Acknowledgements

Thank you to my cover artist, Frauke Spanuth, from Croco Designs for creating the Sons of Sangue covers. I am always thinking…best one yet. Ryder certainly delivers!.

Thank you to my editor, Trace Edward Zaber. Thank you for your help and putting up with me!!

CHAPTER ONE

"*TWENTY-TWO.*

That's how many shots of Patron it took to level the idiot because only someone dull in the head would drink that much tequila. Luis, the name he had heard dropped earlier, seemed to be in charge of a group of soldiers belonging to the La Paz cartel and the one who had boasted he could out-drink anyone, no matter their size. So, when Ryder Kelley had walked into the little seaside tavern, Luis had been easy pickings. The man had no idea when he agreed to the bet to go shot-for-shot that tequila would have little or no effect on Ryder, his vampire DNA preventing him from absorbing much of the alcohol.

Ryder had spent the last six months working his way down to La Paz, Mexico, acclimating himself with the territory. His hair had grown past his collar and he now sported a half-assed beard that itched like hell. Even so, with his light brown hair and whiskey-colored eyes, he wasn't about to pass for a local. Thanks to a cute little *señorita*, though, Ryder had managed to learn a spattering of Spanish along the way, just enough to give him an idea of the conversations going on around him.

Luis's soldiers hooted and hollered over their fallen comrade, who now lay facedown on the wood-planked floor. He'd no doubt have one hell of a hangover when he came to, and maybe a knock to his oversized cranium. Ryder bet the fat bastard couldn't find a decent hat to fit him. Hell, Luis would be damn lucky if he didn't die from alcohol poisoning, the dumb son of a bitch.

Ryder had stopped by Salazar's a couple of times, as it was a known hangout for Raúl's men. The exterior of the building had seen better days, the paint peeling and chipping from extended salt water exposure. Inside, it reminded him of a typical seaside tavern and eatery. Salazar's had the best seafood this side of La Paz. No wonder the cartel claimed it as their own. The crab broil with Spanish chorizo was some of the best he had eaten, while the shrimp fajitas with mango-lime slaw came in a close second. Frequenting Salazar's would by no means be a hardship.

Some of the men had picked Luis's sorry ass off the floor and hauled him from the joint, his booted feet making drag marks along the already scarred floor. The rest of the men went about their drinking and ignoring Ryder. It was obvious, even though Ryder had a serious alcohol tolerance and drank their boss under the table, they didn't consider him deserving of their time. He'd need to find another way into their good graces.

The key would be in earning their respect.

These weren't your typical seaside fisherman. No, the men from Raul's camp killed for a living, assassinated a man without so much as a blink. Ryder figured it was about the only way a newcomer would earn their favor, for which he'd need outside help, someone who wouldn't have a propensity for dying.

Gunner Anderson, vice president of the Washington chapter of the Sons of Sangue, came to mind. He wasn't likely known by the cartel. Oregon had been the chapter on the cartel's radar due to a long history of bad blood. Although his Sons of Sangue brethren were keeping their distance, Ryder had stayed in touch with Grigore "Wolf" Lupei from his own Oregon chapter, so he already knew Gunner was in the area. Several of the Sons from the Oregon and Washington chapters had followed him south for backup, should the situation get hairy. And Ryder trusted Grigore to have his back. Not that he didn't trust his other brothers, but he and the large wolf-like man seemed in tune with each other.

"¿Cómo te va?"

Ryder had been so engrossed in his musings, he hadn't noticed the man's approach. A good way to get himself killed. "Excuse me? My Spanish is lacking."

Although he knew what the man had asked, Ryder would rather they didn't realize he understood some of their native tongue. Better to have them talking freely around him.

"I asked you 'How's it going?'" he repeated himself in English, his accent thick.

The man was a good five or six inches taller than the one they'd carried out. And Ryder would bet, by the way he held himself, he was also high up on the chain of command.

Ryder raised his bottle of water, then took a long pull. "I've had a bit too much to drink, but thank you, I'm holding my own."

"*Sí*, I can see that." He rubbed his well-manicured fingers across his whiskered chin. "Most men would be comatose. But you..."

Ryder shrugged, then took another swig of his water. "I guess I have a high tolerance for alcohol. Blame my upbringing. My father was feeding me tequila when I was nine."

"Your father must have been *muy estúpido*."

"You could say he wasn't much of a parent."

"*¿Y tu mamá?*"

"My mother? Dead."

Ryder wasn't putting much of a spin on the truth. Although his father had raised him alone, he hadn't plied him with alcohol at an early age. Best to stick close to the truth so there would be less chance of a slip up down the road.

The man pulled out a thin filtered cigar from a red pack in his shirt pocket, then grabbed a pack of matches from the bar. He ripped one from the pack, then slid it across the strike pad. Sulfur filled the air as the match burned bright. He took it to the cigar now stuck between his lips and puffed until the end glowed red. He shook the match to extinguish the flame.

"What brings you here, *señor*, to La Paz? You're not from around these parts."

Ryder scrubbed a hand through his hair. "What's your first clue?"

"Besides being a gringo?"

"Other than the obvious." He chuckled. "I'm looking for work."

"There's no work for you here, *señor*."

"Well, that's not very neighborly of you."

The man tilted back his head and laughed, the sound carrying through the room and catching the notice of his comrades. "*Señor*, you're in the wrong town. We aren't very neighborly, as you say, here. Finish your drink *y vete ya*."

"What if I happen to like the food?"

The man stepped into Ryder's personal space, and the vampire inside him started to take offense. "You'll find another tavern in another town. This one isn't for you."

Ryder raised a brow. "Last I checked, this was a public establishment."

He looked back at the men now paying them attention. "*Estúpido Cabron! ¿Tiene un deseo de muerte?*" Placing a hand on Ryder's shoulder, he leaned in close enough Ryder could smell the stench on his breath. "Unless you wish to be carried out of here in a box, *señor*, I suggest you take your bottle of water and move on."

Ryder leveled his gaze. "Unless you want to be carried out of here like your buddy, I suggest you take your hand from my shoulder."

The man narrowed his black gaze, removed his hand, and chuckled again. "You either have a set of *cajones muy grande o eres um imbécil*. Which is it, *señor*?"

"I'm not about to argue over who has the bigger dick, if that's what I believe you said, but don't mistake me for a fool."

"And if I do?"

"Then that would be your second mistake."

"And my first?"

"Thinking you could order me around." Ryder tipped back his bottle, finishing the contents, then slammed the plastic onto the old bar.

Ryder felt the man's eyes on his back the entire way out of the establishment. He may have earned himself an enemy from his blatant lack of respect, but better that than allow them to think of him as anything other than a formable opponent.

Regardless of the man's issued demand, Ryder planned on making another appearance. Next time he'd bring a show.

Stopping next to his Harley Davidson CVO Road King, he grabbed his skull cap from the seat when a shiny black Cadillac Escalade pulled into the parking lot of the old tavern. Normally, back in the States, the vehicle wouldn't have caught his notice. But here in La Paz? Not many could afford the extravagance.

He pulled out a small pocket wrench and kneeled beside the twin cam engine, feigning a mechanical issue. Stealing a glance in the SUV's direction, Ryder hoped to finally catch a glimpse of the illustrious Raúl Trevino Caballero. The man had been harder to find than a fucking needle in a haystack. He supposed Raúl hadn't risen to his position without being careful, as he no doubt had made many enemies along the way.

The Escalade rolled to a stop on the cracked pavement, just to the left of the entrance. The driver hopped out of the vehicle, quickly skirted it, and opened the rear passenger door. A slender hand reached out, definitely not one belonging to Raúl, or any man, for that matter. The driver helped the woman alight, a pair of red stilettos hitting the asphalt. Damn if those heels didn't have "fuck me" written all over them.

Ryder's groin tightened at just the thought of wrapping those muscular calves he viewed beneath the vehicle door about his waist, while those spike heels dug into his ass cheeks. Fuck, he had been without for too damn long. The woman probably had a body to die for and a face only a mama could love, using her bright red shoes to draw the attention south to her great pair of gams. The woman cleared the door of the SUV and Ryder dropped the small pocket wrench with a clatter. He also had to shut his gaping mouth.

Jesus, the woman was smoking hot.

Ryder took back his early thought about her being homely. Hell, this woman was a fucking goddess. Long brown hair cascaded over her shoulders and down to the small of her back. The sun highlighted some of the strands, making her hair appear two-toned. She wore a black pencil skirt that hugged her womanly curves, curves that made his mouth water. Ryder had never been a fan of stick-thin body types, and this woman had a set of hips a man could grab onto.

His gaze slowly rose to a nice set of tits that swayed gently in her halter-style tank with each step she took. Fuck. If the sight of her ample breasts didn't damn near give him a hard-on, imagining her full lips around his dick certainly did the trick.

What the hell was a woman like that doing here?

Her outfit and the way she carried herself screamed "high maintenance." Salazar's wasn't the type of establishment that catered to the wealthy. The red soles of her shoes told him all he needed to know. This woman's monthly allowance was likely more than he made in a year. She was out of his league, but that didn't mean he couldn't appreciate a prime piece of ass.

Just before she entered the tavern, she paused and looked back at him, blessing him with a smile. One that socked him in the gut, leaving him desiring someone he had no business sharing oxygen with. Ryder winked at her nonetheless, his action causing her to wet her full lips.

If he were only in La Paz for another reason, he might be tempted to try and tap that. But he was on a mission, one that required him to romance Gabriela Trevino Caballero. Fucking any other woman was out of the question, especially should the kingpin's niece find out about it. He couldn't chance the bar full of Raúl's soldiers being a bunch of gossips.

After pocketing his wrench, he strapped on his skull cap before stepping over the seat of his tribal orange Road King. He kicked back the stand and turned the key. The engine roared to life. Making a large circle in the parking lot, he took one last look back at the Escalade and saw the word "Gabby" printed in white vinyl lettering on the lower left corner of the dark tinted window.

Fuck me.

GABRIELA TREVINO CABALLERO, or "Gabby" as her friends called her, walked into Salazar's, the little seaside tavern owned by her uncle. He rarely ate there, which was one of the reasons Gabby liked to eat here. Salazar's had the best chef in all of La Paz, only surpassed by her uncle Raúl's private chef. Eating at the fortress he called home, though, required her to sit down and share a meal with him.

It wasn't that she hated her uncle. After all, had it not been for him, she might have wound up in foster care or worse. When her father had been viciously murdered by an American biker gang, it was Uncle Raúl who had taken her in and raised her as his own. Gabby lacked for nothing. The man overcompensated for her losing her father several years ago, and most likely because her uncle hadn't been able to conceive children of his own.

Gabby appreciated all he afforded her, and to say she lived a privileged life would be an understatement. But most days, her home felt more like a glorified prison. She wasn't allowed to leave without his express consent, or without an escort in tow. It wasn't as if she was clueless when it came to what her uncle did for a living. Gabby chose to wear blinders. Uncle Raúl was never going to allow her to move out and live on her own, all for good reason.

Raúl Trevino Caballero had enemies, enemies who would love to get their hands on her. She shivered at the thought of what they might do to her in order to get to La Paz's most notorious kingpin. So instead of the frightful alternative, she allowed herself to be catered to, held a prisoner in her own home because of the family she had been born into.

What choice do I have?

Today, she had been lucky to spirit time away with just one bodyguard. Going to Salazar's, though, didn't require her to be accompanied by an entourage, not when most of her uncle's men frequented the place. None of them would dare touch her, fearing the wrath of Raúl, which made dating pretty much impossible. Gabby couldn't help recalling the last disastrous date she had gone on more than a year ago. The poor man damn near lost his hand, all because he had dared to grab her ass. Her entourage had quickly reported back to Raúl and only her promise never to see the man again had saved him his appendage.

Coming to Salazar's was a good escape and brought to mind the other reason she came here. Her uncle had put her in charge. This little tavern was not only her getaway, but her pride and joy. Her uncle's lackeys were here most days, and usually well behaved. Any insolence on their part would be reported back to Raúl.

"Where's Luis, Sergio?" she asked Raúl's second in charge, meeting him just inside the entrance. "I thought he would be here. After all, we have salmón al pastor as the special today. It's his favorite."

"Some *gringo* drank his ass *estúpido*. We carried him out."

"The American I saw outside a moment ago?"

Gabby's heart skipped a beat over the handsome man she'd spotted fixing a motorcycle. The man had the face wet dreams were made of and the body of a gladiator. His T-shirt stretched over what looked to be a nice set of pecs and abs. Her mouth had watered at the sight of him, reminding her exactly what she was missing.

But dating an American?

His bike's license plate had labeled him as such. Uncle Raúl would have her head ... or more than likely, the American's. She couldn't help wondering what the hottie was doing this far south. What she wouldn't do for just ten minutes unescorted with him.

Sergio nodded. "I chased him out of here just before you arrived."

Gabby stopped short, her glare landing on him. "You did no such thing."

"I did." He squared his shoulders, not in the least embarrassed for his rude actions. "He's not welcome here."

"Says who?" She raised a perfectly plucked brow. "I run this establishment, Sergio, and I won't have you chasing away my customers. This isn't just a hangout for you losers. You got me? I've been working damn hard to make a name for this place ever since Uncle Raúl put me in charge. That means customers."

"We're customers."

"Real customers, Sergio. Not those on my uncle's payroll."

He shifted his stance, his jaw hardening. "I'm sorry, Gabby."

She pointed toward the entrance. "March out there and give that man your apology."

Anger flared in the depths of his dark eyes. "I will not."

"Sergio?"

"*Maldición*, Gabby. Next, you'll be wanting to unman me. I can't have tourists coming here and undermining my, Luis's, or your uncle's authority."

"But you can mine?"

He gritted his teeth and squared his stance. "You don't pay my bills, Gabby. I won't grovel to the *gringo*."

She stomped her foot, then turned and marched toward the kitchen entrance. The driver of the Escalade quickly followed in her footsteps, not allowing her from his sight. For the love of all that was holy. Just once it would be nice to go somewhere without being shadowed.

This establishment was hers to run and she meant to prove so.

Sergio had gone too far.

Just before clearing the double swinging doors to the kitchen, she caught sight of the large man's lit taillight through the large front window as he slowed to a stop at the exit of the parking lot leading to the road. Not glancing back, he picked up his feet, turned the motorcycle away from town and pulled back on the gas. Thanks to Sergio, she'd likely never see the sexy American again. The thought shouldn't bother her, but it did. For the first time in a very long time, a man had actually managed to make her heart trip. Now, she was left with nothing more than wicked daydreams and her battery-operated boyfriend, or as she liked to refer to it, B.O.B.

Deflated, Gabby made her way into the heart of the tavern. Rather than answer any of Sergio's questions, she left the dumb ass in the dining area and passed through the double doors to bake. Making delicious pastries and cakes had become a favorite pastime of hers. Much better than sitting at home and manicuring her nails. Although she had a privileged upbringing, Gabby was far from a socialite. She much preferred getting her hands dirty and working at her restaurant.

After grabbing an apron with a Salazar crab printed on the front, she slipped it over her head and tied it loosely behind her back. Using a hair band she had circling her wrist, she pulled her heavy hair off her shoulders and fashioned it into a messy bun atop her head. Wearing her favorite pair of Louboutin's wasn't ideal to bake in, but then again, when she had stopped by, baking hadn't been on her agenda.

She smiled at the chef. "I hope you don't mind."

"*Señorita,* I am honored with your company. Besides, everyone loves your desserts."

"Thank you, Francisco. I'm happy to hear my efforts pay off."

Once she plucked a mixing bowl from an upper shelf and a bag of flour, Gabby went to work, hoping to purge her thoughts of *Mr. Sexy Americano.*"

CHAPTER TWO

"WE NEED TO COME UP WITH A PLAN THAT INVOLVES ME shooting and Gunner dying."

"Fuck you, Ryder." Gunner jammed his hands deep into the pockets of his jeans. His already dark eyes glossed over, taking on the appearance of obsidian marbles, proving that his vampire DNA was seconds away from emerging.

Guess I pissed off the big guy.

"Hear me out, Gunner."

"What's your plan? You know we're here for you, bro." Grigore planted his backside on the seat of his bike and stretched his long legs, crossing them at the booted ankle. "You're the boss at this rodeo."

"Whatever it is, it's not going to be my fucking funeral. I plan to stay among the living," Gunner grumbled. "I may be new to this whole vampire thing, but I'm kind of liking it. Find some other dumbass to kill."

"Sorry, Gunner, it has to be someone the cartel isn't familiar with. That would be you. And since you're a big guy, it would be far more impressive and work in my favor when I kill you." Gunner flashed his fangs, but Ryder held up a hand to stall him from going completely loco. "Hear me out. You'll survive, I promise. It may hurt like hell, but we aren't ready to ash you ... yet," he added with a smirk.

Grigore chuckled and placed a palm in the center of Gunner's chest. "Down, big boy."

"I need to earn the respect of Raúl's soldiers. I've been down here a few weeks, stopped by their hangout a couples of times, and even drank their boss under the table a while ago. Let me tell you, that son of a bitch can put down the tequila. But other than the fact I'm white, an American, and I don't belong? They barely notice me."

"What the fuck does that have to do with me eating a bullet?" Gunner curled back his upper lip, his fangs gleaming white in the waning sun. "I signed up to keep an eye on your sorry ass, not to become a bullseye for your target practice."

"You show up at their little seaside tavern and cause a ruckus. Be a complete asshole. Pull a gun on one of Raúl's patsies. I'll step in, attempt to calm you down"—Ryder shrugged—"then shoot you. Not through the heart, of course."

"Then what? It's not like I'll really be dead."

"You'll pretend to be, so practice that. These guys aren't stupid and won't be easily fooled. I'll throw your bleeding ass in the trunk of a car with a little help from one of Raúl's men, then drive you away. They'll think I mean to bury you so far back in the woods that you'll become just another missing person." Ryder looked from Gunner to Grigore. "Thoughts, Wolf?"

"Where are you going to get the car?" Grigore's hand indicated the motorcycles sitting in a semi-circle on the dirt lot just outside of La Paz, but far enough off the road not to be seen.

"I'll leave that up to you. Find me one with California plates to match the ones we stole for my bike."

Grigore chuckled. "You aren't asking for much."

"I need it in a week, tops. I don't want these assholes forgetting me."

"You drank their boss under the table, got on your bike, and rode out of there ... without your supposedly drunk ass dumping the cycle, I might add," Gunner said. "I'd say you got their notice, Ryder."

"What's all this going to prove?" Grigore scratched a spot beneath his ear, obviously skeptical of the idea. "I'm not sold on showing our faces and any of those boys knowing we're here. What if someone recognizes Gunner?"

"How?" Ryder asked. "It's not like they will tie him to me. They believe I'm a Devil from southern California. Gunner's from Washington. He belonged to the Knights. And you're not showing your face, Wolf. Even though, I doubt someone would know you."

"This is true," Grigore agreed. "You told them you were a Devil?"

"I didn't announce it. I don't have the Devils cut any longer, as you know. When I arrived here a couple of weeks ago, I stopped in for a drink to get a feel for the place, knowing Raúl's men used the joint as their hangout. One of them threw his beer at me after a brief exchange, told me to go back north. I took off my shirt and mopped my face. I still have the Devils' tattoo on my back. I didn't have to say a word. The fact they think I'm a Devil was the only thing that didn't get me thrown out of the joint outright, because the Devils run the cartel's drugs."

Gunner's brow furrowed. "If you don't mind me asking, why the fuck do you still wear a Devil's tattoo?"

"I'm waiting for Gypsy's sorry ass to pay for the new tat when I get home." Ryder raised his T-shirt, showing Gunner an age-old scar marring half his left pec, traveling up to his shoulder. "This body has so much scar tissue I wasn't sure where the hell the Sons of Sangue tattoo was going to go once I inked over the old Devils' one."

Gunner hissed. "What the fuck happened?"

"You want the long or short version?"

"We ain't got all night," Grigore groused.

"The Devils found out I wanted to leave the MC. My girlfriend wasn't thrilled about me being a part of the club. One day, they told me to meet them, said they had a job that required my help. When I got there, they had doused my girlfriend in gasoline, lit her up. By the time they let go of me, she was engulfed. I tackled her in an attempt to put out the flames, burning myself in the process. I was too late. She died later that day."

Moisture gathered in Ryder's eyes, the pain still raw years later. Every time he looked at the scar in the mirror, he was reminded of the ugliness and the loss. "She was carrying my baby, man."

"Fuck me. That sucks, dude." Gunner shook his head. "Did you kill the man responsible?"

"Didn't have to. One of the Sons of Sangues' mates did me the favor." Ryder took a deep breath, then slowly released it. "I plan to pay back the debt by helping find the man's brother, the one who took Viper's son."

"I don't follow."

"Raúl Trevino Caballero's killed Ion Tepes, Viper's kid, because his mate dared to take on the cartel. Rosalee, Viper's mate at that time, killed Raúl's brother, the one responsible for my girlfriend's death. Raúl, in turn, killed Viper's son. An eye for an eye, if you will."

Grigore chimed in. "That's a story for another day, but it's the reason Viper and Hawk have waited for the chance to take down Raúl. Brea Gotti, Draven's mate and goddaughter of Raúl, enlightened us with a way to get closer to the kingpin, through his niece. Speaking of, Ryder, have you met her?"

Ryder whistled low; just the brief glimpse had tugged at his groin. "Brea was right, the woman is an absolute knockout. I've seen her. I didn't realize who the woman was until I saw the word 'Gabby' on the back of her SUV. It looks as though she might have a bodyguard with her at all times."

"You make contact?" Grigore asked.

He shook his head, adding a sly grin. "Apparently, I'm not her type. She barely acknowledged me."

Grigore guffawed. "Well, Don Juan, you better figure something out to turn her pretty little head if you want an in and to find out Raúl's exact location. Brea said it wouldn't be easy, as he doesn't stay in one location for very long."

"Fuck you, Wolf. I don't have a problem where the ladies are concerned."

"Then why the hell are you still single, pretty boy?"

"Same reason you are, dumbass." Ryder shook his head. "Because it's a choice. I tried that whole 'couple thing' once. Remember? It didn't work out so well for me. And as long as I remain in an MC, I plan to keep it that way. I'll never put another woman I care about in jeopardy again. This lifestyle is *my* choice. They shouldn't have to pay the consequences for it."

"Someday, you'll need to move on, let the past go."

"Yeah? What about you, Wolf?" Ryder all but growled. "What about the one you left behind?"

Grigore stood, grabbed his helmet and straddled his bike, indicating the conversation was over. "We'll get you that car and meet up in a week. In the meantime, why don't you figure out a way to get into Gabriela's good graces and not worry about *my* love life?"

"Touchy much?" Ryder asked.

After snapping the skull cap into place, he started the motorcycle and flipped Ryder the bird. Ryder laughed as Grigore and Gunner circled the dirt lot, leaving him to eat their dust … literally.

He coughed, waved a hand in front of his face, then lifted his leg and straddled his own bike. Grigore had shut down his question before it even had time to formulate. The man certainly didn't like bringing up his past, any more than Ryder did. Kicking back his bike stand, he turned the key and started the engine. The bike rumbled to life. Picking up his feet, Ryder exited the dirt lot and drove in the opposite direction., opening up the throttle to speed down the road toward the tavern.

Time to put *Operation Seduce Gabby* into motion.

THE CELL VIBRATED ON THE table next to Gabby. She dusted the flour from her hands onto the Salazar's apron and picked up the phone. She smiled at the name of her best friend staring back at her. Gabby had thought Adriana was still out of town on a short trip north with her fiancé.

Sliding her finger across the glass to answer, she placed the phone next to her ear. "*¿Cómo estás?*"

"Fucking terrific. You?" Gabby noted sarcasm in Adriana's reply.

"What did the asshole do this time?"

"What *doesn't* he do? I should've listened to you and stayed home." Gabby heard the sniffle and her heart went out to Adriana. "*Pinche idiota*. I swear I am nothing more than dirt under the sole of his boot."

"Nothing I haven't said before." Gabby sighed. "You should start listening to me."

"*Tu puta*. You are no better."

"Me?" Gabby laughed. "I haven't slept with a man in so long, I could hardly be considered a whore."

"I wasn't talking about the sex, sweetie. We both know you need to get laid, your uncle be damned. You're going to grow that cherry back if you aren't careful." Gabby could see the wide grin likely spreading across Adriana's face. "I'm talking about getting away. You can't stay cooped up in that fortress forever. You should've come with us."

"With you and Mateo? Oh, hell, no! Besides, my uncle wouldn't let me out of the country without at least ten bodyguards shadowing my every move. I wouldn't put you through that."

Gabriela shivered at the thought of one of her uncle's enemies getting their hands on her. She couldn't blame Uncle Raúl for watching out for her well-being, except for the fact, had it not been for him, no one would give a damn about her in the first place. She would be able to come and go as she pleased. Why the hell couldn't she have been born into a typical family? She'd give up all the riches her uncle allowed her just to live a normal life.

"Gabby? Hello? Are you listening?"

"I'm sorry, Adriana. What did you say?"

"I said, how about making your way over to my place so we can share a bottle of wine ... or four," she added with a giggle.

"And Mateo?"

"He's not home. Said he had business with your uncle and would be gone for a few days. I have the apartment to myself. I'm thinking we need a little girl time. Besides, I could use my friend."

"Break up with that ass, and you wouldn't need me."

"You know I love him."

"Only Lord knows why," she whispered beneath her breath.

"What was that, Gabs?"

"I said give me an hour and I'll be over. I'm at Salazar's baking up a storm at the moment."

"What the hell did your uncle do this time?"

Adriana knew Gabby too well. "What *doesn't* he do? Besides, I have to tell you about this American I saw today at Salazar's. He's *muy guapo*."

"You found someone you consider handsome in La Paz? Seriously?"

"Why is that so hard to believe?" Sure, Gabriela hadn't dated in a while…

"Because Sergio has the serious hots for you and you don't even blink an eye when he looks your way."

"He works for my uncle," Gabby reminded her. "Luis's second in command."

"And who better to protect you? He's tall, muscular, and as you say, *muy guapo*."

"Says you. Me? I'm not interested in anyone who works for my uncle. Or someone who spends more time in front of the mirror than I do."

"Then who?"

"If it wasn't for causing the poor man trouble, I'd definitely wouldn't mind looking up *Mr. Sexy Americano*."

"He must've been pretty hot if he out-shadows Sergio. Do you know how many women would love to get their hands on that man? Me included."

"You have a fiancé."

"Semantics."

"I don't want him, Adriana. End of story. If you want to ditch Mateo, Sergio is all yours."

Her best friend sighed in defeat. "I'll uncork the bottles. You get your pretty little ass over here and tell me all about this *Americano* that actually turned your princess head."

"Screw you, Adriana, no princess here." Gabby laughed at Adriana's age-old joke about how her uncle catered to her. "There's not much to tell. Probably just a tourist that I'll never see again. I'll be there in an hour."

Gabby ended the call and set the cell on the table when Sergio stepped through the swinging doors, as if her conversation had conjured up the frustrating man. Sergio was persistent, if nothing else, and far too arrogant for her tastes. She stifled a groan.

"What can I do for you, Sergio?" Gabby managed to keep the disdain from her tone. "Don't you have something better to do? Like work for my uncle? He doesn't pay you to come back into the kitchen to fraternize with the help."

"You're far from the help, *cariño*."

Sergio skirted the table until he stood just inches from her. Gabby had to fight the urge to take a step back. She wouldn't show him fear. He pitched one hip against the table edge and braced a hand upon the surface, careful not to touch the flour littering it. His blue short-sleeved work shirt stretched tight across his chest and abs, showcasing his muscular arms. Adriana had been correct in her assessment. On the outside, Sergio had the looks that most women coveted and a body honed by hours in a gym. He never had trouble when it came to women ... until her.

That was not about to change.

Not only did Gabby make it a habit not to date those employed by her uncle, the man had a serious undercurrent that gave her chills. There was a reason he sat second in command. He was a sociopath, having no morals. A man exactly like her uncle.

"You think your uncle would mind me talking to you?" He tucked a stray strand of hair behind one of her ears. "Your uncle has given me his blessing. You're already mine, Gabriela. Stop fighting us."

Gabby didn't doubt that one bit. If her uncle were to marry her off, it would only be with someone he approved. Who better than one of the men he put in charge of keeping his empire intact?

"Too bad for you that I'm not of the same mind."

Sergio righted himself, his hand doing a sweep of his torso. "Come on, Gabby. Seriously? Any woman would be happy, lucky even, to have this."

Gabby didn't bother hiding her eye roll. "Then go find them, Sergio, because this woman isn't interested. There is no us."

"Are you lesbian?" His gaze heated. "I mean, I could be down with that. You and Adriana in my bed? Damn, that's every man's fantasy come to life."

Gabby grabbed a cookie pan and slammed it onto the surface, metal clanging against metal, and started spooning cookie dough onto the sheet. "Because that would be the only reason a woman would turn you down, right?"

"I don't need to beg, if that's what you're getting at."

Placing a flour-covered hand in the middle of his chest, she pushed him back a couple of feet. "Why not go find one of those women and leave me the hell alone then?"

"It's not like you date…"

"Which is a product of my overbearing uncle. It has nothing to do with my sexual preferences, of which you are not."

Sergio's lips turned down when she dropped her hand, leaving a flour handprint in the center of his chest. He tried to brush away the white powder with little luck.

"Do your menial tasks and bake your cookies, Gabby, then go fuck your pretty little friend Adriana. You'll be wishing you had this," he said, grabbing his crotch. "She can't give you what I can."

"Get the hell out of my kitchen, Sergio."

The man turned and stormed through the double doors, but not before knocking a pan from the wall, leaving it to clatter to the floor in his wake. A tremor passed over Gabby's shoulders. She had a sinking feeling had it not been for her uncle, she'd be meeting him in some dark alley … and not by choice.

Francisco looked up from the crab bake he was making. "You would be wise to stay away from him, *señorita*. That man is a *hombre malo*."

"Bad to the core, Francisco. You don't have to tell me that. Thank goodness he fears my uncle." Gabriela walked to the hook near the sink, pulled off her apron and hung it up. After turning on the faucet, she washed her hands, then dried them on the towel before turning back to the chef. "Do you mind finishing up my cookies?"

"Not at all, *señorita*."

"Thank you." She kissed the elderly man on the cheek. His face reddened. "I'm in a sudden urge to get out of here before Sergio adds alcohol to his already inflated ego."

Francisco laughed, the humor twinkling in his eyes. "Go out the back door. Avoid him altogether."

Gabby grabbed her phone from the table and typed a quick message to her driver to meet her out back. Francisco was correct, bypassing Sergio was the best course of action. She wasn't about to let one man ruin her planned girls' night with Adriana.

When she stepped into the alley, the old wooden screen door slapped closed behind her. Her driver stood next to the waiting Escalade with the door open. Seconds later, she was tapping another message on her phone, telling Adriana she would be arriving sooner than planned."

CHAPTER THREE

Ryder sat astride his Road King, just out of sight from the parking lot of Salazar's. After leaving Grigore and Gunner, he had retraced his route and wound up right back where his day had gotten a whole lot more interesting. To his disappointment, though, the black Escalade was missing from the lot. He had returned too late to catch another glimpse of Gabriela Trevino Caballero.

He was supposed to seduce her, get an inside to her uncle and his whereabouts. Hell, he wanted inside all right ... deep *inside* her. He shook his head, picked up his skull cap from his lap, and snapped it back into place. Unless he started thinking with the right head, Ryder was going to seriously fuck this up. He couldn't allow his rising testosterone to cloud his judgment or compromise the mission. Turning the key to his cycle, he ground his teeth as the engine roared to life. Just as he was about to pick up his feet and head back to the little studio apartment he had rented by the week, he caught sight of the black SUV circling from around the back of the lot.

Lady Luck is on my side.

Pulling out of the alcove, he trailed the Escalade from a distance. No way the driver wouldn't spot his tribal orange and black motorcycle. Among the thin copse of palm trees lining the oceanside road, it stuck out like a sore thumb. But instead of heading south to where Ryder knew Raúl's home base to be, the SUV headed for town. People milled about the city center, the nightlife being active in La Paz. Ryder had spent a few nights bar-hopping among the locals, getting a feel for the place. Unlike Salazar's, the town had been welcoming.

Two blocks ahead, he spotted the Escalade taking a right up a slope. Ryder turned one block before and made his way up the incline. At the next crossroad, he saw the vehicle forge ahead. He continued his climb on the adjacent road until he no longer spotted the SUV at the next intersection. Making a quick left, he headed toward the byroad he'd last spotted the Escalade. Stopping at the corner, he caught sight of the vehicle parked in front of a small, colorful, three-story building. The driver helped Gabriela alight from the rear seat. She stepped onto the curb, then turned and held out her palm, saying something to the driver. His face hardened, but he stopped and leaned against the Escalade, crossing his arms over his chest. Gabriela ignored his disapproval and continued on her way into the building.

Ryder's gaze landed on the sway of her ample hips, hips he could easily imagine holding on to, and an ass that would fill out a pair of jeans nicely. Or in her case, at the moment, a black pencil skirt. Damn, but that woman had a killer body. Gabriela opened the door to the stairwell and disappeared from his sight.

Ryder turned the motorcycle in the opposite direction and circled the block. He'd have to approach from the back side, since it was unlikely the driver was going to leave his post or wouldn't notice Ryder's arrival. He parked near an eatery called Seaside, painted in bright blues and greens above the rustic door, and killed the engine. He had dined at the joint a couple of times, though he much preferred the seafood served at Salazar's. Being a vampire meant he didn't need human food, but he still enjoyed an occasional meal even if it offered him no nourishment.

Quickly backtracking on foot, he skirted around the buildings, sticking to the alley. Once he reached the rear of the three-story building and determined Gabriela wasn't on the first floor, he took the wooden stairs that led to a wooden deck off each unit. Each level contained a single dwelling. On the second deck, he stayed out of view from the French doors and peered in, careful not to be seen. The lights were off in the unit, telling him she had likely gone to the top floor.

Ryder stealthily moved up the stairs, praying the wooden creaks wouldn't give him away. Once he reached the final deck, he moved quickly to the side of the wide-open double doors. White lacy curtains were pulled to the side, giving him a clear view of the interior. With lights illuminating the unit, it was easy to see almost the entire living space.

A woman with waist-length, straight black hair sat on a worn leather chair next to Gabriela, facing an unlit fireplace. This far south, he doubted the woman used it at all. Where Gabriela was rounded in all the nicest of places, this new woman looked as if she could use a good meal or two. Some men were attracted to thin, but Ryder preferred a little more meat on a woman's bones.

Gabriela had curves to rival the sexy Latin actress Jennifer Lopez. Though similar in looks, Ryder would take Gabriela over JLo any day of the week. The smaller woman sat with her back to the door, while Gabriela took the chair facing him. Thankfully, the doors had been left open, giving him the opportunity to eavesdrop on their conversation. Soft Latin music filtered through the unit.

Gabriela tucked her legs beneath her in the chair while her friend leaned forward and poured them each a glass of red wine, handing Gabriela a wineglass large enough to be a fishbowl.

"To friends," Gabby said, clinking glasses with her friend before taking a sip. Her pink tongue swept her lower lip, making Ryder, to his chagrin, aware of the increasing tightness of his pants.

"To *best* friends," the woman added before lowering her glass and cradling it between her palms. "You're always there for me, Gabs. What would I do without you?"

"You don't have to worry about that. I always will be." Gabriela's smile lit her face, instantly warming Ryder's blood. "What's Mateo gone and done to piss you off this time?"

"The usual. The *hijo de tu puta madre* thinks he can order me around."

Gabriela's eyes widened. "He hasn't hit you has he, Adriana? I could—"

Adriana waved a hand in the air. "Oh, hell, no. You aren't telling your uncle anything. Mateo needs that job."

"*Por el amor de Dios*, doesn't it bother you what he does for a living? My uncle's men kill people."

"Is that why you keep putting off Sergio? You were born to this life, Gabs. You live quite comfortably because of it, I might add. You can't judge your uncle or his men."

Gabriela has a conscience.

Ryder stored away that little tidbit for later, along with the fact Raúl's second in command had a thing for his boss's niece.

"It's not because he works for Uncle Raúl, though that's reason enough." Gabriela harrumphed. "Sergio and I are never going to happen. I'd be surprised if he ever made time in his life for a girlfriend. Truthfully? He probably only wants me in order to get in good favor with my uncle. Don't use me, you know? In my book, that's unforgivable."

Well, that certainly killed any warm fuzzies he might be feeling for the gorgeous brunette. When he seduced her as the mission called for, she'd never forgive him for using her to locate her uncle. He'd do well to remember that.

"SO, TELL ME ABOUT this sexy *Americano*?"

Heat rose to Gabriela's cheeks just at the mention of the man. She had only gotten a quick glance, but she wouldn't mind getting a longer look ... a *much* longer one. Unfortunately, either her uncle's men had run him off, or he had stopped by the tavern on his way through town. There weren't many Americans this far south of the border, and surely not in La Paz.

"Seriously hot, like sizzling."

Adriana giggled. "I haven't heard you talk about a man like that since, well ... he who shall not be named."

And just like that, it seemed a bucket of ice water washed over her. "Thanks for being the mood-killer, Adri."

"Ah, come on, Gabs. It's been over two years. You can't deny yourself companionship because of one bad relationship."

"We were supposed to get married. He was fucking my uncle's maid, for crying out loud." Anger bubbled up the back of her throat at the reminder. "They're both lucky the only thing my uncle did was fire them. Thankfully, I haven't seen either of them since."

"And in all of that time, you've dated only one other man." Adriana winced. "Poor guy. Your uncle threatened to cut off his hand if he ever grabbed your ass again."

"See? And you wonder why I don't date."

Even though she found the American extremely datable, at least when it came to his appearance, she wouldn't dare put him on her uncle's radar. Not when she knew it couldn't possibly end well.

"I get it." Adriana took a sip of her wine. "But if you dated Sergio—"

"Not even if he was the last man standing." A shiver passed down her spine. "I won't date any of my uncle's men again, especially Sergio."

"Mateo works for your uncle."

Gabriela disliked her friend's fiancé, just as she had most of those employed by her uncle Raúl. She couldn't fault Adriana for loving a man who was capable of following her uncle's directives, but it wasn't in her own DNA to do so. Yes, she was raised within the cartel lifestyle, though her uncle had done his best to keep her separate from his business dealings. That didn't mean she agreed with how he ran his business, or how he had profited off selling drugs and weapons. Not to mention the many who had died as a result.

"We aren't talking about your relationship, Adri. Just because I made the decision to no longer date those in my uncle's camp doesn't mean that's the right decision for you." Gabby leaned forward and placed a hand on her knee. "It's your life to live. I just don't want to see you hurt. I swear if he lays a hand on you again, nothing you say will keep me from telling Raúl."

"He's changed."

"Really? Then why did you call me? I believe it was something about being 'nothing more than dirt under the sole of his boot'?"

Adriana drained her wine, then refilled her glass, offering to refill Gabriela's. Gabby took the bottle and emptied the remains into her overlarge glass.

"Okay, so you're correct."

"Call off the wedding before I have to walk down the aisle with you. Hard telling what he will do once he gets a ring on your finger."

The breeze picked up, ruffling the white curtains, drawing Gabby's attention to the deck. The sun had begun to set, casting a beautiful orange glow across the horizon.

"Why on earth are we sitting inside on a gorgeous night like this?" Gabriela stood and headed for the deck, where two wicker chairs flanked each other. "Are you coming?"

Adriana grumbled something, but followed anyway. Footfalls sounded on the stairs below, but by the time Gabby reached the doors, whoever had descended had disappeared.

"Do you have a neighbor?"

Adriana plopped into one of the cushioned chairs and placed her bare feet on the iron rail. "One. The unit beneath me is rented. The other is vacant. Why?"

Gabby shook her head. "It's nothing. I heard footsteps on the stairs is all. It must've been the one beneath you leaving."

"Huh … he must've gotten home early from work. Usually, he doesn't get home for another hour."

"You know him?"

Adriana shook her head. "Only in passing. He's older. In his fifties, I think. We haven't spoken much, other than in greeting."

"I find it curious he would leave from the back of his apartment and not through the front door." Gabriela sat in the other chair, shaking off the odd feeling of having been watched. "So what are you going to do about Mateo?"

Adriana chuckled. "You're like a dog with a bone."

Raising a brow, Gabby smiled. "As I recall, you begged me to come over."

"I did."

Settling into a comfortable silence, they watched the sun disappear beyond the horizon, leaving behind an orange halo. Gabriela couldn't think of anyone else she'd rather spend such a night with. Adriana and she had been friends going on five years, ever since Adriana started dating the ass she was now engaged to. Gabriela's thoughts traveled back to her earlier years of growing up and a friend she had long since lost, Brea Gotti, her uncle's godchild. Since Brea's father's passing, Adriana had seen less of her best friend as the months grew into years, to the point she no longer came around.

Her heart panged.

She wished things had ended differently between her uncle and Brea. Whatever had happened, Uncle Raúl had forbidden Gabriela from reaching out to her. She supposed it was just as well; Brea hadn't bothered contacting her either.

"Do you think you will see him again?" Adriana broke into her musings.

Gabriela looked at her friend, furrowing her brow. "Who?"

"The *Americano*."

"Not likely." She rolled her eyes. "I'm sure Sergio made sure of that. The man infuriates me to no end. He can't be chasing away my customers just because he might not like them."

"Your uncle employs him to protect you."

"I get that." Exasperation left her in a huff. "But he also employs him to kill people. Sergio got where he is because he's ruthless. And if you don't want Mateo to turn out like him, then I'd suggest you find your fiancé a new job."

Anger flashed briefly in Adriana's eyes. "I really hate it when you get self-righteous, Gabs. Seriously? What do you expect him to do to make the kind of money he's making here in La Paz? You may not have to worry about where your dinero comes from, but it pays my bills."

Gabby gripped Adriana's hand and squeezed. "You're right and I'm sorry. It was insensitive of me. There aren't a lot of jobs here. I just don't want to see you hurt. Maybe if Mateo treated you better."

"You'll get no arguments from me there." Adriana dropped her hand to the chair and stared out across the deck. "Maybe someday we'll both be free."

"Now, that's a dream I could get behind."

Gabriela drew in a deep breath and settled into her chair, staring out across the lights of the city now filling the sky, listening to the drone of conversation from the nightlife picking up in the streets. What Gabriela wouldn't give to walk free among them, to not worry about an entourage following her or an unknown enemy of her uncle's snagging her.

Taking a deep pull from her glass, she willed the numbness of the wine to take hold. Most people would kill for the lifestyle her uncle afforded her, while Gabriela dreamed of throwing it all away and living a life of anonymity.

Sitting up as a plan formulated, she turned to Adriana. "Let's get out of here."

"Where to?" Adriana's eyes lit with a genuine smile. "I'm sure your driver—"

"No." Gabriela laughed. "We're going to do what your neighbor did and take the back stairs."

"But your uncle—"

"Won't know." Gabriela stood, placed her wineglass on the table next to the full bottle of wine they had yet to touch. "I want one night where you and I can go party among the locals and not have my uncle's soldiers following my every move, reporting back to him."

"Are you sure?"

"Absolutely." Gabby smiled, bubbling with excitement. "Let's party."

CHAPTER FOUR

Ryder crossed the main drag of La Paz to a little place called Los Diego, where the nightlife spilled into the streets. The crowd buzzed with conversation while Latin music provided a pleasant backdrop. His rented second-floor apartment was situated across from the bar. Normally, he didn't mind watching the goings-on from his window, being comfortable in self-isolation. It was these times he did his best thinking. But after hearing Gabriela's confession about the "seriously hot" *Americano*, he was too keyed up to stay in.

Not only did his body want a little action, Ryder needed to feed.

Los Diego would provide him the perfect cover to find a young *señorita* looking for a little extracurricular in the human anatomy. Of course, he'd need to hypnotize her into forgetting the part that involved fangs and all things vampire.

He took the three steps leading onto the front cement patio, skirting the patrons lining the establishment and sitting at outdoor tables. After ducking his head beneath the doorjamb, he moved along the outer wall in the darkened tavern. Ryder headed for a table at the rear of the club, more specifically next to the back door with a glowing EXIT sign.

Easy access to the alleyway.

After he claimed a stool at a high-top table, his back to the wall, a waitress with a saucy smile sauntered over. Too bad she was working or he might've been tempted to give her an invite to what he had in mind. She wore a peasant-style blouse with off-the-shoulder sleeves and a hem that barely covered her ass, while a pair of skin-tight leggings hugged her thighs and calves. She was cute, he'd give her that, though not nearly as stunning as Gabriela.

Fuck, I need to get my head out of my ass.

Gabriela Trevino Caballero was a job and he'd do well to remember that.

"What can I get you, *muy guapo*?"

"A shot of tequila to start." Ryder winked, causing her cheeks to blush. "Can you also bring me a chelada with a Modelo Especial as well, *hermosa*?"

"Coming right up." She turned and walked away with an extra sway of her hips that Ryder could appreciate.

Damn, too bad she was on Los Diego's time.

Scanning the crowd, Ryder looked for a nice little *señorita*, one who wasn't seeing a lot of action, as they tended to be less noticeable. His exact modus operandi when seeking women outside of the donor society he used in Oregon. The society consisted of women who knew about the existence of vampires and allowed them an artery tap for nourishment. It was the Sons of Sangue's preferred way to feed. Ryder hated taking what wasn't freely offered, but this far south, he had little choice.

His gaze landed on a short, pleasingly plump woman, sipping a cocktail through a straw while her pretty friend chatted with a guy near the bar. The straw-sipper chewed on the end of the green plastic as her gaze traveled the room before landing on him. Even from the distance between them, Ryder could see the growing interest in her warm brown gaze.

His waitress returned with his order, setting down the shot and a glass rimmed in lime and salt. She opened the beer and poured it over the ice. Ryder stood, dug dinero from his pocket and handed it to the waitress, giving her a healthy tip. He quickly slammed back the tequila, then grabbed his beer and headed for the short, rotund woman, hoping for easy pickings.

Ryder was hungry and had a hard-on that needed appeasing. Not a great combination when there were no donors available. He'd have to make do.

The door to the tavern swung outward, drawing his gaze. In walked Gabriela and Adriana, without Gabriela's ever-present bodyguard. Ryder couldn't help wondering how she had managed to give him the slip. The man no doubt continued his post by the Cadillac, waiting for her return. Ryder bet the two women had slipped down the back deck stairs.

Doing a quick turnabout and returning to his table in the darkened corner, he'd hoped to go unnoticed. So much for taking care of his needs.

"Despacito" by Luis Fonsi filtered throughout the club, while patrons danced and moved together on the dance floor. Laser lights shot about the small room, though lucky for him, never quite reaching his corner. It was obvious the song was popular with the crowd.

Gabriela and Adriana chatted animatedly as they approached the bar. Men parted, giving them room to pass, though certainly not out of politeness. More than likely so they could ogle the women's asses without being caught. Even the man chatting with the friend of the woman he had been seconds away from approaching, stopped talking and watched the two walk by. The taller woman leaned down and whispered into her straw-chewing friend's ear. They placed their empty glasses on the bar and exited the club.

Damn, now I'll need to find another blood host.

His gums ached with the need to feed. Ryder had already gone three nights without any real sustenance. With the arrival of Gabriela and her friend, finding a new artery would be a whole lot trickier.

The women ordered drinks, then ignored the leering men to find a table near the already packed dance floor. Ryder had a good view of them from where he sat drinking his beer. The waitress returned and asked about a refill, but he declined. She hustled off, and when his gaze returned to the table the women had occupied, he found them missing. He scanned the dance floor, finding Adriana easy enough. She sidled up against a man he had never seen before. But Gabriela—

"Careful, I might think you're following me."

Ryder jerked his head in the direction of the sexy voice, bringing his mouth inches from the deep red-painted lips of Gabriela. Fuck if he didn't want to taste them.

Play dumb.

"Do I know you? I mean, I sure as hell wish I did, but—"

Her lips tipped upward as she sat at the table. "Buy me a drink?"

Ryder raised his hand, motioning over his waitress. "What's your poison?"

Gabriela raised her glass to the waitress. "Another paloma please."

The waitress nodded, barely acknowledging Gabriela. Instead, her gaze landed back on Ryder for longer than necessary. He ignored the waitress, his gaze quickly returning to the gorgeous woman now seated at his table. Well, he had wanted an in and Gabriela had just handed it to him.

"Paloma?"

"Grapefruit, lime, and soda, topped off with tequila." She smiled warmly, the gesture arrowing straight to his groin, reminding him that his feeding mission had been prematurely aborted. "You aren't from around here."

"What?" Ryder widened his gaze. "Born and raised. *Mi casa es su casa.*"

Gabriela chuckled. Ryder found he liked the sound. "Spanish 101."

"Guilty." Ryder leaned back as the waitress brought Gabriela's drink. He dug out a few dinero and placed them on the waitress's tray. "What gave me away?"

"For starters? Your motorcycle has American plates."

He raised a brow, continuing to act as if he hadn't spotted her earlier. "I walked here."

"That may be true, but you didn't walk to Salazar's. I saw you leave there earlier today." She took a sip from the salted rim of her glass. "I hope you weren't … run off."

Ryder shrugged. "More or less."

Gabriela laid a cool hand atop his warmer one. Fuck, just the feel of her skin caused the temperature in the club to rise. It was already hot as Hades inside. Now it felt like a fucking inferno.

"Don't let them bully you."

Ryder flipped his hand on the table so their palms aligned. He laced fingers with hers briefly before withdrawing his hand. "The man who told me not to come back didn't seem like he was looking for an American friend."

"I'd say he's all bite, but…"

"He's not." Ryder took a sip of his beer. "I've known men like him. He doesn't scare me."

"You don't want to be on his bad side."

"Look… I didn't catch your name."

She smiled again. Damn if he couldn't get used to that. "My friends call me Gabby."

"And me?"

Her small pink tongue swept the salt from her lower lip. Ryder wanted to do the same, his blood heating with need as she held his gaze. "What about you?"

"Am I a friend?"

She shook her head and laughed. "If you want to be. But I come with a warning."

"What's that?"

"Don't get too close."

"I'll take that under advisement." Ryder rubbed a hand over his whiskered jaw. "Back to the man at Salazar's—"

"Sergio."

He had a name. "Yes. He won't stop me from getting what I came here for."

"And that is?"

"You." Ryder watched suspicion take over her gaze. He placed a hand on her forearm to keep her from rising. "Gabby, I'm kidding. How the hell would I know you before coming to Mexico? Although, I must say I'm quite glad we met. Maybe next time I head south, that statement will hold true."

THIS MAN MIGHT HAVE her libido in overdrive, but that didn't mean she shouldn't proceed with caution. Truth of the matter, she didn't know him, nor had she asked Sergio why he had tossed him out of her restaurant in the first place. Gabby had allowed the stranger's ruggedly handsome face to cloud her good judgment. And with his announcement of coming down to Mexico for her, in jest or not, it triggered her warning bells. She needed to learn more about him if she intended to allow the second part of his statement to be accurate.

"Where are you from...? I'm sorry, I didn't catch your name either."

He smiled warmly, the gesture causing her heart to skip a beat. "The name is Ryder. I'm from southern California."

Gabby traced a water droplet path down her glass, noting he hadn't exactly been forthright about where he called home or given his last name, though to be fair, she hadn't given him hers either. California damn near filled the west coast of the United States, so he had basically danced around her question.

"What brings you to La Paz?"

"A change of scenery." His whiskey-colored eyes gave away nothing, telling her he was quite good at schooling his features. "Too many reminders back home. My girlfriend passed away some months back. I thought leaving town might be therapeutic."

"I'm so sorry. How did she die?" Gabby tamped down her pity, sensing this type of man wouldn't welcome it. She laid her hand back on his. "That was incredibly insensitive of me. It's really none of my business."

He turned his hand, so their palms aligned again and twined fingers with her for the second time in the span of a few minutes. "It's okay. Life happens. Sometimes it sucks. If it taught me one thing, it's that none of us get out of here alive and you need to live life. I had stopped doing that."

"And now?"

"I'm here, trying to move forward." He pulled the left side of his T-shirt over his shoulder, revealing an ugly scar that appeared pretty large in size. "I got this as a reminder. She died in a fire and I tried to save her, but..."

He shrugged his shoulder back into his shirt, dropped her hand, and sat back in his chair. After grabbing his drink, he took a long pull, then set the empty glass on the table. He picked up the bottle of Modelo and poured the rest over the remaining ice.

Moisture gathered in Gabriela's eyes as she watched him hide his pain behind a cavalier attitude. What he must have endured she couldn't begin to imagine. Her heart went out to him as she sucked back the tears.

"It was a while ago," he continued. "The wounds are healed, though the scars remain. The physical and emotional. And because of it, I haven't really dated since."

"I can see why."

She picked up a napkin from the table and blotted her eyes, feigning having something in them. Gabby refused to cry in front of him. Hell, she hardly knew the man. And yet here she was nearly shedding tears over his heartbreaking story. She had always been an ugly crier, fat trembling lip and all.

Ryder took a swig from his drink before asking, "So what about you?"

Gabby furrowed her brow. "What about me?"

"I assume you have no significant other since you're sitting here. At least, I would hope not." He ran a knuckle down her cheek, causing a shiver to snake down her spine. Not in a bad way, of course, but in a very ... *very* good way. Dropping his touch, he leaned back in his chair. "You said you come with a warning. Care to elaborate?"

Damn, I did say that.

Not ready for full disclosure, she said, "Let's just say my life is complicated."

"Sergio?"

She laughed, rolling her eyes. "He wishes, *pero es imposible*. It's not going to happen. Like you, I'm currently not dating."

He raised one of his tawny brows. "Would you be open to it?"

Gabby drew her lower lip between her teeth. "Depends on who's asking, I guess."

There would be no getting around her uncle or bodyguards if she agreed to see him again. It was by pure luck she had gotten out this time without her driver's notice. The poor guy might already be combing the streets looking for her. But Antonio wouldn't call in the troops. The repercussions of losing her whereabouts would be horrendous. Sooner or later, though, she'd have to throw the man a bone and text him to let him know where she and Adriana had gone, that was, *if* he had noted them gone at all.

"I'm not sure—"

"There you are." Adriana stepped up to the table, grabbed Gabby's drink, and finished the contents. "We should probably head back, Gabs. Don't you think?"

Disappointment flooded through her. If only her life was different and she had been born to another family. Ryder certainly didn't need that kind of trouble added to everything he was running from. He deserved a normal relationship. Besides, Adriana was correct, they did need to get going. She'd already pushed Antonio's limits by making him stay by the car earlier. If he had found them missing, he'd be livid.

Gabby slid off her chair. "You're right. We better head back."

"Before the troops come looking for us," Adriana added.

Gabby laughed off Adriana's comment, knowing it wasn't far from the truth, hoping Ryder thought her off-handed comment was in jest. Should Antonio decide to call Sergio about her disappearing act, all hell would break loose.

"Wait." Ryder stood, his hand slipping around her waist. His mere touch upped the temperature of the club. That or she was suddenly prone to hot flashes. "I don't have your cell number."

Gabby stood on her tiptoes and bussed his cheek with a kiss. "No, you don't."

Then, just like Cinderella, she wove through the packed nightclub, following in Adriana's path. She didn't dare look back to see if Ryder watched, not wanting to show more interest than she already had.

Moments later, they were back on Adriana's deck, giggling like a couple of school girls on how they had stolen a short time away. A quick check out the front window of the apartment proved Antonio had dutifully stayed put.

Adriana grabbed her corkscrew and quickly opened the other wine bottle, then refilled the glasses they had used earlier. "Do you want to see the *Americano* again?"

Heat rose up Gabby's neck and warmed her cheeks. Of course, but that didn't mean she would. "It can't happen, no matter what I desire. You know that. He doesn't deserve the trouble I'd bring into his life."

Adriana sat in the wicker chair flanking Gabby's and curled her legs beneath her. "You'd be stupid not to see him again if the opportunity arises. Why not let him decide what he wants? It was so obvious he's into you."

Gabriela wasn't as open to the idea. Her suspicions continued to bubble beneath the surface. "What if he works for one of my uncle's enemies?"

"That could be said for any man you meet, Gabs." Adriana sighed. "It's no way to live. You deserve to be happy."

"And yet here I sit, worried if this guy is on the up and up."

"He didn't come on to you. You sat down with him. *You* made the initial first step."

Gabriel tipped back her glass and drained some of the contents, then rolled the stem between her fingers as she contemplated Adriana's remark. She *had* been the one to approach Ryder and not the other way around.

"If you're so worried about his intentions, then try running into him a few more times. Get a better feel for him." Adriana grinned. "Besides, that *Americano* is *muy guapo*."

"You won't get an argument from me."

Gabriela hoped she hadn't blown her one chance with Ryder by not giving him her number. After all, Adriana was correct; not only did she deserve to be happy, she deserved a little romance. Ryder was the first man in a long while to make her desire more than just a conversation. But if Gabby wanted a chance with him, then her uncle and his men needed to be kept in the dark. After all, Sergio had already had one run-in with Ryder. Having another wouldn't bode well. Gabby didn't want to be the reason Ryder sucked on dirt from six feet under.

CHAPTER FIVE

THE KNOCK ON THE BACK DOOR OF HIS APARTMENT STARtled Ryder. He had yet to make friends in La Paz, nor had he told anyone where his home base was located. Well, other than his brethren, and they had yet to visit him within the city limits, not wanting to blow the mission. The lights hadn't been turned on for good reason, making the residence appear momentarily uninhabited and giving him a covert view of the street below.

The exact way Ryder preferred it.

When the knock came, he had just begun to unscrew the top from a bottle of Jack Daniel's and partake while he waited for the nightlife to get into full swing. Ryder preferred to mingle among the crowds, giving him a better chance to blend in. Though this far south, there weren't many Americans, he stood out like a beacon in the masses.

So much for commingling.

Pushing away the bottle from the table's edge, he stood. His front door had the security peephole, but there wasn't one on the back entrance. Ryder had no choice but to open it in order to see who had come calling by way of his rear-facing porch.

Sticking his Sig Sauer P226 Legion into the waistband of his jeans at the small of his back, Ryder crossed the few steps of his studio. No, he didn't need the gun for self-defense, but the person on the other side wouldn't know that. Aged wood creaked beneath his feet, no doubt alerting the person he was at home. Keeping one hand on the grip of his gun, he opened the door a crack.

"It's about fucking time." The door slammed inward, knocking into Ryder's shoulder and causing him to step back. "What are you afraid of the boogeyman?"

"You're damn lucky I didn't shoot your sorry ass on sight." Ryder shook his head, removed his gun from his waistband, and laid it on the table. "What the fuck are you doing here, Gunner?"

"Wolf's on his way, too. We raced by foot. I won." He guffawed. "I thought he was supposed to have superior speed and all because he's my elder. Hell, he's just old."

Grigore walked in through the door and slammed it closed behind him. "I'm not too old to kick your ass. Besides, forty-five ain't old in vampire years."

"Can't you two do anything quietly?" Ryder picked up the Jack, used the pad of his thumb to finish twisting off the cap and brought the bottle to his mouth, swallowing a good couple of fingers of the amber liquid. "If you two idiots don't knock it off, I'll kick both your sorry asses."

"Why don't you throw your primordial strength in our faces, for fuck's sake? You just got lucky being related to Radu." Grigore snatched the bottle of Jack from Ryder's hand and took a large swig. He set it on the table and wiped the back of his hand across his bearded face. "We're here to finalize our plans."

"You could've called," Ryder grumbled.

"And what fun would that be?" Gunner slapped Ryder on the shoulder. "If I'm going to get my dumb ass shot, I might as well have fun with it."

"You know once I shoot you, you're done down here, right? That you'll need to head back to Washington and I won't have to see your ugly mug again?"

Gunner shrugged. "Why the hell do you think I'm so anxious to get on with the plan, Ryder? To get back home. This heat is enough to turn a fucking vampire into a melted pile of goo."

Ryder couldn't blame him. Sweat ran down the center of his back, even with the poorly working air-conditioner chugging away on the wall, making the heat barely tolerable.

Grigore picked up the T-shirt draped across the table's chair and tossed it at him. "Put that on, for crying out loud. Cover that shit up before my muscles get jealous and expect me to do something ridiculous like work out."

Ryder caught the shirt. "There's got to be a jelly donut somewhere in the city with your name on it, Wolf."

"Damn straight there is."

Pulling the shirt over his head, he stuck his arms through the holes and draped the material across his abs. "What prompted this visit? You two buffoons don't have anything better to do than harass me?"

Grigore pulled out a chair, stepped over the seat, and straddled it, crossing his arms over the back. Despite his earlier jest, Grigore was built like a beast. His forearms were massive and covered with tattoos. He wasn't classically good-looking, but women seemed to dig the rugged vibe he had going. The sheer size of him made him a formable opponent without vampire strength.

A few days had passed since his run-in with Gabriela and Sergio. Ryder wasn't convinced they should go in with guns blazing just yet. He needed to give Sergio a chance to cool off lest he toss out Ryder upon arrival. Not to mention, he needed a little more time with Gabriela. Ryder could tell he had her interest, but it wasn't without a bit of mistrust. Winning her over wouldn't be easy, especially once he "killed" Gunner in cold blood. Gabriela would view him no better than the men who work for her father, which certainly would not gain him brownie points in the romance department.

"We were bored."

"*You* were, shithead." Grigore stood and slapped Gunner on the back of the head. Gunner might have been a few inches taller, but Grigore made up for it in mass.

"That's because you're old. Look at those grays."

Grigore chuckled, and sat down again, patting the few grays threading the hair at the sides of his head. His beard was salt-and-peppered, with more white centered at his chin. "The ladies like it. They call the look 'distinguished.'"

Ryder shook his head, knowing Grigore was anything but old. He had gotten the grays in his early thirties before he had turned. "I bet they do."

With a wink, Grigore said, "Don't count me out, boys. I get my fair share of the ladies. Now, enough of the 'what's fashionable' lesson, let's get this plan ironed out. If we're going to shoot Gunner, we need to make sure this goes off without a hitch. We can't have one of Raúl's men taking aim and *actually* shooting our boy here."

"Boy? Fuck you, Wolf."

Grigore laughed again, the sound deep and rumbling up from his gut. "What do you have in mind, Ryder? Spell it out. We can't afford mistakes."

"Let's give this a week, then we can put this into action. I need a little more time with Gabriela to make sure I have her interest before this goes down and blows any chance with her. She doesn't seem too fond of her uncle's men." Ryder scratched the back of his head and blew out a steady stream of air. "Hell, this might blow any chance I have anyway, but I don't see any other way to get in with Raúl's soldiers. I need them to open the door and I won't get that without their respect. Getting an in with Gabby? That might not get me an audience with Raúl if she's not too keen on me meeting her uncle. We need his whereabouts. I believe Luis and Sergio might be my straightest line to the big guy."

"I can't help but agree," Grigore said. "Gabriela might be a bit more protective over that side of her life. Not like she'd be using Raúl for bragging rights."

Gunner walked to the window and looked down on the busy street. "Not that all this isn't fun, but if my time is limited, we might as well get this show on the road. If it's all the same to you, I'd rather not spend my time thinking about it."

One of Grigore's eyebrows raised. He smiled. "You don't like the idea of getting shot?"

"No, smart ass." Gunner turned around and glared at Grigore. "I don't. I've been shot a few times before and it hurts like hell. I don't suppose being a vampire changes that."

"Not at all. You'll just heal faster and the bullet won't leave a scar." Grigore looked at Ryder. "Which means, after you shoot him, we won't have hours to bury him. You'll need to get his big ass in the trunk and to the woods before anyone notices the bullet wound is missing amongst all of the blood."

"Is burying me necessary? Can't you just toss me in a shallow ditch or something?"

"Worry much?" It was Ryder's turn to chuckle.

Gunner seated himself on the windowsill. "I'm claustrophobic, okay?"

"If all goes to plan, and it's just me leaving with your body, then we won't need to bury you. We'll designate a pickup point for Grigore and the guys, and then you get to hide out for a few days. Once we're in the clear and everything goes according to the plan, you get to head back to Washington. Your job will be done since we can't risk you being seen."

"What if one of Raúl's goons wants to tag along?" Grigore asked.

"That's when I'll have no choice but to bury Gunner. So, make sure there's a shovel in the trunk of that car. We'll meet in the same place, but you'll need to stay out of site. Once we're out of there, then you and the rest of the guys get to dig him up."

Grigore appeared deep in thought. He grabbed the bottle of whiskey and took another swig. "You know, now that I'm thinking about it, we'll need to bury Gunner, either way, leave him there for a short time."

"What the fuck for?" Gunner's tone rose.

"Don't worry, you'll survive. I'll make sure you get enough oxygen to breathe." Grigore rubbed the white of his beard. "If they let Ryder go on his own to bury you, they aren't likely going to trust him. They'll follow, make sure Ryder does as he says. They aren't about to take his white-ass word for it."

"You're right."

Gunner grumbled. "Not only do I get shot, but now I get to eat dirt from six feet under."

"Seriously?" Ryder laughed. "You think I'm going to bother burying you that fucking deep? I don't want to be there all night digging. It will be shallow. And if we need to, Wolf will be ready with a straw. You'll survive and you'll get to go home. So, quit your fucking whining. The rest of us will be down here for the long haul."

"For however long it takes," Grigore added, giving Ryder a high-five. "We're going to get this son of a bitch. We won't stop until we allow Viper his vengeance. Raúl's days are fucking numbered."

Grigore was correct. They wouldn't stop until they found Raúl and called in Kane and Kaleb Tepes so they could finally get their retribution for Kane's son. It was a long time coming for the twins. But after meeting Gabriela, he fucking hated the idea of using her. She was innocent in all of this, born into a family of reprobates. You couldn't fault her for her family tree.

Ryder needed to keep his head on straight where she was concerned, not allow his heart to get tripped up, no matter how good-looking or incredibly sweet she was. If the situation was any different, he might consider getting to know her on a personal level, and not just because he wanted to fuck her.

GABBY STOOD IN THE KITCHEN of Salazar's, baking up a storm. She had already created a pan of sopapilla cheesecake bars and a tres leches cake to add to the night's menu before starting the caramel cinnamon apple enchiladas the restaurant was famous for. Her spicy chili chocolate cookies she had baked the other day had gone over quite well. When she was finished with the enchiladas, Gabby planned to make another batch.

All because she had needed to keep her mind occupied.

Francisco and his sous chef had a handle on the evening entrees, so Gabby stuck to desserts whenever she entered their domain. She could bake, but she wasn't much of a cook. Normally, she ran the business side of things, oversaw the schedule, balanced the books, and managed the staff. But on days like today, she baked. Francisco never complained because it left him perfecting the evening's menu and worrying less about the pastries.

"What has you worried, *señorita*?" Francisco approached the long stainless table, wiping his hands on a white-ribbed terrycloth bar towel.

"Why would you think anything is bothering me?"

His hand swept the desserts already prepared. "Because you have enough here to feed our patrons three times over and yet you're making more."

"Then we will have enough for tomorrow as well." Gabriela placed her sugar-coated hands on the table and leaned toward the chef, standing on the opposite side. "You go mind your fish and not my love life."

"Ah"—he pointed his index finger toward the ceiling—"so this all has to do with a man."

Heat rose up her neck. "I said no such thing."

"But you did. I asked what had you bugged. You, *señorita*, brought up your love life."

Gabby hung her head and laughed, before giving her attention back to Francisco. "You caught me there."

"Anyone I know?" His face darkened. "Surely not Sergio."

"No." Gabby gasped, a hand covering her heart. "Goodness, I think I'd abstain from sex altogether before I'd ever give in to Sergio. Besides, the truth of the matter is he wants me only because of my uncle. That man desires power, not women."

"You certainly have him pegged. You'd do well to stay away from that one." Francisco picked up a knife and cut a small piece of the tres leches cake and plopped it into his mouth. He moaned. "*Delicioso*. No one has the touch to make such desserts, *señorita*, not even me."

"You flatter me because I save you work." Gabby held out a chunk of the cheesecake bars, which he promptly took. "But in all seriousness, I love to do this. It's therapeutic. I should be thanking you for allowing me to invade your kitchen."

Francisco gave her a wink, turned, and left her to her baking. As she reached for a large container of sugar, Gabby's mind flitted back to the bar. She had been the one to approach Ryder, not the other way around. And yet she still mistrusted him. Her life demanded she be suspicious of anyone entering into it, leaving her lonely more times than not.

Ryder had made it clear enough he was interested. She hadn't mistaken the intrigue in his light brown eyes. Nor the flirtation.

"*He won't stop me from getting what I came here for ... you.*"

Could she trust him? He had said the phrase in jest, hadn't he?

She wanted to think so. Adriana was correct about Gabriela wanting companionship, someone to cuddle with, to tell about her day. She had been alone for far too long. Bringing someone into her life, though, was always messy. If her uncle found out about Ryder, every aspect of his life would be placed under a microscope. Raúl would no doubt have him followed, see if he was a threat to his business first, his niece second. Gabby couldn't stand the thought of Ryder being put through what every other man in her life had. Not to mention Sergio, who would likely make Ryder's life a living hell. If for nothing more than his mean spirit. The man hated to lose.

Bottom line, if she intended to see Ryder, she'd need to see him off the grid. Getting away from her bodyguards was never an easy feat, but she had done so the night Antonio had stayed put by the SUV. Next time, she might not be so fortunate. If she was going to see Ryder, she would need Adriana's help.

Decision made, she quickly dusted off her hands and grabbed her cell, finding Adriana's number, and clicking on the glass. Gabby placed the phone to her ear and waited for her best friend to answer.

Three rings and Adriana answered. "Hey, Gabs. What's up?"

"Are you free tonight? Or do you and Mateo have plans?"

"He's still out of town. What do you need?"

Gabby drew her lower lip between her teeth, wondering if she was making a huge mistake. Her stomach fluttered at the thought of seeing Ryder again. What if he wasn't even in the country any longer, had gone back to California? There was no guarantee she'd run into him again if she and Adriana went to the same club, making her instantly regret not getting his number. Finally, a man she could see spending some time with, and she had no idea how to contact him.

"Gabs?"

She took a deep breath. "I want to go back to the dance club near your place. Are you free later?"

"Absolutely. You know me, I hate sitting home alone. Are you at Salazar's?"

"Guilty. I'm baking."

"Of course, you are. What's got you bugged?"

Gabriela chuckled; her friend knew her too well. "I was thinking about—"

"The Americano," Adriana finished. "He's *muy guapo*. You should have gotten his number."

"Tell me about it. I was just thinking the same thing. Hindsight."

"I'm game if you are. We can go for drinks, if nothing else. How about I meet you at Salazar's in an hour and we can have a light supper first? I'm dying for some of Francisco's crab cakes."

"Sounds like a plan. I could go for some of his crab cakes, too." Gabby smiled, hoping their night would go as planned. "See you in a bit."

She placed her phone on the table. With the knife she had used earlier, she cut off a small chunk of cheesecake and plopped it into her mouth. The cookies would have to wait for another day. For now, she needed to finish the dessert enchiladas, then clean up the mess she'd made. Francisco would do so without complaint, but she'd made it.

Forty-five minutes later, Gabby sat at a tall table near the front window, waiting on Adriana, who was notorious for being late. Taking a sip from her wine glass, she caught a glimpse of the black Escalade in the parking lot. There would be no getting out of Salazar's unless she was in that vehicle. Her uncle would have her head if she even thought to get in a car that hadn't been, what she liked to call, "Raúl proofed." If it wasn't approved by him, then neither of them left the house in it. He took every precaution at home and while on the road. Hell, most of the time, even his own men had no clue as to his whereabouts. While Luis and Sergio always knew his location, the rest were on a need-to-know basis. Gabby, of course, always knew in case she needed to get a hold of him in an emergency. She was the one person he always made himself accessible for.

Riding back to Adriana's apartment in her friend's small sedan would be out of the question. Gabby would have her driver follow Adriana. Once there, she'd need to convince the driver to stay by the SUV once again. Antonio had been a pushover, always having had a soft spot where she was concerned. But today's driver? Her gaze went to the bar where he stood talking with some of Raúl's men. A "yes" man. Convincing him was going to be much trickier.

Adriana's brown sedan pulled in front of the restaurant. She opened the door and got out, spotting Gabby in the picture window and waving enthusiastically before heading for the entrance. Thirty seconds later, seated across from her, Adriana grabbed Gabby's glass of Pinot Noir and took a healthy swallow, draining half the contents.

Gabby waved at the waitress and ordered an open bottle with another glass. Once the woman returned with the wine, they placed their order of crab cakes and salad containing romaine lettuce, black beans, corn, tomatoes, and avocado, tossed with the house dressing.

"So glad you called, Gabby. I hated the idea of sitting home alone and channel-surfing the television, without even a good movie to watch."

"Going dancing is certainly preferable to that." Her gaze flitted to tonight's driver. "I'm going to need your help. This one's going to want to follow me inside your apartment if he can. Losing sight of me, he'd consider it a personal failure to my uncle."

"Oh, don't worry. I got this. He can stand in the hallway outside the door if he wants, but he isn't coming inside."

The waitress set their plates before them, then excused herself when they both said they didn't require anything else. Adriana wasted little time as she cut into her crab cake, dunked it in the chef's special sauce, then plopped the morsel into her mouth. A look of pure pleasure crossed her face as she moaned over the delicacy.

"*Tan bueno.*" Adriana licked her lips, then quickly cut another bite. "So damn good. I wish I could hire him for all my meals."

Gabby laughed. "You couldn't afford him."

"Don't remind me."

"You know you can always get a free meal on me here." Gabby picked up her glass and took a sip. "So, what's the plan? How are we going to keep my driver from following us everywhere?"

"You leave that to me. I'll have him so flustered, he'll be begging to stand watch from the landing outside the apartment, leaving us to escape via the back door." After stabbing an avocado slice, she bit into the fruit. "Let's just hope he stays there. If not and he discovers us gone, we'll apologize later for the oversight. Not like he's going to tell your uncle you gave him the slip. You think your guy will be there?"

Gabby shrugged. "It's a long shot ... but unfortunately, it's the only one I have."

CHAPTER SIX

Kane took his seat at the table, glancing around at the men who filled the room. Gone were the obvious Sons who had followed Ryder south of the border. He brushed the hair, mussed from his motorcycle ride into town, back from his forehead. Cara, his gorgeous mate, was busy at the Sheriff's Office, working on some case with Cara's partner Joe Hernandez. Cara had confided a few nights ago that Sheriff Ducat was looking to retire and would not run for reelection.

The bad news?

It appeared as though Hernandez might be the one running ... unopposed. If that were the case, then the Sons of Sangue would need to learn to play nice with her partner, make sure he had their backs just as Sheriff Ducat did. The Sheriff's Office and the Sons had existed side-by-side for years with very few problems. Kane hoped to keep it that way.

The second reason for the called church meeting?

Red, the president of the Washington chapter, had been decapitated in a motorcycle crash last night. The Sons of Sangue, at least all present and not those in Mexico, would be expected to attend the man's memorial, ride with him to his final destination, where he would be ashed. Those in

Mexico wouldn't be given the option as to not jeopardize the mission. They couldn't risk pulling them, even for a couple of days.

Gunner Anderson, the chapter's VP, would need to be told. He was next in line to take over for Red. Of course, there would be a Washington chapter meeting on the subject, but Kane doubted any of them would have an issue with Gunner stepping into Red's shoes. Gunner may have been the VP for only a short time, but from what Kane had gathered, the man was honorable and his brothers seemed to like him well enough.

According to the last report from Grigore, Gunner would be headed home soon. Kane hoped to hell they knew what they were doing down there. Losing Gunner to an accidental fatal shot from friendly fire could cause unwanted mayhem between the two chapters. Following today's meeting, Kane would head north to keep an eye on things until Gunner made his long trek home.

Kaleb banged the gavel onto the strike plate and conversation around the room died. The two had already discussed the day's proceedings and were on the same page. Kane was the obvious choice to go since Kaleb resided as president in Oregon. They could do without their past P for a short period.

"We're calling this meeting for a few reasons." Kaleb took his seat at the table. "One of which will require immediate action on our Past P's part. We have some unfortunate news to share with you. Red, Washington's chapter president, was in a fatal motorcycle crash that beheaded him. We'll need to clear our schedules to show our respect. This isn't negotiable. And unless you're lying nearly dead somewhere, you have no excuse not to be at his ashing."

"Sorry to hear that, man. That sucks." Grayson rubbed his short-cropped beard. "I may not have known him as well as Viper, but he seemed like a good dude."

"He was one of the good ones," Kane agreed, his gaze traveling the table. "I've spent a lot of time with him over the past few years. I trusted him enough to bring his boys onboard with the Sons."

Bobby raised a brow. "And now, Viper?"

"We'll find out, Preacher. I'm staying north following the memorial. I want to spend time with his men. Get a feeling for them. I was there when we turned them, stuck around for a few weeks. They seemed onboard with being our sister chapter while those who weren't, left before the turning. I don't think we'll see trouble from them now."

"I'll volunteer to go with you," Alexander spoke up.

"Not a chance, Xander. You have a new mate who needs your attention." Kane grinned. "By the way, I don't think I've said it yet. Congrats on the pregnancy. India's going to need your support here."

Alexander's cheeks reddened, the vampire likely still getting used to the idea of being a daddy. He sure as hell didn't waste any time getting her with child. Kane thought of Cara and their empty house. Hell, not like they hadn't been practicing, but Cara hadn't been ready to become a mother. He, on the other hand, wouldn't mind getting started. Suzy, Kaleb's mate, frequently bugged his twin to give Stefan a brother. Kaleb's words had gone from a big "Hell, no," to a "Let's wait and see what this year brings." Kane figured Suzi was starting to win Kaleb over to the idea.

Maybe it was time to start working on his mate. The way Kane had it figured, he had a couple of extra bedrooms that needed filling. Watching Grayson with Lucian and Kaleb with Stefan was making him want a son or two of his own.

"She's pregnant, Viper. Not delivering." Alexander chuckled. "We have plenty of time."

"Still not going with me, GQ. I think I'm best doing this alone since they already know and trust me."

"I agree with Viper," Kaleb said. "He can handle this by himself. The rest of you can return here after the wake in case we're needed in Mexico. Ryder has his hands full. From what Grigore has said, he's no closer to getting an in with the cartel soldiers. They don't trust him and already ran him out of their known hangout once. Hence the reason Gunner's going to take a bullet.

"Plan is, he and Gunner will arrive together. When the locals try to throw Ryder out of the tavern, Gunner's going to step up and threaten the life of one of them. Ryder will shoot him, haul him out of there in the trunk of a car, and bury his ass. Not a lethal shot, of course. Once they leave, Wolf and the other Sons will dig him up and send him home. Ryder's hoping it will go a long way in earning him an in with the soldiers."

"Good plan." Grayson gained their attention. "As long as someone else doesn't shoot his sorry ass first. I'm not sure how the Washington boys will react to us killing their new P."

Kaleb's lips lifted on one side as humor twinkled in his gaze. "I don't think that would sit well with our new chapter."

"Sorry to hear about Red, Viper," Anton said, seated between Grayson and Bobby. "I know the two of you were close."

"Thanks, Rogue."

"Spread the word to the prospects," Kaleb continued. "Everyone is required to be there. No excuses. Now, onto the second reason for our meeting. Joe Hernandez will be running for sheriff."

"What the fuck, dude?" Grayson narrowed his gaze. "Just what we need. Someone who doesn't exactly see eye-to-eye with us, sitting at the head county chair. What happened to Ducat?"

"Cara said he's retiring and Hernandez is running unopposed," Kane filled in.

"Why not have Cara run?" Anton picked up the paper coffee cup he had brought with him and took a sip. "She would make a better sheriff, in my opinion. Nothing against Hernandez, but I agree with Gypsy. We aren't his favorite people in Lane County."

"Cara actually brought it up. She thought it might be best for us if she did run."

"And?" Bobby asked.

"Absolutely not from me, Preacher. She works hard enough as it is. I like her as a detective, keeps us having eyes and ears in the Sheriff's Office. But no way in hell am I letting her turn into a fucking politician."

"Can't blame you, bro." Kaleb toyed with the mallet. "These mates are certainly changing things around here. Suzi wants another baby. I told her she'd have to quit her job first."

Kane laughed at the idea, knowing how much Suzi loved helping the elderly at the nursing home. "How did she take that?"

"She put in her fucking two weeks." Kaleb shook his head. Chuckles resounded around the room. "Looks like I'll have to keep up my end of the bargain."

"Stefan needs a brother."

"Sure, Viper. How about a couple cousins while we're at it?"

The laughter rose in volume until Kaleb had to use the mallet to regain everyone's attention.

"Contrary to what you all think, I'm not opposed to the idea. I'd love a couple of sons," Kane continued. "Another reason Cara isn't running for sheriff. I'm ready to start filling those extra rooms at the farmhouse. You all laugh, those of you with mates, but you aren't far from joining the ranks."

"I, for one, am looking forward to it," Alexander said. "I couldn't be happier that India and I are expecting."

"We're all happy for you, GQ." Kaleb reined in the conversation. "Back to the subject at hand, though, I think it's perfect

Cara keeps her job for now. She'll go a long way at keeping Hernandez on our side. He likes Cara."

"How about we just turn his ass?" Bobby asked.

"While I'm not exactly saying it's a bad idea, Preacher"—Kaleb tapped a forefinger on the table—"I'm just not sure what his wife and kids would think. I'd have to say using Cara to earn his favor is the better idea."

"Agreed, Hawk." No way in hell did Kane want to bring on Hernandez as a vampire, positive nothing good would come from it. "We'll figure it out. Let's just be thankful one of us is already in the office."

"Anyone hear from Grandpa?"

"You really do have a death wish, Gypsy." Kaleb chuckled. "I think the only ones he doesn't mind that term of endearment from is Suzi and Cara. You certainly aren't on that short list. But to answer your question, no, Vlad headed back to his island. He's taking care of his untrustworthy brother at the moment. Word has it, Mircea's no longer happy with his surroundings. Vlad thinks Mircea might try an elaborate escape, so he's better off staying close to home for the time being."

"Of course, unless we need him," Kane added. "He wants Raúl dealt with as much as we do. We don't need miscreant vampires on the loose."

"Does Ryder detect any vampires in Mexico?" Anton asked.

"He hasn't made contact yet with Raúl, Rogue," Kane said. "And unless the kingpin keeps any turned vampires close, Ryder hasn't scented any in the area or among the soldiers hanging at Salazar's."

"Well, let's hope this plan works and he gets in there before Raúl comes up with any crazy ideas like turning his band of killers into vampires. There will be no stopping him." Bobby's lips turned down, his long beard concealing most of his mouth. "There are only so many of us and we already know Raúl has a lot of foot soldiers."

"I agree, Preacher," Kaleb said. "Ryder has spent a few months acclimating to the area. Let's hope his plan is solid. Raúl is slipperier than a damn snake. If Ryder can't get an in via Raúl's men, then let's hope he's making headway with Gabriela Trevino Caballero. She may be his ticket in. If anyone knows the kingpin's whereabouts, it would be his niece."

"Any word on her?" Anton asked.

"Only that they've officially met." Kaleb stood, walked to the side table, and started pouring a few glasses of whiskey. He slid a glass across the table to each of them before retaking his seat. "We're keeping in touch as good as we can with what's going on down there. Wolf reports back daily. But so far, there isn't a lot to report. My hope is Ryder charms the pants right off Raúl's niece. She's our best hope. Anyone else have anything to report before we end this meeting?"

Everyone shook their head, no one commenting further. Kaleb picked up his glass, the rest of the Sons following suit. "Then this meeting is adjourned. Salute!"

"*Salute*," traveled the room.

Kane took the glass to his lips, downing the two fingers of the amber liquid and welcoming the answering burn.

Tomorrow they would all make their way to Washington and pay Red his proper respect.

CHAPTER SEVEN

Ryder had broached the idea of Gunner accompanying him for a few beers at the nightclub where he had last seen Gabriela. It took little convincing to get the Washington biker onboard, but Grigore was another story. It made sense to be seen with Gunner beforehand, instead of showing up at Salazar's as complete strangers. Shooting someone you know to protect a cartel soldier? That took balls and would go a long way in his mission to gain their trust. In the end, Grigore had acceded to the plan.

Music blared through the opened glass and steel doubledoors. People spilled onto the patio, circling the tall tables covered by umbrellas. Lights beneath the canopies illuminated the evening sky since the sun had long since set. Conversation could barely be ascertained over the speakers. No one seemed to mind, huddling closer to be heard. Thankful for his enhanced hearing, Ryder could still pick up most of the conversations. A popular Shakira song had patrons moving to the cadence. Even those standing at the tables tapped their fingers along with the beat.

Gunner crossed the threshold and easily parted the crowd. The man stood head and shoulders above most. Finding a couple of empty stools at the end of the long bar, he took one and motioned for the bartender. Before Ryder claimed his seat, a couple of Modelos and two shots of whiskey sat in front of them.

"Thanks, bro."

Gunner held out his fist and Ryder complied, bumping his outstretched hand. "Anytime, man. I appreciate you getting me the hell out of there. I'm not cut out for solitary confinement. Apparently, I'd suck at a stakeout. Not being able to party was starting to drive me bat-shit crazy."

Ryder chuckled. "I can imagine. Been doing a lot of sitting myself. These things take time. As it is, these soldiers don't have any faith in me. They aren't your normal type. These guys have some serious trust issues, and rightfully so. If I'm ever going to get in with the kingpin, I need to be patient. Bide my time."

"Well, thank the good Lord you're shooting my ass. Much more of this waiting stuff and I might flip my lid." Gunner held up his shot glass and clicked it with Ryder's, before they both downed the whiskey. "How long are you going to be down here, man?"

"As long as it takes. It's simple, I owe the Tepes brothers and Gypsy for saving my ass. Not to mention what happened to my girlfriend."

"Sorry, man. That's got to suck."

"It does. There isn't a day that goes by I don't hate myself for putting her in that situation." Ryder took a sip from his beer. "She shouldn't have gone out like that, not when it was me they were angry with. But that's how the cartel does things. They go after your family. The suffering lasts a lifetime. And now that I'm a vampire? I have an eternity to remember I was the cause."

"You can't control what others do, man."

"No, but I shouldn't have put her in that situation to begin with, which is why no mate for me."

Ryder took another sip of his beer. There was no way in hell he'd chance putting another person he loved in jeopardy. The lifestyle he lived was not conducive to having a serious relationship. Losing someone he loved sucked. Losing them because of his choices was unforgivable.

"Lonely existence, man. Being a vampire, you could live a good long life."

"I'm content with the donors we're provided." Ryder shrugged. He had used quite a few of them, spent the night with some of them as well. Who was he to complain about variety? "You ready for a mate?"

"We're talking about you." Gunner laughed. "But yeah, I think if the right woman came along, I wouldn't have a problem with it. Until then, I'll party my ass off. Maybe I'll think about it after I've lived to see a couple hundred years."

"We could all be so lucky."

"How old do you think the Tepes twins are?"

"Viper and Hawk? I've never asked. But the real question is, how old is their great-great-grandfather?" Ryder thought about the old ruler, Vlad, trying to remember his history. "He has to be near five-hundred-and-eighty or so. As far as I know, he's the eldest vampire."

"I thought he had an older brother."

"He does, but Mircea was turned *after* Vlad."

Gunner's smile grew. "Well, if that old man can still get the ladies at over five hundred years, who are we to settle down before him?"

Ryder chuckled. "You do have a point."

Turning in his stool, Ryder observed several patrons taking to the dance floor, bodies moving seductively to the samba. His gaze toured the room, looking for one woman in particular. Gabriela would no doubt be easy to spot, drawing his gaze like a heat-seeking missile. Fuck, but she knew how to turn up the heat just by entering a room.

Gunner and Ryder fell into a comfortable silence, watching the array as they sipped from their bottles of Modelo. Ryder would much rather partake from an artery, which he needed to do soon. Find a cute little *señorita* to dine on and maybe a little horizontal performance as well. He was getting damn itchy for some action. Ryder normally didn't abstain, nor did he have to back home. He had his choice of donors to have sex with since many of the Sons in Oregon were mating up. Finding a bed partner had never been a chore.

A long black-haired *señorita* approached Gunner, her dark eyes looking up at him, even from his seated position. Once he stood, she'd be lucky to be chest high on him. She smiled, her white teeth showing bright in the lights from behind the bar.

"¿*Te gustaría bailar?*"

"I don't dance." Gunner responded, surprising Ryder, having no idea Gunner knew the language.

"It won't kill you." Ryder nodded toward the dance floor. "Just follow what they do."

The woman gripped Gunner's hand, urging him out of his seat. Gunner complied, following the cute, much-shorter woman to the dance floor. Ryder couldn't help but chuckle. Gunner couldn't move to the rhythm to save his life. Not like he could hide on the dance floor either. The crowd parted like the Red Sea, giving him plenty of room to one-step the samba.

"What has you chuckling?"

Ryder turned to find the one woman he had been looking for. For the second time, she had snuck up on him. He really needed to up his game. His flesh heated and his gums ached with the need to emerge. Ryder bit back the vampire in him and shifted in his chair.

"To what do I owe the pleasure again?"

"I was hoping to run into you." Her admission left her blushing. "I only got your name. I had no idea how I might find you again, except go back to the scene of the crime."

His hand indicated the barstool Gunner had vacated. "Have a seat."

"Are you sure? There's a half-empty beer—"

"My friend is busy doing what he hopes looks like dancing." Ryder chuckled.

He called over the bartender and ordered her a paloma. Throwing a few dinero onto the bar, he turned back to Gabby.

"I'm impressed. You remembered."

"I'm pretty sure there isn't much I'd forget about you."

She laughed, the sound making Ryder smile. "Do women usually fall for your lines?"

"Are you kidding? With a face like this?" He grimaced. "I'm lucky if a woman pays me any mind at all. They are more than likely to go for my friend."

"Which one is your friend?"

Ryder nodded toward the dance floor. "The tall one."

Her gaze went in the direction of Gunner before returning. "I don't know what the other women are thinking, but I'm pretty sure I prefer you."

One of his brows rose. "Do you?"

The admittance shouldn't have pleased him, but it did. Gabriela was his mission, not his fuck-buddy. He'd do well to remember that. But sitting this close and scenting her desire had the vampire in him wanting to devour. If her blood tasted half as good as it smelled, he was in deep shit should he make the mistake of tasting it. He'd likely be an instant addict.

"Most definitely."

"Now who's feeding who lines?"

"It's not a line if it's true." She took a sip of her drink that the bartender had left, hiding her grin. "Besides, I came looking for you, didn't I?"

"You did."

"And..."

Her pause left him wondering what she wanted. What the hell had her searching him out? A quick look around the club and he spotted Gabby's friend, now dancing with Gunner. Ryder wasn't sure what happened to his other partner, but Gunner seemed more into Gabby's friend, if the hand on the small of her back was any indication.

"And I found you."

Ryder laughed at the way she dodged his question. He still had no clue as to why she'd seek him out. It wasn't like he was model-handsome like Alexander "Xander" Dumitru of the Sons of Sangue, who had earned the moniker GQ. Someone as gorgeous as Gabriela deserved a pretty boy. Not someone more on the rugged side, who had their share of scars. But damn if his body didn't care, reacting to her nearness, kicking up his own desire. His jeans became constricting. Much more and he'd be spouting a full-blown erection in pants that had no hope of hiding it.

Vampires were sexual beings, damn it. He wasn't used to curbing his appetite. He needed a change of subject.

"What do you do for a living?"

"Why?" She took another drink from her glass as she watched him over the rim.

"Look at you. You're dressed in clothes I couldn't possibly afford. You wear Louboutins."

Gabby set down her drink and chuckled. She laid a hand on his knee, shooting heat straight up his thigh to his groin. Much more and the entire club would know he sported a hard-on. Everything about this woman heated his blood, from the soft waves of her hair, to her brown eyes, and full lips.

She had killer hips and a nice set of tits, too. It was all he could do not to ogle her.

"I'm surprised you've heard of the brand of shoes."

"It's not like I live under a rock," he grumbled.

Maybe he had said too much already. His mouth could sometimes get him in trouble. And this might be one of those times.

"I meant no disrespect. It's just, most guys don't know fashion."

"Would you believe me if I told you I have a foot fetish?"

Placing the perfectly manicured hand that had been on his knee over her lips, she laughed again. "Oh, please ... no. You aren't getting nowhere near my toes."

Ryder shared in her humor. "I can think of better things to... Maybe I should shut up while I'm ahead."

Gabby drew her lower lip between her teeth and looked down, her cheeks reddening. By the scent of her rising desire, he could tell her mind had gone to the same place as his. He wouldn't mind suggesting they take it back to his place, but it was better he kept that under wraps for the time being. He didn't need anyone knowing where he stayed. As for Gabby, he'd bet she wouldn't be offering to head for her place any time soon. Her uncle wouldn't be too happy knowing she'd divulge where he hung his coat either. Although, thanks to Brea Gotti, they already knew the location. What they didn't know was if Raúl happened to be there at the moment.

And it wasn't like he could ask.

"You never answered my question. What is it you do?"

"I manage my uncle's restaurant, Salazar's."

"Where I first saw you?"

She nodded. "It's a great little place."

"I agree. They have the best seafood I've found down here."

"Thank you. I'll be sure to let Francisco know." She tucked one side of her hair behind her ear. Ryder's fingers itched to touch the silken strands. "What do you do?"

Ryder rubbed his jaw to keep his hands to himself. "I'm between jobs, at the moment. Looking for work."

"Maybe I can help, see if Francisco needs more hands in the kitchen."

Oh, man. He really needed to get a handle on his runaway mouth around her. Although, setting it up that he was looking for work played right into his mission. Getting a job washing dishes did not. And right about that time, Gunner reappeared and put in his two cents.

"Not sure you're cut out for dishpan hands, bro." Gunner winked at Gabby. "Although, he can cook a mean omelet."

Ryder shook his head and smiled. "As much as I appreciate the offer, Gabby, I had another type of work in mind. I'm working on some connections. I'm sure it's only a matter of time before I find something."

"Does that mean you're sticking around?"

"Absolutely."

Her eyes held his, the interest evident. "Awesome. That means I'll get to see you again. Are you going to give me your phone number? Or do I have to keep stalking you?"

Ryder held out his hand. Gabriela unlocked her cell, opened her contact app, and handed him the phone. Ryder quickly typed in his name and number before handing it back.

"Send me a text so I know your number as well."

She took her phone from his hand, their skin making contact. Christ, there was so much heat in that brief touch he felt it clear to his gut. He'd need to get laid, and soon, for fear of sporting an ever-present hard-on around this woman. His phone dinged. Ryder took it from his back pocket and slid his thumb across the screen.

Next time some place more private. Your place?

CHAPTER EIGHT

MY PLACE?

Hell, no, Ryder thought the following day. He needed a safe haven, one where he could lay low should the heat get turned up. If Raúl's men found out where he was staying, he might wake up with a knife at his throat or a gun to his temple should he further piss off Sergio or any of the other men. Putting his trust in Gabriela wasn't something he should do, no matter how much he wanted to get her between the sheets. Or up against a wall. Hell, he wasn't picky, Ryder thought with a wry smile. Banging her, though, wasn't on his list of to-dos, no matter how much the idea appealed to him. He needed to get her attention, get her trusting him, but he also needed his head in the game, so he couldn't let his dick do the thinking for him. His pad needed to be a backdoor spot where he could meet with Grigore and the other Sons. Not a place for a booty call.

Her text could be used to his advantage, nevertheless, finagle him an invitation to her place instead … meaning Raúl's fortress. Eventually, the kingpin had to make an appearance. It was his home, after all. Following tonight's meet and greet, he'd send Gabby a text and tell her he wanted to get together, but his place wasn't going to work since he had been sleeping on friends' sofas until he managed to secure a paying job. Getting to spend time with her was hardly going to be a tribulation. Truth of it, Ryder found he enjoyed her company. Too bad they hadn't met under better circumstances. He wouldn't have minded getting to know her a whole lot better. But due to the situation, he'd need to keep his pants up and his hands to himself.

Christ, with his vampire genes and her smoking hot looks, that task would be damn near impossible.

Zeroing in on the job at hand, Gunner sat beside him in the old clunker Grigore had drummed up. The sedan rattled and rumbled down the highway, making Ryder fear the bucket of bolts might fall apart before they ever arrived at their destination. Fucking Grigore. It'd be the last time Ryder put him in charge of finding a vehicle. Hell, he probably would've been better off throwing Gunner over the bitch seat on his motorcycle and bungee strapping his ass to the leather, before carting him off to his shallow grave. At least then he knew they'd get to what was to be Gunner's final destination.

Ryder glanced across the bench seat at Gunner. "You ready?"

"Let's get this shit over with. What I'm ready for is to head north where I can get back to Red and the rest of my brothers." He wiped a hand across his sweat-beaded brow. "I'm so over this fucking heat already. No wonder I live in Washington, man. No getting away from this humidity."

"What's the matter? Having a bad hair day?"

Gunner ran a hand through his unruly curls. "Fuck you, man."

Ryder chuckled as they pulled into the parking lot of Salazar's. "No thanks. You might take a liking to me."

With a roll of his eyes and a shake of his head, Gunner said, "I like you, man. You're one crazy motherfucker."

Adrenaline coursed through Ryder's veins, making the vampire in him dance dangerously close to the surface. The power of ten-plus men vibrated through him. Primordial power Ryder was still getting accustomed to, something he had yet to use. Should he unleash the beast, no one inside the tavern would walk out alive. He'd drain every last one of the cretins before they even knew what had hit them. But tonight wasn't about taking out as many men as he could. Tonight was about earning respect, securing a job, and finding Raúl, no matter how much he'd enjoy wiping the earth of the scum.

"It's showtime," Ryder said. "We have only one chance to get this right. We fuck up, and we'll both be heading for an early grave that neither of us has a snowball's chance in hell at coming back from."

Ryder parked the car around the side of the building. They had a better chance of concealing Gunner being tossed into the trunk from the view of the road.

Gunner glanced at him, giving him a wink. "I got this, boss. I hope you have a damn good aim."

Exiting the vehicle, Ryder slammed the door, rocking it on its four bald tires. He shook his head. Next time he needed something, he'd rely on his own fucking skills. Gunner followed Ryder through Salazar's entrance. They stepped up to the bar, Gunner clapping his shoulder.

"What're you drinking, man? It's on me."

"Seriously?" Ryder gave the bartender a nod. "Not about to pass up a gift. I'll take a Modelo and a shot of tequila before my friend changes his mind."

The man's lips turned down as he looked at Gunner. If Ryder was to guess, he'd say they weren't welcome here anymore than the day Sergio had thrown him out.

"*¿Y tu, gringo?*"

Ryder wasn't sure if Gunner even understood he had been insulted. "I'll have the same."

Though they weren't here to pick a fight with the bartender, the man had certainly set the mood as conversation died down around the room. Without turning, Ryder felt the eyes of the locals glaring into his back. Good thing he wasn't here to make friends.

Two beers and shot glasses were set in front of them. Gunner dug into his pocket and laid more than enough dinero on the bar, tipping a man who didn't deserve their thanks, let alone the extra dinero. The man scooped up the money and walked to the end of the bar. He'd not likely offer to serve them again. It didn't matter. Ryder wasn't planning on staying long.

After picking up his shot glass, he downed the liquid, then chased it with a swig of beer before turning and giving the joint a once-over. Sergio hadn't missed their entrance. Luis sat on a high barstool to his right. *Good*. They were both in attendance. Better for Ryder. He was pretty sure he had already earned some of Luis's respect. Palming his beer bottle, he held Sergio's stare. He wasn't about to show any sign of weakness where the man was concerned. Sure, Sergio was deadly, could kill a man without so much as a second thought. But Ryder? He was downright lethal.

The fucker doesn't stand a chance one-on-one.

It didn't take long for Sergio to push off the wall and head in their direction. Luis watched from his perch. Sergio's stride was slow, cocky even. He might intimidate a weaker foe, but his swagger didn't faze Ryder. In fact, Ryder welcomed it, reveled in the day he'd get to drain the motherfucker of every last drop of his blood. Surely, it would be bitter.

"You really do have a set of *cajones muy grande*."

"Nice to see you again as well." Ryder smiled. "I don't believe we were introduced last time."

One of the man's dark brows rose. "We weren't."

"I'm Ryder. This is my friend Gunner."

It was Sergio's turn to smile. "You think I give a fuck? Why don't you and your *amante* hit the door? You're not welcome. This is your last warning, *pinche idiota*."

Gunner rose to his full height, squaring his shoulders. He stood damn near a head above Sergio. Ryder bet had he not had an entire room full of men backing him, Sergio's bravado might slip. Hell, Ryder's money was on Gunner, even without his vampire genes. Gunner's biceps bunched as his fists clenched. The muscles in his jaw ticked. He looked ready to pummel Sergio. Ryder would pay to see that. Unfortunately, Gunner would be the one going down tonight, leaving Sergio for Ryder later. He couldn't help but smile at the thought. He'd glory in taking down Sergio, Luis, and their fucking boss.

"You own this fucking joint?" Gunner asked, his tone deep and threatening.

To his credit, Sergio didn't show any sign of backing down. "As far as you're concerned, I do. *Ustedes dos idiotas* would do well to hit the road and never come back. *No son bienvenidos.*"

"Your last name Salazar?"

Sergio's brow creased. "No."

"Then I think I'll stay and have another beer here with my *amigo. Vete a la mierda.*"

Sergio fisted Gunner's shirt, his free hand pulling a switchblade and holding it to Gunner's neck. "You just fucked yourself, *Americano. Eres un hombre muerto.*"

Gunner laughed, then spit in Sergio's face, using the gesture to pull the gun from his waistband and stick the barrel in the center of Sergio's chest. "Looks like you're the dead man, *hombre.*"

The color drained from Sergio's face. Several guns appeared from the men surrounding them. Sergio held his arms out to his side in a Jesus-like pose and dropped his knife to the wooden floor, where it clattered.

"Put down your gun, *amigo*, and we all walk away," Sergio instructed.

"I don't think so." Gunner raised a brow as his gaze swept the room. "I drop my gun and your men take me out. *Yo no soy estupido.*"

Sergio took several steps back, giving every man in the joint a clear shot. Ryder had to act or fuck up this mission royally with Gunner winding up dead for real.

Ryder pulled out his Sig Sauer, sticking it against Gunner's spine. Careful where he aimed, the shot would blossom from the front, looking like a heart shot, when in fact, Ryder would just miss the vital organ. Gunner would crumble to the floor after the bullet traveled through him. If Ryder aimed it just right, it would go straight through the front window, missing any other person.

Eyes widened around the room and guns lowered. Maybe not all of them, but it was a sign they trusted Ryder to take care of his friend. Respect would hopefully come when he took out Gunner, rather than side with him.

He pulled the trigger.

Gunner jerked, staggering forward as the exiting bullet shot through the window, missing anyone else in its path. Gunner dropped his gun. It thudded against the floor next to his feet. He turned slowly to look at Ryder, his hands covered the gaping wound on his chest, blood seeping through his fingers, before he collapsed.

GABRIELA FALTERED BACKWARD, gasping, her hand flattening against her chest in the exact spot where the man was bleeding out. She had watched in horror through the square window on the swinging door as Ryder shot Gunner in cold blood. Sure, the taller man had held a gun on Sergio, but her uncle's goons would've protected the arrogant ass. It hadn't been necessary for Ryder to step up and do so. Not to mention, the two men had arrived together, the dying man having bought Ryder a drink, the same man she had met at the dance club with Ryder.

What sort of person did that?

A damn cold one.

Spotting Ryder by the bar, she had been about to exit the kitchen, let her presence be known. Gabby had been worried what Sergio might do, figuring she needed to keep a close eye on things. Sure as the sun would shine, Sergio had approached the two before she'd had a chance to stop him from causing a scene. All of this could've been avoided had Sergio heeded her warning the last time he chased Ryder from the premises.

Now, she had a man bleeding out on her restaurant floor.

Gabby needed to call for an ambulance, hoping she wasn't too late to save the man's life. Cell phone in hand, she pushed through the kitchen door. Ryder turned his head in her direction. He had hunkered down to check for the man's pulse. His face blanched.

"Is he...?" Gabby asked, stopping just shy of the pooling blood.

Ryder gave a quick nod, his mouth a stern slash across his handsome face. "Put down the cell, Gabby. There's no help for him."

"We can't leave him here." Her voice trembled. "We have to—"

Sergio approached, a quick glance at the dead man. "He's right, Gabriela. We take care of our own. You know we don't bring in the authorities. Go back to the kitchen and mind your own business."

Her mouth gaped as she glanced from Sergio to Ryder, who all but dismissed her with a turn of his head. He was no different than the men who worked for her uncle, dashing her hopes that he was somehow better.

Gabby licked her dry lips, glancing at the bullet hole in the front window. She squared her shoulders. "I take it that will be fixed?"

"Before the night is over." Sergio laid a palm on her shoulder. She shook it off. "Go back to the kitchen where you belong, Gabriela. Let us handle this."

Anger rose up her spine and heated her cheeks. "This is *my* restaurant."

"No." Sergio's grin could only be described as evil. "It belongs to *your* uncle."

He was correct, of course, but the comment was like tossing gasoline on an already raging fire. Her uncle may own the place, but Gabriela had taken pride in running it the last couple of years. With a final glare in Ryder's direction, she turned on her heel and hurried off.

She heard Ryder's deep timbre say, "He's my friend. I'll see that he's taken care of."

"Make sure no one finds his grave," Sergio instructed. "When you get back, we'll talk."

She left the main room and entered her sanctuary. Francisco looked at her with pity. He knew what kind of man Raúl was, knew the type of men who frequented the restaurant. But even so, it was the first time a man had been killed in the establishment. Until now, Gabby had managed to keep the violence from entering her domain.

Ryder had brought the violence to her doorstep.

He was at fault.

Placing a hand over her lips, she let out a shaky breath. He was no better than Sergio. How the hell had she been so wrong? Gabriela had always prided herself on being a good judge of character. And yet Ryder had blinded her to his true nature.

She pulled the apron over her head and tossed it to the flour-coated table. "I have to get out of here."

"You go ahead, *señorita*. I'll clean up."

"Thank you, Francisco. And out there…" She couldn't even bring herself to ask who would clean up the carnage.

"You head out and don't worry yourself. I'll take care of everything."

Gabriela crossed the floor and hugged the chef before kissing his cheek. "*Gracias*," she said, grabbing her purse from the back counter.

Taking a final look at the swinging doors leading to the front of the tavern, Gabby opened the back door, welcoming the warm breeze caressing her skin. Once outside, she sucked in much-needed oxygen.

He is no different.

Straightening her spine and her resolve, she vowed to stay away from him. Gabriela headed for the Escalade, her insides still shaking. Antonio opened the rear passenger door and assisted her crawling into the cool interior, where she sank against the dark leather. Her driver walked around the vehicle and settled himself behind the wheel. After starting the SUV and pulling the gearshift into drive, they circled the back lot before heading around the side of Salazar's, just in time to see the dead man slung over Ryder's shoulder. With no more than a quick sympathetic glance in her direction, he popped the trunk of a beat-up sedan and tossed in the body.

"Where to, Miss Gabriela?"

"Home, Antonio. And please, don't tell anyone where I have gone. I'll be in no mood for company."

He gave her a quick nod. "Home it is. Your uncle will be pleased to see you."

Her gaze jerked to the rearview mirror. "Uncle Raúl is there?"

The driver smiled. "*Sí, señorita.*"

CHAPTER NINE

"WELL, DEAR BROTHER, ARE THE RUMORS I'M HEARING from my staff true?"

Mircea smiled, one that told Vlad Tepes that his sibling was about to feed him a line of bullshit. "Whatever do you mean?"

Vlad slammed the door to Mircea's room/temporary confinement. The walls shook from the force, causing the picture frames to rattle against the plaster.

"I traveled back here because someone tried to claw their way out of this room." Vlad jabbed a finger toward the far corner where the pristine wall looked as if a sledgehammer had been taken to it. "You realize the walls in this room have been reinforced so that not even I could break through them? The plaster is nothing but a facade. Who the hell is going to pay for the repairs?"

Mircea chuckled, his eyes rolling damn near to the back of his head. "Dramatic much?"

"Me?" Vlad roared, causing the picture frames to shudder again.

"It's not like you can't afford the renovations."

"If only it were a mere remodel, not damage to my home, you ass." *Breathe.* Lord, but he wanted to tear his brother's head clean from his shoulders. "If the accommodations aren't to your liking—"

"Seriously?" It became Mircea's turn to raise the roof. The high pitch in his tone rang in Vlad's ears. "If you're so worried about your precious fortress, then let me the hell out of here."

"It's not that fucking easy and you know it."

"Tell me why you continue to hold me hostage when all I wish to do is return to my home in Italy and live out my life in peace."

Vlad chuckled, feeling none of the humor. "So, you're saying you have no desire to hunt down my kin and eliminate them one-by-one?"

Mircea shrugged. "I do owe you, brother. You stole my lovely Rosalee from me."

"I ended her life because she was a bitch. And besides, she wasn't your blood daughter to begin with."

"No. Thank heaven for that." Mircea reached for an opened bottle of wine and poured himself a half glass. After swirling the contents, he brought the crystal to his lips and downed the entire glass in one gulp. "But she would've made me a beautiful mate in time."

Vlad shook his head. "She wouldn't have been faithful to you on the best of days. Arm candy, maybe. But a bitch is still a bitch. Surely, you know that."

Pouring himself another glass, he neither agreed nor disagreed. Vlad would've been better off allowing his grandson, Kane, to take this one's life. For some reason, though, he had felt the need to spare his brother. Now, he was stuck with the insufferable ass.

"I should've let you die, you arrogant fool."

One of Mircea's brows arched. "And you think your grandson could have done the job? You merely spared his life."

"Normally, I might've agreed with you, given your primordial strength. But never underestimate the power of my blood, Mircea. My money was on Kane that day."

Mircea set down his stemless glass with a thud, red wine spilling over the edge, splattering to the table. Vlad was reminded of blood, the very blood he was tempted to spill of the man standing before him.

Fangs jutted beneath his brother's upper lip as his eyes blackened over. Mircea's face not only contorted with the vampire springing forth, but with his mounting rage. A mighty roar escaped his lips, one surely loud enough to be heard well beyond the room had it not been soundproofed. Vlad had pissed off his brother yet again, but he wasn't about to apologize for it. Mircea needed to know where he sat on the food chain, well beneath Vlad's grandsons.

"Your grandsons wouldn't stand a chance against me. That is why you have me locked up in here like a common criminal."

"Because you wouldn't fight fair." Vlad heavily sighed. "Which is why you'll continue to sit in here, trying your damnedest to claw your way out. When you tire of this ridiculous vendetta, I'll let you go. Today you have proven quite the opposite. You're still gunning for my relatives and I simply can't allow that."

Mircea's glare would have chilled a lesser opponent. "You're saying I'm stuck here?"

"Yes. Tear down the plaster if you must, but you aren't getting out of here."

"I'll find a way."

Vlad laughed, this time the humor tickling him. "You will try, I'm sure. Mark my words, Mircea, you'll die in here first if I have to withhold sustenance from you."

Mircea's grin was pure evil. "You wouldn't have bothered saving me from Kane's wrath only to starve me to death."

"True, but then I thought there was something worth saving." Vlad took out a key and unbolted the self-locking door. "Today, I'm not so sure. Think about that if you ever want to leave this room again."

Vlad walked out, slamming the door behind him, snuffing Mircea's cry of outrage. What the hell was he going to do with him? Vlad needed to make a decision soon. He couldn't keep Mircea behind lock and key forever.

"How much farther?" Ryder heard the mumbled words from the trunk of the sedan.

He supposed Gunner was tired of being cramped in the small space. Good thing for him the sedan was older, thus making the trunk larger than on most of the newer models.

"Only a couple more miles. You'll need to feign being dead a while longer. We got company."

"Who the fuck?"

"We have a tail. Apparently, Luis sent a few of his goons to make sure I finish the job."

"I texted Wolf," Gunner said. "He'll be out of sight when we arrive at the predetermined spot."

"Good. I promise not to bury you too deep, and with any luck, the two jerks won't leave their air-conditioned car for fear I'll make them help dig."

He heard Gunner chuckle just before he turned down the dirt and gravel road, heading farther into the woods. Ryder drove about three miles before he stopped at a particularly dense thicket. Rolling to a halt, he glanced in his rearview mirror, noting the second vehicle stayed dozens of yards back.

"Looks like we're in luck. Our eyes stopped far enough back to keep us in view, not close enough for me to enlist their help."

Ryder didn't wait for a response. After exiting the car, he popped the trunk. Gunner lay curled and unmoving. Picked picked up his brother with little effort, though putting on a pretense of a struggle. After all, a man of his size should have trouble lifting one of Gunner's girth, especially when the body was dead weight.

Spotting a defoliated area, Ryder dropped Gunner to the ground with a thud. Points to the big guy for not so much as grunting. Ryder returned to the sedan and extracted a shovel before closing the trunk, rocking the car on its threadbare tires. Ryder chuckled with a shake of his head. He might just grow attached to the beat-up piece of shit.

Not bothering to acknowledge Luis's lackeys, he put shovel to dirt and started clearing away debris. He took his time, and after about an hour in the insufferable heat, he rolled Gunner into the shallow grave and began quickly covering him with dirt. He had wasted enough time. Finished, he patted the small mound with his shovel, then tossed dried leaves onto the surface, camouflaging the newly dug area.

Just as he was about to walk away, his vampire hearing picked up Grigore's whisper. "About fucking time."

Ryder resisted the urge to smile and headed back to the sedan. He popped the trunk again, tossed in the shovel, then closed the lid. Crawling behind the wheel of the car, he started the engine, then did a three-point turn to aim the sedan in the direction they had come. Passing the second car, he saluted the men before heading down the road.

CONVERSATION DIED WHEN Ryder walked through the door of Salazar's. Luis stayed seated, his expression schooled, while Sergio approached him in a slow, confident stride. Ryder had been uncertain the type of reception he'd receive, their actions giving nothing away.

The goons assigned to follow him walked through the door. The hairs rose on the back of his neck, his vampire DNA shimmering just beneath the surface and at the ready should all hell break loose. Sergio said nothing to the two.

They simply nodded, then headed for the bar, where the bartender immediately offered a couple of beers. The good news? They had arrived too quickly to have investigated the grave.

His heart slowed its beat, no longer feeling as though every man in the place was about to draw on him. If they were, he'd already be dead. Ryder glanced around the room, most of the men going back to their meals, drinks, and conversation, leaving Sergio and him to the business at hand. At least that was Ryder's hope, an open invitation to join them.

His gaze flitted to the swinging kitchen doors as a smaller guy in chef's garb came through to speak to one of the waitresses. Ryder's heart panged, knowing Gabriela had come through those same doors and witnessed the crime he wasn't exactly guilty of, no doubt thinking the worst of him. Things couldn't be more fucked up where she was concerned. Hearing what he had done secondhand would have been one thing, but seeing him kill a man in cold blood was another. While by appearances it looked as if he had possibly gained the trust and respect of men he disliked, he had lost the same from Gabriela.

And that sucked.

Sergio clapped a hand on Ryder's shoulder, giving him no time to spare Gabby another thought.

Keep your head in the game.

"I owe you a drink, *amigo*," Sergio said.

"You owe me nothing."

Ryder shook off the man's touch. Appearing too eager could foil his attempt to further win the man over. The fact remained, they weren't friends. Not by a long shot. And these men were suspicious by nature.

"You killed your amigo to save my life. And yet I get the feeling you don't like me."

He shrugged. "He wasn't my friend. More like an acquaintance. We met several weeks ago when I came to Mexico. We had drinks, hung out a few times."

"Why are you here, *amigo*?"

"I told you before. I'm looking for work."

Sergio walked him to the bar, spoke to the bartender in Spanish, and ordered them both a michelada. "You drink them? There's a bit of a kick."

"Never had one."

He smiled as two Bloody Mary-looking drinks were set in front of them. Sergio held up his glass. "You will like. *Salud*."

Ryder clicked glasses with him, then took the rim to his lips, taking a good swallow. The shit was spicy, he'd give him that much. But with the mix of beer, he found he liked it. Somehow the mix jelled well.

"It's good. *Gracias*."

"*De Nada*." Sergio set down his glass and turned toward Ryder. "Now tell me why you came to Mexico looking for work. Surely, there are jobs where you came from."

Ryder knew his answer hinged on whether he'd be shown the door or not. "I left town to get away from old memories. I figured new scenery might help."

"What are you running away from, *amigo*?"

Ryder leaned his forearms on the bar, cupping the glass between his palms. "My girlfriend died because of me. The reminder was killing me. So I left."

"How did she die?"

"Fire." Ryder pulled his T-shirt off his shoulder, revealing the ugly scar. "I tried to save her. I was too late."

One of Sergio's dark brows arched. "You set the fire?"

"Fuck, no. I was in a motorcycle club. I wanted to leave. Apparently, they decided to teach me a lesson."

"Which club?"

"The Devils. I'm sure you're aware of them. We ran drugs for La Paz cartel."

Sergio nodded, his expression flat. "They still do. Why leave them and come to me?"

"Tank and I had a disagreement. I was supposed to be the next VP. He thought otherwise." Ryder shrugged, turning back to his drink. "With Tank and Spike now gone, I suppose I could go back. But I'm ready to put the past behind and move on."

"So you came here looking for us." It wasn't a question.

"I want a job."

"You have a tattoo proving you were with the Devils?"

Ryder pulled his shirt over his head, revealing more ugly scars and a back tattoo labeling him as a member of the MC.

Sergio glanced at Luis, then slapped Ryder's bared shoulder. "Put your shirt back on. Luis and I believe you've proven yourself. *Eres uno de nosotros.* Welcome aboard, *amigo.*"

Ryder hid his grin as he pulled his shirt over his head, once again covering the Sig still tucked in the waistband of his jeans. He'd bet every man here concealed. "The pay?"

"Depends on your worth." Sergio smiled. "We'll give you thirty thousand pesos a month to start."

"Sounds fair." In truth, Ryder expected a lot less.

"We also have odd jobs from time-to-time. For those, you'll get paid extra."

"All of this is under the table?"

"*Sí, amigo.*" Sergio laughed. "I'm thinking you won't want to claim this on your taxes next year. How much did you make with the Devils?"

"I didn't earn a wage. We got paid for jobs done."

"With La Paz money."

Ryder nodded. "That about sums it up."

"How did you make a living?"

Ryder shrugged. "Besides the Devils? Odd jobs. That's why I'm here. It's time I make some serious cash now that I'm no longer with the club. Thought I'd head south."

"So you came looking for us," he repeated.

Ryder took a sip of his michelada, then set down the glass. "I did. I had hoped I might find you. But you weren't exactly sending out the welcome mat."

"*Sí*, we don't trust many."

Ryder turned, crossing his arms over his chest, and faced Sergio full on. "And you trust me now?"

Again, he grinned. "No, *amigo*. We're offering you an income because you proved useful. Trust comes in time."

CHAPTER TEN

Lord, she was a mess. Gabby couldn't stop the tremors from wracking her body. Thankfully, Adriana hadn't been busy and dropped everything to head out to her uncle's palace. The eight-thousand-square-foot house could only be thought of as such. The Spanish style home sat just yards from the beach, giving million-dollar views from almost every window. Much like her uncle's beach house further up the coast, only larger.

Raúl's staff kept the mansion pristine, not a grain of sand in sight. Interior designers had custom-made furniture brought in, every inch looking as if it graced the pages of a magazine. Only the best for Uncle Raúl, she thought with a sigh. In truth, she could be happy in a one-bedroom apartment, for all she cared. All of the riches her uncle afforded her had not bought her happiness. In fact, the older she got, the more downright miserable she became.

For the most part, Gabby stuck to her wing of the estate. She had access to the pool and spa via her personal balcony and didn't have to see her uncle if she didn't wish to. Even though Raúl was in residence today, she had yet to see him, which was fine with her.

Gabby wasn't about to seek him out either. Seeing him would only be a reminder of what had gone down at Salazar's, everything she detested about her uncle and the men who worked for him. Sure, Raúl could be a good man when it came to doting on her. He had provided for Gabby, gave her a home when her father had been murdered, treated her like a princess, made sure she wanted for nothing. Unfortunately, she also knew where his money came from. Being born into the cartel did not mean she had to approve of the way they did business.

The door to her sitting room opened and Adriana breezed in. Her waist-length black hair had been tied up into a messy bun, her deep brown eyes holding compassion. She instantly pulled Gabby into her embrace.

She stepped back and studied Gabby's face. "What's your uncle done this time?"

Gabriela rolled her eyes, too mad to even shed a tear. "Hired the wrong man."

"I'm not sure I understand. Who did he hire?"

They moved to a pair of wicker chairs facing the picture window that overlooked the ocean and each took a seat. Gabby tucked her legs beneath her as she grabbed the iced cappuccino she had been sipping on from the center glass-topped table. Even a good coffee wasn't helping her feel any better.

"Can I have Maria bring you an iced cappuccino?"

Adriana shook her head. "I had a coffee on the way over. Who are we talking about if not Raúl?"

Gabby traced the side of her glass with her forefinger. "Ryder."

"The hottie *Americano* from the bar? Are you sure your uncle hired him?"

"No, I'm not positive, but Ryder's been looking for work. I'm only surmising Sergio offered him an option to join up."

Adriana's gaze narrowed. "Why on earth would you think that?"

"Remember the good-looking *Americano* you were dancing with the other night?"

"The tall one?" Her friend's cheeks reddened. "He gave me his number. If not for Mateo, I'd be wanting to spend a lot more time with that one."

"You won't be calling him anytime soon, Adri. He's dead."

"What?" Adriana's mouth gaped. "How?"

Gabriela inhaled, hoping to further calm her nerves. It wasn't as if she had to worry about any harm coming to her. But witnessing a murder? That was all new. Just when a man finally held her interest, it turned out he was no better than her uncle. Her hopes of finding someone outside of Raúl's circle wasn't going to happen. Neither was falling for a cold-blooded murderer.

Gabby palmed her iced coffee and informed Adriana of the string of events leading up to Ryder dumping the big guy's body into the trunk of the car. She shivered at the remembrance.

"I'm not sure what happened after I left, but I'm going to assume Ryder buried him in some backwoods or desert where he'll never be found. It wouldn't matter anyway. My uncle and his money control the *policía*. They'd turn a blind eye on anything occurring at my restaurant."

Adriana shook her head. "I don't even know what to say. This is bad ... really bad. He killed his friend? Why would he do that?"

She shrugged. "To be honest, his friend drew on Sergio first. Ryder shot him before he could shoot."

"In defense then?"

"Surely, but Sergio or any of his men could've taken him out. Why did Ryder feel the need to do it? He shot his friend in the back. That's cold, not to mention cowardly."

Gabriela glanced across the horizon. The ocean appeared calm, not much of a sea breeze coming in. The opposite of the storm brewing within. Gabby was sure there was a black cloud hanging over her head.

Adriana placed a hand on Gabby's forearm, gaining back her attention. "What would've happened if Sergio had shot and killed Gunner instead?"

Gabby thought about that and how it might've changed her feelings had Sergio shot Gunner instead. "I don't know. At least I wouldn't be thinking of Ryder as cold-blooded."

"No, Gabs." Adriana tightened her grip on Gabby's forearm before letting go. "You might have been watching Ryder's murder as well. Think about it. They arrived together. Sergio would have made sure they buried both men. That's how they work. Don't leave any witnesses. You know this.

Regardless of whether Raúl has the *policía* in his back pocket or not."

Gabby thought about it, knew Adriana was correct. Had Ryder not acted, he'd have followed Gunner to that grave. She wasn't sure if it made up for his actions or not, but it certainly lent a better understanding. She sighed, leaning her head against her hand, feeling defeated. She'd never get out from underfoot of the cartel and their dealings.

Putting her glass on the table, she stood and padded to the floor-to-ceiling windows. Her sitting room overlooked the ocean, while her bedroom afforded her a view of the spa and pool. Waves gently rolled over the sand, making her wish for the tranquility, a peace of mind. Her cell phone pinged behind her on the stand, but Gabby didn't bother looking.

She heard the rustle as Adriana, true to her nature, picked up the phone. "It's Ryder."

Adriana's bare feet pattered across the marble and pearl glass-tiled floor as she approached. She held out the cell. "Are you going to text him back?"

Gabby took the phone and stared at the display with his black typed words: We need to talk.

"I don't know. Honestly, Adri. I had hoped he was different."

"Maybe, he is. How will you know if you don't give him a chance?" Adriana gently placed her hand back on Gabby's forearm. "Let him explain, Gabs. He was in a room full of your uncle's men. If he hadn't taken Gunner's life, he'd also be dead right now. You know that. He may have killed Gunner out of defense for Sergio, but it was likely also out of self-preservation. Don't hold it against him. Not if you think he's someone worth getting to know better. Don't live with regrets."

"I swore I'd never get in a relationship with anyone like my uncle's men," she whispered. Dare she take a chance? "I don't know. On one hand, I really want to get to know Ryder. There was something about him that made me want more. On the other, if he's nothing more than a cold-blooded, hired killer? I can't do this."

"Meet with him. What's it going to hurt?"

Gabby used her thumbprint to open her cell. She clicked on the message icon and read his text again. It certainly wasn't going to hurt to hear him out. If anyone was to blame for the situation, it was Sergio. From what she had witnessed, her uncle's man had started the argument.

Which also brought up another issue: Sergio.

He wouldn't take it well if Gabby was interested in someone Sergio thought of as an outsider. He had wanted to cement his position in her uncle's home, in the La Paz kingpin's family. What if he set out to kill Ryder? Gabriela wasn't about to put him in a position that could get him killed.

Besides, what would she even say?

"You're putting way too much thought into it, querida amiga. Where are you hiding my best friend?"

Gabby couldn't help but laugh. "Right here, Adri. I'm trying to be honorable. I don't want Ryder to get hurt because of me. You know Sergio believes I belong to him. He's not going to step aside for some Americano."

"Why not let Ryder take care of himself? If what you told me is true"—she tsked—"then I'm betting he can hold his own against the *gilipollas*. Sergio is a blowhard and one day his ego will trip him up. Maybe Ryder's the man to do it. Tell him the truth, let him decide if he still wants to get involved with you. Stop trying to be everyone's savior."

Adriana was correct. Gabby had always tried to do the right thing, making up for her uncle lacking the gene. She needed to trust that Ryder could take care of himself. After all, he had already had run-ins with Sergio and had come out alive. Gabby prayed it stayed that way. Any other outcome and she'd not be able to live with herself.

Gabby typed on the screen: *Meet me*. Before she hit the arrow, she glanced at Adriana. Her smile encouraged Gabby to hit SEND.

KANE SAT IN ONE OF THE high-backed chairs circling the meeting room table at the Washington chapter clubhouse, awaiting Gunner's arrival. Kane had been in Seattle for nearly a week, following Red's ashing, and was starting to get a bit restless. He hadn't been away from his mate for this long since he and Red had headed south looking to help Anton with his undercover work, while hoping to find Joseph "Kinky" Sala's killer. Not that they had been needed. Anton had gotten the job done.

And Joseph's killer?

Raúl would be dealt with soon enough. Kane and his brother planned to personally take care of that piece of work once Ryder located him. The pleasure would be all Kane's, and a long time coming. Losing his son due to Rosalee pissing off the kingpin, had been the single worst thing to happen to him. The second had been being strapped to Rosalee as a mate following Ion's demise. Thankfully, Vlad had finally put her scheming ass to rest. Kane had shed no tears when he'd heard the news.

But Red? That bastard was one of the good ones.

It sucked seeing his old friend going up in flames. According to his men, it had been a freak accident. His motorcycle had blown a tire. And at the rate of speed he was traveling, when he hit the cable median barrier on the side of the road, it had taken his head clean off.

He and Red might not have started off on the best of terms, back when he was the president of the Sons' Oregon chapter and Red's chapter was the Knights. He now looked back fondly at how the robust man had stood up to him.

In the end, Kane had allowed Red and his boys to run guns through their state, while the Sons profited quite nicely from the deal. His twin hadn't been quite so onboard and promptly cut off Red's route when he had taken over the reins as President of the Sons.

There were times Kane missed being the decision maker. He wouldn't mind stepping back into those shoes someday. But plain and simple, he had broken rules when he and Cara had gotten together. Rules were put in place for a reason and breaking them wasn't an option. Given the choice, he'd do it again. His mate had been the best damn thing to happen to him. And lately, he had been thinking about adding to that union, though he had yet to broach the subject with Cara.

He had watched his mate around the other infants. It was no secret she loved babies. When he returned home, he was going to talk to her about having a brood of their own. If she worried about her job and taking care of the baby, Kane had no problem stepping up to the plate and helping out.

Alexander and India were about to add to the growing number of baby boys within the club, while Kaleb and Suzi might be heading for baby two. At this rate, they were going to have to add on a daycare to K&K Motorcycles, Kane thought with a chuckle.

The door to the meeting room opened, ceasing his baby musings. It was time to get to business. Gunner Anderson sauntered in, followed by the club secretary, Adrian "Smoke" Wellman. Kane stood and greeted both with a shake of their hands. Gunner and Adrian took their seats. Red's seat would remain unoccupied until Gunner was voted in as president by the club. The Sons of Oregon had already given their blessing, following Gunner's stint down in La Paz. After all, he had taken a bullet for them, literally.

"Glad to see you back in one piece, Gunner." Kane poured them each two-fingers of the Gentleman Jack he had purchased for the occasion and slid the tumblers across the table. "*Salute.*"

The men clinked glasses then each downed the whiskey. Kane refilled their glasses then set the bottle on the table.

"How was your trip back north?"

"Could have been better, Viper. Hot as hell, for one thing." Gunner chuckled. "I healed pretty quickly, but I still felt the discomfort most of the ride back. By the time I hit Washington, the pain was gone."

"Thanks for taking one for the team," Kane said. "You have the Sons of Oregon's backing to become chapter president. We appreciate you helping Ryder."

"Yeah, well I can't say it was my pleasure. But I'd do it again for the MC." Gunner used his thumb to indicate the man to his left. "I brought along Smoke today. I'm going to present it to the boys that we vote him in as VP. I was hoping to get the Oregon brothers' blessing on this as well."

"I'll vouch for Smoke." Kane nodded. "I'll let Hawk know. I'm sure you'll have both our blessings. Look, this club is now yours, Gunner. You make the changes as you see fit. You and Smoke send Hawk your proposals. You on board with being VP, Smoke?"

Before joining the MC and becoming a vampire, the man got his moniker from his past stint as a fireman, having left his career some time ago. He had almost died on the job from inhaling too many toxic fumes when his mask and regulator were knocked from his head by a fallen beam. By the time his senses had come back from being knocked silly, he had inhaled a good deal of smoke.

"Completely." Adrian took a drink from his highball glass, then set it on the table. "Not like I have anywhere else to be. I've also been putting some time into helping build the new K&K Motorcycle shop. Looking forward to learning the ropes and building some kick-ass custom bikes."

"We're definitely looking forward to that as well, and the added revenue," said Kane. "We have more orders than we can handle in Oregon. So the sooner the shop is up and running, the better. With training, we should be able to accommodate enough jobs for all of the men in your chapter."

"How long you here for?" Adrian asked.

"I plan on heading back tomorrow at the latest. I'd like to call a church meeting and get the hierarchy set up before heading back." Kane looked at Gunner. "You get that shit set up, call me, and I'll take it to Hawk for his approval, then I'll be back for the final vote. You think you can get that taken care of by tomorrow?"

"Sure." Gunner rubbed his thumb over the smooth surface of the tumbler. "I'll give you a call once we're ready for a vote."

"Sounds great." Kane smiled. "I'll be anxious to get back to work at K&K myself. I've been away far too long as it is."

"Not to mention getting back to your mate." Gunner laughed. "No thank you to that."

"Laugh, smart ass." Kane shared in his humor. "You'll meet someone one of these days, and I'll be back to tell you I told you so."

"You old guys can have your mates." Gunner winked. "Me and Smoke? We'll stick to variety."

Kane stood, shaking his head with a chuckle. "I'll remind you of that when you come looking to us for permission to mate."

Gunner stood. "Whatever, man. Ain't a woman out there that could convince me into fidelity yet. I got a lot of years ahead of me to play the field."

"I hear you. It wasn't that long ago I was of the same mind." Kane shook Gunner's hand, then reached for Adrian's as the other man rose. "Sorry about Red."

Gunner's gaze softened. "A damn shame is what it is. Red knew his way around a motorcycle, man. Hard to believe he was taken out by a fucking tire."

"He was a good man." Kane couldn't help but agree. Surely, Red kept an eye on the condition of his treads. But sometimes, freak accidents happened. "See you boys tomorrow."

CHAPTER ELEVEN

GABBY HAD JUST BROKEN HER UNCLE'S RULES BY GIVING Ryder directions to his house. Well, technically, it was her home, too, and she was allowed guests ... just those Raúl pre-approved. Gabby figured she'd sneak Ryder into her suite without her uncle being the wiser. If they were found out, she would say she thought Ryder worked for Raúl. His soldiers were already authorized to be on the property.

Her cell pinged, alerting her to a text message. Gabby jogged to the accent table between the chairs facing the ocean and picked up the phone, reading the text: *I'm at the gate*.

She nearly skipped to the panel on the wall and punched a few buttons on the number keypad, allowing him access to the grounds. Her stomach fluttered, and her pulse pounded in her ears. No matter what she had witnessed, or the very real possibility he now worked for her uncle, her body's betrayal spoke of her infatuation. It didn't help her mouth practically salivated at the sight of his well-toned body. Damn her traitorous hide.

Besides the few texts they had sent each other, they had yet to discuss what had gone down in her restaurant. She had watched him shoot a man in cold blood and toss him into his trunk, for crying out loud. A shiver passed down her spine.

Gabby needed an explanation for why he had gone to Sergio's defense. Adriana's reasoning came back to the forefront of her mind.

"You might have been watching Ryder's murder as well."

Gabby sucked in a deep breath, hoping to calm her nerves. Even knowing Adriana was correct didn't make it a pill easier to swallow. Her reason for not dating anyone who worked for her uncle was solid. The men were ruthless killers. And rightly so. Her uncle wasn't in the business to make friends. She despised what he did for a living. Sure, she benefited from his riches, wanted for nothing, but that didn't mean she had to like where it came from.

Living on my own?

Wasn't going to happen. If her uncle didn't have so many enemies, who would jump at the chance to get to him through her, she would've moved out long ago. Gabby was in a no-win situation, which made finding a love connection damn near impossible.

After walking to the French double-doors facing the pool, she watched Ryder pull his motorcycle to one of the twin stairs leading to her balcony, and parked it to the right of the railing, concealing it from a direct line of view. She hoped her uncle was taking his normal midday siesta, keeping him from hearing the soft rumble of the motor, the exact reason she had picked this particular time of day.

Not wanting to appear too anxious, she waited for Ryder to ascend the semi-circular, red-tiled stairs before she opened the double doors and met him on the veranda. The cool breeze thankfully kissed her heated skin.

Ryder's gaze raked over her, not helping the blush she had hoped to ward off. "Gorgeous as always."

"Charming as ever." Gabby raised one brow before offering him one of the patio chairs, leaving the doors to her suite open. She wasn't ready to invite him inside. "Can I get you something to drink? Water? A beer? Tequila?"

He shook his head, continuing to stand and cocking one hip against the cement railing. "I'm good. But please, help yourself if you're thirsty. It's quite warm out here."

Gabby pivoted on her heel and entered the cooler exterior of her sitting room, opened her beverage refrigerator, and withdrew a bottle of water. She returned to the patio and sat in one of the chairs. After unscrewing the cap to the bottle, she took a cool swig to hopefully help her frayed nerves, then set the bottle on the glass-topped table next to her.

"Thanks for letting the goons at the gate know I was coming. They didn't look too inviting."

She smiled, looking up at him. His eyes were the color of whiskey and just as warm. Gabby swore she could almost see his soul. Regardless of what she had witnessed, she knew Ryder was a good man, could see as much in his eyes.

"I had to. Otherwise, you wouldn't have gotten past the gate I opened."

Ryder crossed his arms over his chest, his lips tipping down. "We can pleasant-talk all day and avoid the elephant in the room, but I'd much rather get it out in the open."

Gabby took another drink from her water bottle. While she didn't approve of his actions, she wasn't quite ready for him to walk away from her either.

"It is warm out here." She fanned herself with her hand. "How was your ride over?"

"The ride was fine." He chuckled, obviously aware of her dancing around the real topic. "Would you prefer to go inside?"

She shook her head. Taking him inside might have the guards alerting her uncle. "It's better if we talk here."

Ryder gazed around the grounds before returning to her. "I'm sure there are at least a half-dozen men with me in their sights. If it makes you feel more comfortable, then we can say what needs to be said out here. Is he here?"

"Who? Uncle Raúl?"

"Yes." Ryder raised a brow. "I'd like to know what I'm walking into, Gabby. You invited me, remember? I don't like being blindsided."

"He's here, but as I recall, *you* wanted to talk. *You* texted me."

"I did." He sighed, shifting his stance. "Yet here we stand pussyfooting around the exact topic that needs to be discussed."

"We're talking."

Lord, the man made her more nervous than a pig in a bacon factory. Part of her wanted to run for her sanctuary and shut him out. The other part wanted to drag him in and jump his bones. That part ... had some really good arguments.

Ryder leaned forward, obviously detecting her indecision, his lips scant inches from hers. Gabby couldn't help but hold his heated stare. She licked her lips. *Well, just in case he decided to close the gap*.

"We're skirting the issue, sweetheart. I think you should know that I detest small talk. I shot a man. You saw me do it."

Heat sizzled through her, causing her to cross her legs. Gabby couldn't help it, his nearness had her libido going off the charts. "Why did you do it?"

"Gunner was a fool." Ryder stood up straight, much to her disappointment and started pacing the red-tiled decking. "The dumb-fuck was going to get us both killed. You of all people should have seen that coming when he opened his big mouth. Had I not killed the man, I would've been right next to him in that grave. You think I'm fucking happy about that?"

"So, you took the coward's way?" That wasn't fair of her and she knew it, but he responded before she could rescind.

Ryder stopped pacing and glared at her. Gone was the warmth. *Shit*. Not how she had wanted this to go.

"Whatever you want to call it, sweetheart, I prefer to think of it as self-preservation."

"I'm sorry." Gabby grimaced. "That was mean-spirited."

"Look, I get it."

"That's where you're wrong, Ryder." Anger itched up her spine. No one could pretend to understand what it was like to grow up in the kingpin's household. "I grew up here. I saw bad men daily. I have an uncle I love, and yet hate at the same time. He took me in, gave me a home after my own father was killed. Do you have any idea how his death scarred me as a child? Regardless of what my father did, I loved him. He was my world. He shielded me from the violence ... that is, until he was murdered. Then my whole world changed."

Ryder's gaze softened, but he said nothing. He stood but a foot from her.

"My best friend moved on as soon as she could get out from under this life. I hated Brea Gotti for a while for cutting ties and leaving me behind. But what really upset me was the fact she was able to move on and leave behind the bloodshed and crime. I didn't have that luxury. I'm stuck here, Ryder. Like it or not."

"No one is stuck, sweetheart. Least of all you. The amount of money you have could take you anywhere in the world. Most people here in Mexico? They can barely afford food on their table, let alone fly to other countries of their choosing. You can't play the sympathy card. Not with me."

Gabby stood and shoved Ryder back a few feet. He stumbled, his backside hitting the railing.

"Go to hell, asshole." Gabby's neck and face heated. "You were the one who wanted to talk. I was the one who wanted to forget the day I laid eyes on you. Go back to Salazar's, kiss Luis's and Sergio's feet. Do my uncle's dirty work. Just know, that also means you don't ever get to touch me. Now, please leave before I have you removed from the grounds.

That won't look very good for you if you did take a job with my uncle's men."

Without bothering to see him gone, Gabby pivoted and marched into the cooler interior of her suite, pulling the doors shut behind her. When they swung back open, the thought crossed her mind that maybe she should have locked them, too.

FORGET THE DAY SHE laid eyes on me?

If it were only so fucking easy. He should've walked away, should have crawled onto the back of his bike and hightailed it out of there. Christ, at the least, he should've called Grigore and let him know Raúl was somewhere in the fortress.

Technically, his job was done. Locate Raúl and get out. Instead, he opened the doors she had used to shut him out and entered her space ... uninvited. Ryder didn't make a habit of going where he wasn't wanted. And surely not when it came to women. He didn't need to, not when there were enough willing to share his bed or let him sink his fangs into a carotid.

I need my fucking head examined.

This woman infuriated him, and at the same time, consumed his every thought. He wanted her beneath him to the point of madness, the erection in his pants evidence of that desire. His vampire DNA slowly simmered like electricity sizzling through his veins.

Ryder had fed a couple of nights prior, but it might've helped his cause had he fed before making the trek out here.

Not only was his dick demanding appeasement, the scent of her blood called to his very nature.

Yep, I'm fucked.

His eyes heated, knowing full well they were about to become black, fathomless pools. Hypnosis was his only option. There was no stopping the emerging vampire. The sharp points of his fangs scraped the inside of his lips as they filled his mouth. When the twins informed him he was not just a vampire, but a primordial one, they forgot to mention he felt things all the more acutely as such ... which included his sexual cravings. This shit needed a fucking manual like Vampires for Dummies.

Ryder's nostrils flared, scenting Gabriela's mutual desire. She could spout a hundred different reasons for hating him, but he affected her in a more primal way. If he gathered the skirt she wore and slipped his fingers beneath her panties he'd bet she was already wet.

Her stern lips drooped, her mouth now gaping. No way to hide the fucking changes to his face. Gabby's eye rounded and she gasped. Quickly grabbing her by the biceps, he backed her against the wall before she had time to scream and covered her mouth with his free hand. Her eyes filled with fear as they held his. He'd need to hypnotize her fast, before she alerted the entire staff, not to mention Raúl.

Ryder had been damn lucky upon arrival. Whatever they'd used to build the house, he couldn't detect the scent of Raúl on the grounds, which meant the man couldn't discern him either.

"Hear me now." He framed her face between his palms, giving her little choice but to hold his marble-like gaze. "You will not remember everything you see. You'll feel me, know me, but my face will remain a mystery. You won't comprehend the changes you see in me. Nod if you understand what I'm saying."

Gabby slowly nodded, her pink tongue wetting her plush lower lip. His gaze held fixed on hers. As much as he wanted to, kissing her was a really bad idea, considering her current state of fury.

Her anger returned in full force once her confusion diminished and the hypnosis took root. She shoved at his chest. Had Ryder not allowed it, she wouldn't have been able to budge him. He stepped back. She continued to strike him with her hands. Gabby had a lot of anger and passion needing to be burned. He had been the one to invade her space, so he supposed he deserved her animosity.

"Get out of my room ... and get the hell out of my life. You aren't wanted."

"Are you sure about that?" Ryder grinned. His nostrils flared again. "I have a feeling if I reach beneath your skirt, I'll find you wet and a liar."

Gabby slapped him hard across the cheek. Ryder didn't so much as flinch. The vampire in him wanted to toss her on the bed and prove to her the truth in his statement. The man in him knew he deserved her fury. He had been out of line.

"You don't get to talk to me that way."

Ryder took two steps in her direction. She took one back. "And you don't get to be a tease."

Her perfectly plucked brows drew inward. "What? When did I ever tease you? I've only been upfront with you since we met."

"Sweetheart, I can scent your desire and it has me hard enough to drive through these concrete walls."

Ryder almost laughed as she turned up her nose, trying to detect what the hell he was talking about. He took another step forward, backing her against the wall again. He gripped her hand and placed it over the erection straining the front of his jeans.

"You can't play with fire if you don't want to get fucking burnt, Gabriela."

"I never ... that is, I ... oh, hell," she whispered, slowly withdrawing her hand and holding it to her chest as if it had been singed.

Some of the anger left her eyes. Her breathing became shallow. Her pulse hammered at the base of her throat, drawing his gaze and calling to his fangs. It would be so easy to dip his head and take his fill. He nearly salivated at the idea of tasting her on his tongue.

"You do want me, Gabby." It wasn't a question. He already knew the answer.

She shook her head. "No."

Ryder smiled. Sinister, but a smile nonetheless. "Yes."

She placed her hands on his chest, searing his flesh as if she touched his skin rather than the shirt he wore. She drew her lower lip between her teeth and shook her head with a little less force.

Ryder leaned in, his nose nearly touching hers. "Yes," he whispered.

He should walk away before it was too fucking late. He was losing control. What started out as a way to prove a point was turning the tides against him. He wanted to pull up her skirt, rip off her panties, and bury himself to the hilt. She wouldn't fight him, of that he was sure. Ryder needed to be the one to walk away, to put distance between them before she hated him forever. For once she discovered he had used her to find Raúl, she'd never forgive him and he wouldn't blame her.

When he meant to step back and increase the distance between them, Gabby stood on her tiptoes and kissed him, stopping him in his tracks and numbing his thoughts. Good Lord! All admirable intentions flew right out those double doors he had left open for his speedy retreat. The warm breeze caressed his back, not doing a damn thing to cool his ardor. Even a primordial vampire had only so much constraint. He needed to get the hell out of there before things spiraled out of control.

Sure, they were grown-ass adults and could do as they pleased, including respecting each other in the aftermath. Something told him, though, Gabby would quickly regret her brass actions. He had to be the bigger person. Rather than deepen the kiss, he released her, wiping a hand across his lips. Shit, she tasted like a slice of Heaven.

"Gabby, I—"

"Look, I don't know what just came over me. I'm sorry…" She placed her hands on her hips and glanced at the floor. She took a deep breath, then looked back up. "You know what? I'm not sorry I kissed you. What I am sorry about is you joining up with my uncle's men and being a disappointment to me."

He could still detect her desire, and as long as he continued to note it, the vampire in him would war within. He wanted to do the right thing, walk away and call Grigore. Not take advantage of the situation. That guy was quickly losing out because his befuddled brain could think only about the hard-on straining the front of his jeans and wanting to take her against the fucking wall.

"I'm sorry I'm a disappointment to you." And he was. In the end, he'd be an even bigger disappointment to himself. "Maybe, I should go. You'll never understand—"

"I'm angry with you. Hell, I'm pissed at myself for still wanting you. But understand?" She advanced a few steps, closing the gap between them. "More than you know. I live this life every damn day. I can't walk away, even if I want to. I guess I had hoped … needed you to be different."

Ryder couldn't help it. The dirty part of his mind had focused on one thing. "You want me?"

Gabby nodded, her tongue wetting her lips.

Ryder snaked his hands around her back lightning quick, holding her flush, and crushed his mouth to hers.

CHAPTER TWELVE

INSANITY. THAT'S EXACTLY WHAT KEPT HIS ARMS WRAPPED around Gabby and his mouth fused to hers. It didn't take much to deepen the kiss. Once she moaned, he took the invitation. His fangs grazed her flesh, nicking the soft pad of her tongue. He tasted the smallest amount of her blood ... mind-blowing. Ryder didn't think he had ever savored anything so exquisite, like the finest ambrosia. It was nothing short of sheer willpower that kept him from moving to her neck and sinking his fangs gum-deep.

Christ, if he thought Gabby was pissed at him before, she'd not only be livid with him but furious at herself for allowing things to go this far once passion no longer factored in. Ryder needed to be the bigger person. Hell, he *was* the bigger person, by weight and the strength of many men. And yet, this little slip of a woman made him weaker than any woman had in his past. One taste of her blood and he no longer had the power to step away. The vampire in him growled, roared to life, and damn if it didn't want to be gratified.

If they were going to go no further, then she'd have to be the one to put a stop to it. Ryder backed her against the wall. Using his hand, he gathered her flowing skirt, bunched it to her hip, and slipped his fingers beneath her thong. Fuck, she was smooth as silk. His fingers slid between her folds, finding proof she had wanted him.

Gabby broke the kiss. Ryder waited for her to tell him to get the hell out, rail at him for taking such liberties. Instead, she tilted her head to the ceiling, baring her neck and moaned.

Fuck!

His fangs ached with demand. He could always partake, then mesmerize her into forgetting, except Ryder had fed two nights prior. Drinking from her wouldn't be about sustenance. It would be for pure pleasure. He'd not violate her trust by taking something she didn't freely offer. She may not recognize his vampire traits now that she was hypnotized to disregard them, but Gabby was well aware of what they were doing and had the will to say no at any time. He wasn't about to cross that line and obtain from her what he'd later have to scrub from her memory.

He dipped his head, his nose scenting the very blood he had tasted running through her veins. After licking a path from the hollow of her throat to the soft flesh of her ear, he nicked the small lobe, savoring her essence again as he drew it between his lips and suckled. Damn, but he could easily become addicted to the delicacy.

Pure torture.

Another moan escaped her lips. He slid a forefinger into her, slowly gliding along her inner velvety flesh. Her thighs quivered against his hand. His breath hitched; his balls ached. The phrase "Minute Man" came to mind as he feared having no more discipline than a schoolboy with his first peek at a great set of tits. And damn if she didn't have a beautiful set.

For what he had in physical strength, his self-control could use a little work. Ryder's need for a release increased, making his options limited to fucking her and suffering the consequences or using his own damn hand. Either would get the job done, but the former held more appeal. Stopping? Yeah, that was no longer an option.

Using his thumb, he traced the tight bundle of nerves between her legs, added just enough pressure to her clit to make her breath catch. Gabby arched her hips, pressing against his palm.

"Oh ... Ryder ... I—"

Withdrawing his fingers, he said, "Not yet, Gabby. When I make you come, I want you wrapped around my cock. Before we go further, though, I need to know you're okay with this."

The scent of her desire wasn't enough. Her vocal confirmation was a necessity. And although he wanted her to affirm she wanted this, Ryder needed her to tell him to get the hell out for the good of his mission. Kaleb was going to have his head and rightfully so. If Raúl left the house before any of the Sons arrived, losing the kingpin's whereabouts would be on Ryder. His number one priority was the mission, not getting under Gabby's skirt. He'd be damned, though, if he could do what was right in his present state of hard-as-fuck.

Her tongue wet her lips.

"What's it going to be, *ángel*?" And she was. She was his angel.

Gabby placed a palm against his whiskered cheek. "I should throw you out on your ass, you know."

He wasn't about to argue. He chuckled. "You should."

"But it's been so damn long."

"How long?"

"A couple of years."

Ryder blew out a stream of air. "Then you deserve better than me."

"You joined up with my uncle's men?"

"Yes."

"Then you're correct. I do deserve better, but it doesn't stop me from wanting you."

Gabby gathered his T-shirt in her hands, pushing it over his abs and up his chest. Ryder gripped it between his shoulder blades and pulled it over his head, tossing it to the chair.

"What will it be, *ángel*? Yes or no?"

Her smile warmed his soul. He could easily lose himself. "I thought I made myself clear."

Gabby's gaze went to the scar on his left pec, following it up to his shoulder. She raised her hand, trailing her fingers over the disfigured flesh, heating a path in their wake.

Ryder placed a hand over hers, stopping her exploration. "It's ugly."

She lifted her brown eyes. "On the contrary. I find the scar *hermoso*."

"Now you humor me. There is nothing beautiful in disfigurement."

"Then you have no idea what it represents."

Ryder shook off her touch, wondering why the hell they were talking at all. "What is that, *ángel*?"

"*Amor.* That you loved someone so deeply you were willing to die to save her."

He had loved her, more than life itself. Not to mention his baby she carried, who had died with her. "It was a long time ago."

Gabby placed a kiss on his left pec. Ryder hissed. The simple act added gasoline to the fire that already burned, touching his cold, dead heart. He had no business inserting feelings into an already dire situation. They'd both walk away from this emotionally scarred, worse than the physical one marring his shoulder. Instead, he ignored the latter, drowning it out in the desire pulsing through him.

"What's your answer, *ángel*?"

"Please."

Not exactly a "yes," but an affirmation just the same. Ryder backed her against the wall again. He didn't need to be told twice. His cock strained painfully against the zipper of his jeans. Fuck, he needed to be inside her. He wouldn't last long.

Ryder fumbled with her flowy skirt, bunching it at her waist, then ripped her thong from her as if it were no more than a mere thread. Before she could reach for the button on his jeans, Ryder crouched, placing a palm on one cheek of her ass and drew her forward. He used his free hand to spread her thighs, baring her to him.

He leaned in, softly blowing on the folds before slipping two fingers inside. Using the pad of his tongue, he licked a path from her center forward before circling the tiny clit. Damn, but nothing had ever tasted so sweet. He could go on forever, not seeking anything in return. All that he cared about was giving her pleasure, a pleasure she was no doubt missing from her life.

A couple of years.

Lord, who the hell could go so long without being physically touched? Without life's simple pleasures? Gabby was about to end her dry spell and he was only too happy to be the one to lay it to rest.

Her hips arched off the wall; her legs trembled. Her breath shook from her chest and her sheath tightened around his fingers. She was close to reaching her release, but he'd be damned if he'd allow it just yet. Ryder not only wanted to draw out her pleasure, but he wanted to feel her from the inside while her body contracted around him. Only then would he allow his own release.

Ryder stood, earning him a few curse words from her lips, causing him to chuckle again. "We're far from done, *ángel*."

He flipped open the button on his jeans and gently slid down the taut zipper. Gabby hastily pushed the denim over his hips. His cock sprung free, with him having gone commando. Ryder hissed as she fisted his erection. If she did much more the already strained leash he had on his control would snap like a fucking twig.

"Condom?" she whispered.

Not that he needed them as a vampire. He couldn't get a human pregnant, nor get a disease. Ryder had used them in the past to put his non-donor partners at ease. Donors already knew the score.

"I'm sorry. I'm at a fucking loss. I didn't come here with the intention of fucking you."

Gabby drew her lower lip between her teeth. "I've been on the pill for a few years even though I haven't slept with anyone."

"I'm clean, Gabby. I never go without condoms."

He was just about to concede and get her off, his blue balls be damned, when she nodded. It was all the permission he needed. Gripping her waist, he easily lifted her from the floor, one hand anchoring her delectable backside. Her legs wrapped his waist, ankles crossing at the small of his back while her heels dug into his ass. Ryder's erection lay trapped between them as he braced her against the wall. He used his free hand to guide his penis along her folds, wetting the tip, then slowly pushing inward, giving her time to accommodate his large size.

Her gasp echoed throughout the empty room. Her breath hitched and her head lulled back against the cement wall. Fuck, she was tight. No way in hell was he going to last long, but he'd be damned if he allowed himself a release before giving one to her. He moved slowly at first, not wanting to hurt her since it had been so long for her. Gabby's back rode the wall with each of his thrusts. Her fingers dug into the flesh of his shoulders.

"*Ángel*, look at me."

Doing as she was told, her warm brown eyes nearly swallowed him whole. Fuck, he had it bad, making him go against his own code of honor. His better judgment had told him what he was doing was all sorts of wrong. And yet, he didn't care. He paid mind only to the woman in his arms, watching her come apart in pleasure. Knowing he was the one she chose after two years of abstinence was a heady thought.

Instead of standing there fucking her, he should've been having a chat with Grigore. A definite buzz-kill. This was far more preferable, regardless of it being wrong on so many accounts.

Her breath hitched, bringing his focus back to the gorgeous woman in his arms. Her pupils dilated and her mouth rounded. Ryder increased his rhythm, slamming into her, no longer able to hold back. Gabby cried out, her fingernails biting into his shoulders. Her walls contracted around his cock, pushing him toward his release.

"Ryder," she whispered as her head tilted forward. She rested her forehead in the crook of his neck. Her breath fanned over his flesh.

Her actions were enough to send him over the edge. His ass muscles tightened as he thrust a final time, spilling his release into her. *Fuck!* They had certainly complicated matters. He thought of the mission again as the euphoria of desire crashed down and reality sank back in.

Once Gabby found out about him bringing the Sons of Sangue to her uncle's doorstep, she would never forgive him. He was a fucking snake in the grass and rightfully deserved her disgust.

Christ! Forgiveness would be hard-won, if at all.

And Ryder couldn't say he blamed her ... not one fucking bit.

GABRIELA SMOOTHED DOWN her skirt the minute her feet touched the floor, the soft material swishing about her ankles. Tugging at the hem of her form-fitting top, she pulled it back into place. She had no words. Her breath sawed out of her as if she had run a marathon. Dear Lord! She certainly couldn't say she regretted it, not when Ryder had given her an award-winning orgasm. One she certainly wouldn't mind repeating.

Finished righting herself, she glanced at Ryder who pulled his T-shirt over his head and covered his mouth-watering abs. His longish curls were pleasantly mussed. Gabby wouldn't mind running her fingers through the strands, but she had a feeling it might start another round of awesome sex. Not that that would be a bad thing.

A sly grin curved Ryder's very kissable lips. "What?"

Heat rose up Gabriela's neck, surely reddening her cheeks. She tipped her chin toward the floor. "I'm sorry, staring was rude."

Ryder laughed as he closed the distance, his booted feet echoing across the marble and pearl-glass tiles. He didn't quite fit the room in his vintage concert shirt and worn jeans. Her uncle had designed the room for a princess. She'd bet had he found Ryder there, he wouldn't think the biker was ever good enough for his niece.

And yet, Ryder was exactly her type, what she wanted in a man. Right down to his worn, brown leather boots. Gabby hoped to ride on the back of his motorcycle one day. A shiver ran down her spine at the thought of the open road and clinging to him like a second skin. The man was all sorts of *delicioso* and then some. Her girly bits already craved round two.

Using the pads of his fingertips on her chin, he brought her gaze up to meet his whiskey-colored one. "*Ángel*, feel free to look all you want. I'm flattered you'd even want to. Does this mean you're no longer pissed?"

"I'm not thrilled that you joined my uncle's camp, or the fact you killed a man, even if it was out of self-preservation." Gabby stepped back from his touch and walked to the open French doors, giving him her back. "You have to understand, Ryder. I've lived my whole life disapproving of my uncle and his men. I can't go anywhere without the ugliness of his chosen profession touching me in some way. I guess I had hoped you'd be different. I wanted you to be."

Ryder gripped her shoulders and turned her. "I am different, Gabby. You'll have to trust me on that. I have to go now, but promise me we'll talk later."

"Even if my better judgment says to walk away, I can't. Not now, not after what we did."

His smile returned, this one cocksure. "You liked it, huh?"

Gabby chuckled. "Maybe just a little."

"A little? Well, that sounds like a challenge if I ever heard one. I can certainly fix that."

Ryder's jaw hardened. He tilted his nose toward the ceiling, his nostrils flaring. Gabby followed suit but didn't detect any scent out of the ordinary.

"Fuck." Ryder moved her further into the room, then returned to the exit and began to shut the double doors. "I have to run before it's too late. I'll text you."

Gabby couldn't formulate a proper sentence prior to his taking the steps two at a time down to the grounds, so she said nothing. He stepped over his motorcycle seat, started the engine, and sped off down the driveway. His helmet stayed strapped to the back seat. Ryder had been in such a hurry to leave, he hadn't bothered with his own safety. She couldn't help but wonder what had spooked him.

A knock sounded on the door, causing her to jump. She turned and looked at the heavy wood, wondering who was calling now. When she didn't answer it straight away, the knock turned into incessant pounding.

"I'm coming," she grumbled, angry with the sudden interruption.

"Gabriela! Open this door immediately or I swear I'll pull it from its hinges," Raúl growled.

Gabby was unsure what had her uncle so fired up, but she wasn't about to test him. She jogged to the door, flipped the lock, and opened it. Raúl's eyes were damn near black in his rage. What the hell?

"Uncle Raúl?"

"Where the fuck is he?"

Her brow furrowed. How had he known? Had the guards tipped him off? If that were the case, he certainly would have come long before now. "Who?"

"Don't play coy with me, Gabriela." Her uncle tilted his nose upward, just as Ryder had done before he sprinted down the cement steps as if the hounds of hell were nipping at his heels. "The man who was in here."

"It's really none of your business, Uncle." Her own temperament hit a high note. How dare he tell her who she could entertain? "You forget, I'm an adult."

"Who were you just fucking, Gabriela? I can smell the bastard. You know I'll find out. I have eyes everywhere."

Her gaze traveled the room. He wouldn't have dared put cameras in her room. How had Raúl found out what they had been up to? Ryder wasn't the first man she had brought home, despite the infrequency of it. Her uncle had never seemed to care before.

"Relax, *princess*." He hissed the term of endearment. "There are no cameras in your private quarters, but don't tempt me to add them. Out there, though, I have men and cameras on every entrance, yours included. All I need do is ask. So tell me, who was here fucking you like a common *puta*?"

Gabby gritted her teeth. Her uncle had gone too far. "How dare you?"

"I dare because I own you." His hand indicated the room. "I own all of this."

Raúl struck her so hard across the cheek, he knocked Gabby to the marble flooring. Stars floated in her vision as she lay at his feet, fearing she might just pass out from the pain. Touching her cheek, she could feel the swelling, praying he hadn't broken anything. As it was, she'd be sporting a large bruise. Tears sprung to her eyes. She had never been struck by her uncle before. He had been angry yes, but never to the point he hit her.

"Tell me his name, or I swear to the bowels of Hades, I'll have my men hunt him down and slaughter him like a rutting animal."

Gabby glared at him. "You touch one hair on Ryder's head and I promise you'll never see me again. You may *think* you own me, but you don't. I will see whomever I please."

Raúl's jaw tightened as he looked at her. He didn't bother to help her off the floor, nor show remorse for striking her. "This Ryder, the new guy Luis and Sergio hired, you better hope he doesn't fuck up. If he even gives me reason to not trust his motives, I'll fucking kill him myself. You don't know what you're dabbling in, little princess. There may be more to Ryder than he's allowed you to know."

"Leave him alone, Uncle."

"Ryder and I? We'll have a talk. I promise I won't harm him ... yet. But we'll have a long conversation, you can count on that."

Raúl turned and quit the room, his back rigid. The tears she held at bay now slipped down her cheek. What had she done? If her uncle hurt Ryder because of her, she'd never forgive herself.

Gabby stood and retrieved her phone. She typed a quick message, then hit SEND.

Raúl knows. Be careful.

CHAPTER THIRTEEN

THE CELL VIBRATED IN THE FRONT POCKET OF HIS JEANS AS he walked through the door of his rental. Likely Grigore, since Ryder had texted him upon leaving Raúl's fortress. Holy smokes, there had to have been at least eight or nine thousand square feet of Raúl's estate. Touring the place? Yeah, that wasn't about to happen, but judging by the size and appearance of Gabby's suite alone, he'd bet the rest of the house was just as impressive, if not more so.

Fuck, he couldn't believe he'd allowed himself to get caught on the premises. The kingpin may not have known who was there, but he'd be well aware another vampire had been in the room with Gabby. Although Ryder's primordial sense of smell would be superior to Raúl's, there was no doubt the bastard had detected him through the heavy oak doors.

Plain and simple, Ryder had fucked up and had allowed his dick to do his thinking. Not that he regretted what had happened between them. Hell, no. Given the chance, he'd want to fuck her again, taking his time to do a more thorough job. Ryder had treated her no better than a whore, taking her up against the wall when she was so much better.

Hell, she consumed his thoughts, had him acting out of character and doing things like compromising the mission when in a million years he wouldn't have ever thought he'd let his brothers down ... not for a piece of ass. And yet, Gabriela meant more than that, had endeared herself to him in the short time he had gotten to know her.

I need my fucking head examined.

Turning over the phone, he pressed the HOME button at the bottom of the screen, figuring it was likely the big, wolf-like man telling him he was running late. Grigore seemed to always be about three steps behind the ball.

Before he had a chance to actually see the message, Grigore walked through the door. Right on time. Then who the hell had texted? Glancing back at the cell, the words: *Raúl knows. Be careful,* glared back at him. What a stupid son of a bitch he had been. Not only would Raúl know a vampire had been in her suite, he'd know that vampire had fucked his niece as well. The scent of their mingling desire would be stamped all over the room.

"Motherfucker," Ryder hissed.

"And hello to you as well." Grigore's concerned gaze dropped to the cell Ryder held. "Bad news, I take it."

Scratching the back of his neck, Ryder blew out a steady stream of air. "You want the good first or the bad?"

The big man crossed the scarred flooring and dropped into a kitchen chair. It groaned and creaked from the added weight. He crossed a booted ankle over one knee. "Regardless of the good news, judging by your reaction, I'm betting the bad far outweighs it. Care to tell me what's going on?"

"I found Raúl."

"Halle—fucking—lujah." Grigore's smile split his beard. "So what could possibly put a damper on that news?"

Ryder grimaced. This was not going to go well. "I fucked his niece and I'm pretty sure he knows it."

Grigore sobered, his booted foot hitting the ground as he sat up straighter. One of his heavy fists struck the table, bouncing the legs off the floor. "I don't recall that being part of the mission. What the hell, Ryder? You're a damn primordial and you couldn't keep your dick in your pants? At what point were you aware Raúl was on the premises?"

Ryder ran a hand through his hair and started pacing the small space. What was it about Gabby that had him compromising his principles? "When I first got there. Gabby ... Gabriela invited me to her uncle's massive estate. I jumped at the opportunity. She informed me straightaway that Raúl was in residence."

The larger man shook his head, censure lacing his deep brown eyes. "And yet you stayed and fucked her instead of coming to me with the news? Fuck, Ryder! I don't know ... maybe you could have *called*."

"It wasn't that easy, man."

"The fuck it wasn't." He used finger quotes to drive home his point. "'Oh, Gabby, sweetheart, I forgot I was supposed to be meeting with someone ... oh, I don't know ... but I have to go. We'll get together and fuck at a better time.' You were being a self-centered son of a bitch, Ryder."

"Tell me something I don't know."

"You think Raúl hightailed it out of there already?"

He shrugged. "I'll text Gabby back, feel her out. See where the hell that asswipe is."

"You do that. I have to piss anyway."

Grigore stood and headed for the lone restroom. Ryder supposed he deserved the ass-chewing he just got and more. The "and more" would come from Kaleb once he found out Ryder had fucked up. Pushing the HOME button again, he opened his messages and began typing to Gabby.

Ryder: *You alright?*
Gabby: *I've been better.*
Ryder: *Did he hurt you?*

There was a long pause before she answered back: *I'm okay.*

Ryder: *Where is he now?*
Gabby: *I don't know. He left. I'm betting he's headed to see Luis about your employment.*
Ryder: *He knows I was there?*
Gabby: *Yes. I'm sorry. I told him he's not to harm you.*
Ryder: *Don't worry, ángel.*
Gabby: *What are you going to do?*
Ryder: *Talk to him.*

The door to the bathroom opened and Grigore reentered the room. "Well?"

"Raúl left. She's not sure where to, but she thinks her uncle went to talk to Luis about his employing me." Ryder grimaced. "Looks like I should head over to Salazar's and see if I can't straighten this mess out."

"What if Raúl wants to take you out? He already knows you're a vampire, he could scent it, so he'll know how to kill you. What the fuck are you going to tell him?"

"That Spike turned me. Dead men can't talk."

"You might want to come up with a good story as to why Spike felt the need." Grigore started opening the cupboard doors until he found a bottle of Jack. He unscrewed the lid, grabbed a tumbler, and poured a couple of fingers. He downed the fiery liquid in one gulp before pouring himself another. "You want one?"

Ryder snatched the bottle from Grigore and took a healthy swallow.

"You could use some fucking manners." Grigore rolled his eyes. "There are more clean glasses, you know."

"It's my pad. I'll drink straight out of the bottle if I want." Ryder set the bottle on the table and had a seat. Grigore took the chair opposite. "The way I have it figured, I'll tell Raúl that Spike was looking to make me VP and we planned to take over the Devils. That he was having issues with some of them not liking him as pres, which we already know to be true. He turned me so we'd have vampire strength in our favor. When Spike got himself killed, I figured I needed a change of scenery ... and I still needed a job."

"Sounds like a solid story. While you do that"—Grigore pulled out his cell—"I'll call Hawk and Viper and get their asses down here ASAP. If Raúl sticks around like I think he might, we should be able to get at him. He won't know what hit him. Maybe with you poking his niece, it will give him more of a reason to stay put for the time being, to make sure you're on the up-and-up. Especially since he knows a vampire is fucking her. I'm assuming he'll want to keep a real close eye on you, make sure you aren't one of the Sons of Sangue vamps."

"If he checks with the Devils, they still think I'm dead."

Grigore nodded. "Right. So, tell him you laid low until Spike came across you, making you an offer to be VP. They never got the chance to talk to the Devils before he bit it."

"Let's hope the story holds up. Most of my old motorcycle brethren aren't going to take too kindly to a snitch being brought back to life."

"Spike wasn't always the brightest bulb in the box. Hopefully, they'll shrug it off as another idiotic move. Since he's dead, and you aren't trying to ride with them, they might just let the account stand as it's told. Dead men can't tell no tales. Looks like you didn't fuck up this mission after all." Grigore reached across the small table and slapped Ryder on the shoulder. "Now let's do what we were sent here to do and take down this fuck."

"The rest of the La Paz cartel?"

"We aren't here to kill the lot of them. Raúl is our target. We take him out and any other soldier that gets in our way.

Let the rest of them decide their own fate. We cut off the head. They'll either grow a new one or scatter like rats. Either way, we don't care.

"With the amount of money and power the La Paz cartel has over this region, my bet is on them finding a new kingpin. We leave them up to the Feds. Cara can fill them in from the Sheriff's Office."

"I agree, Wolf. Even though I'd like to see all those motherfuckers pay, we can't single-handedly take down the entire cartel. Leave them to the authorities." Ryder picked up the bottle and took another swig. "With Raúl out of the way, they'll likely be a lot easier to catch anyway."

Ryder thought of Sergio. Kane and Kaleb may be coming down to La Paz to see that Raúl gets what was coming to him. But Sergio? Yeah, that motherfucker was all his.

RYDER PULLED ONTO THE GRAVEL lot of Salazar's, circled a few parked cars, then stopped his motorcycle near the entrance. Turning the key, he paused as the rumble of the engine cut short. Glad for the smaller crowd, Ryder stepped over his seat, lifted his helmet and dangled the chin strap from the rubber handle grip.

A quick glance around the lot told him Gabriela didn't appear to be there. Thank the good Lord for small favors. He'd rather deal with her uncle without her present. A black Cadillac Escalade, one absent of Gabby's name, sat near the side entrance of the restaurant, providing Ryder with proof that

Raúl was meeting his men. The man no doubt had his own fleet of Escalades.

The wooden door creaked as he opened it and stepped into the dim interior, waiting for his eyes to adjust. Even though he had great night vision, it took a fraction of a second for the adjustment to occur. He spotted Sergio sitting alone near the rear of the joint, Luis nowhere in sight. Ryder didn't glimpse Raúl anywhere within the dining area, but he could smell the son of a bitch. Thankfully, the kingpin hadn't scheduled the meeting with his number-one-in-charge elsewhere. He'd rather get this over with and confront the kingpin now, rather than later.

Sergio acknowledged his approach with a nod, though his expression gave nothing away as to his temperament. Ryder couldn't tell if the man was about to go apeshit on him or if he was completely in the dark about what had happened mere hours ago. Surely, Sergio wasn't going to be happy with Ryder achieving what he had spent months trying to accomplish. Ryder wasn't positive of Sergio's motives, but he was pretty sure it had nothing to do with Gabby. Most likely, Sergio wanted to become part of the Trevino Caballero household on a more permanent basis.

Ryder wasn't going to be around long enough to see if the motherfucker managed to get the job done or not. But the thought of him laying his grubby paws anywhere on Gabriela, yeah ... that wasn't going to happen. He'd take him out first.

As a matter of fact, the thought alone had the vampire simmering just beneath the surface. Speaking of someone wanting to go apeshit.

Ryder skipped a greeting. "What are you drinking, *amigo*?"

"*Amigo*? Since when did we become friends?" One of his dark brows rose. "But if you're buying..."

"I asked, didn't I?"

"You got a set of *cajones muy grande* coming here, I'll give you that." He rubbed a hand down his jaw, eyeing Ryder, no doubt wondering why he had offered to spring for the drinks. "I'll take a michelada. I could use a serving of daily vegetables. Helps keep up my strength," he added, patting his biceps.

Ryder stifled a laugh and motioned over a waitress, ordering two of the Bloody Mary-style drinks before addressing the earlier part of Sergio's comment. "What makes you think I'm not welcome here? I'm assuming I still work for Luis. Speaking of, where is he?"

"He's talking to the boss ... about you."

Raúl had wasted no time talking to Luis. Ryder would need to do damage control and fast, try to get in the kingpin's good graces, at least until the Tepes brothers arrived in Mexico. Then all bets were off. These motherfuckers were going down. "Not sure why I'd be the topic of their conversation."

Sergio shook his head and laughed, his humor not quite reaching his eyes. Ryder got the feeling the man held a lot of animosity toward him, more so than the day they'd met. He'd bet the entire mission it had to do with Gabriela. Guess saving his life by taking out Gunner no longer held merit.

"You can't be serious," Sergio hissed.

The waitress set the micheladas before them. Ryder dug into the pocket of his jeans, then dropped enough dinero onto her tray to pay for both drinks, leaving her a generous tip.

"Why the fuck would I know?"

"Word has it you hightailed it off Raúl's grounds a couple of hours ago." Malice filled Sergio's dark gaze. The son of a bitch likely didn't know know Ryder had fucked Gabriela. If he did, Ryder assumed they wouldn't be talking. So Sergio must have suspected an entirely different reason for Ryder being in her suite. "Any reason you'd be running like a little bitch?"

"Why would my whereabouts be any of *your* business?"

Sergio gritted his teeth, his cheek muscle ticking. "Because, you *pinche idiota*, you work for me."

"Last I checked, I work for Raúl. Besides, Luis hired me, not you."

He held his tongue to keep from calling Sergio all the names running through his head, which wouldn't help his cause. Ryder reminded himself that he was the one at fault for his present troubles because he hadn't been able to keep his dick in his pants. So for now, he'd play nice.

"Same difference, *pendejo*."

Luis and Raúl exited the kitchen, entering the main dining room of the restaurant, keeping Ryder from decking Sergio for his latest insult. Due to his primordial keen sense, Ryder had detected Raúl's scent the minute he entered the restaurant. But obviously, by the look on Raúl's face, he hadn't noted Ryder's arrival until clearing the metal swinging doors leading from the kitchen. His black gaze landed on Ryder. If Raúl thought for a minute he could compete with Ryder's primordial strength, he was in for a rude awakening.

"This *pendejo*—"

"I'm not interested in what you have to say, Sergio." Raúl easily dismissed the man, his gaze never leaving Ryder's. Sergio stood, his booted feet clunking on the wooden floor. His hushed grumble made it evident he was none-too-pleased over the brush-off. Raúl ignored his tantrum. "Leave us. Take everyone with you and place the CLOSED sign on the door. I want to talk to Ryder ... alone."

Luis rounded up the few men lazing about and herded them out the door, Sergio complaining the entire time. Ryder was quickly learning the man had undoubtedly pissed and moaned his way into position. He might be heartless in his pursuit to follow orders, but one-on-one, Sergio was gutless.

Ryder squared his shoulders and stiffened his spine once he and Raúl were alone. He wasn't about to cower in front of the kingpin. Ryder stood a good eight inches taller than the asswipe. Raúl's eyes became marble-like as he flashed his fangs. Ryder didn't bother turning. Raúl wasn't worth the effort. Besides, this wasn't a "my dick is bigger than yours" pissing match. This was about his niece Gabriela, and Ryder wasn't going to make things tougher on her.

"We need to talk."

"So, talk." While Ryder was all about respect for Gabby's sake, he wasn't going to show weakness. "What's got your vampire panties in a bunch?"

"I was told you were from the Devils. And yet, no Devil that I know of has vampire DNA except for Spike ... who's dead. Care to elaborate?"

"Spike turned me before he was taken out."

"That fuck didn't have my permission."

Ryder smiled. "Spike answered to no one. No disrespect meant, but he did things his way, regardless of the consequences."

"He was a fucking coward. He wouldn't dare cross me."

Ryder nodded. "To some extent, I'd agree. But when he didn't think anyone would take notice—"

"You want to tell me why you're here?" Raúl interrupted, telling Ryder he wasn't much of a fan of the fallen vampire.

"We were supposed to head the Devils. That was his plan, anyway. He'd remain pres and I'd be VP. In the long run, he wanted to make them all vampires. The Sons of Sangue had cut his plan short. Some of the Devils aren't fans of mine either. Most think I'm a dead snitch. Having no friends in the MC, I came down here looking for work in your camp."

His gaze narrowed. "You hoped to get to me through my niece?"

"Not intentionally."

"Then tell me why you're fucking her."

"I met Gabby before I knew she was your niece. I like her ... as it happens, I like her a lot. I'm sorry if that's not okay with you." Ryder leaned down, driving his point home. Raúl wasn't going to respect a man who wouldn't stand up to him. "But to be totally honest, I don't give a fuck what you think. I'll continue seeing her whether I have your permission or not."

"You do realize you work for me."

"What the hell does that have to do with your niece? I'll do what's required of me and not involve Gabby in the business side of things."

He harrumphed. "Gabriela won't date someone who works for me. She's made that clear on numerous occasions. So, why you?"

"Maybe"—Ryder shrugged—"it's because I'm not like most people you employ."

"How so?"

"Because I would never use her to get to you."

Raúl's fangs flashed brightly in the dim lighting as his lips curved up. "Be sure that you don't."

Ryder arched a brow. "You're giving me permission?"

"I won't get in your way where Gabriela is concerned, for now anyway. She's an adult and can make her own decisions. She'd never forgive me if I threatened another of her ... friends. Regardless of what she thinks, I do have her best interest at heart. And I'd rather know who she's sleeping with." Using a beefy hand, he wrapped his fat digits around Ryder's neck and backed him against the nearest wall. "Fucking break her heart and I'll stop yours. *Comprender?*"

Ryder's eyes heated as he clamped down on his rising vampire DNA. Raúl's life was not his to take. Otherwise, he'd rip the fucker's head off where they stood. He'd bide his time, allowing Kane to exact his revenge. The vamp had been waiting a good long time for his day to come.

Ryder shook off the fat man's hand and shoved away from the wall. "I'll mind Gabriela's heart, you mind your fucking claws. Touch me again and it won't be my heart I'd be worrying about, if I were you."

Raúl laughed, his belly shaking. "I like you. Someone who's not afraid to stand up to me. I think you might just be a good asset. One thing is for sure, I won't need to worry about Gabriela when she's with you."

"Damn straight."

Raúl slapped him on the back. "Don't let my Gabby walk all over you, amigo. She can be a ball-breaker. I taught her well."

"I'll take care of her." Hoping that much was true.

The last thing he wanted was for her to get caught in the middle of the shit about to go down. Once her uncle was ashed, it would be anything short of a miracle if she didn't hate him.

"Does she know?" Raúl brought his attention back.

"Know what? That I work for you?"

Raúl shook his head. "That you're a bloodsucker?"

"No, and I plan to keep it that way."

"You hypnotized her when you fucked her?"

Ryder nodded. "So, she wouldn't remember my vampire traits? Yes."

"You can teach me?"

He smiled, knowing Raúl's time was limited and it would never come to pass. Ryder wasn't about to teach the kingpin anything. "I can."

Thinking Ryder could help him would also go a long way in keeping Raúl in residence, not to mention gaining his trust. Once the Tepes brothers arrived, the kingpin would be dead anyway.

"Back at your place, when we have spare time, I'll teach you."

Raúl slapped him on the shoulder. "I think I'm going to like having you in my employ, *amigo*."

"I have a feeling Sergio doesn't feel the same way."

"You let me worry about him." Raúl led them toward the entrance. "He'll cause you no problems."

The door swung open, startling them both. Gabriela walked into the restaurant, her worried gaze swinging from Ryder's to Raúl's. Rage filled Ryder. It was all he could do to pretend he didn't see the purple bruising on her cheek. He'd kill the motherfucker who dared to strike her.

"Uncle?"

"Everything is fine, Gabby." He placed a brief kiss on the opposite cheek of the swelling. Before he headed out the door, he looked back. "Oh, and get this place open for business, will you? We don't make money with the CLOSED sign up. If Sergio comes back and has anything to say, tell him to take it up with me."

Ryder's teeth ached with the need to drain someone. His gaze swung from the closed door back to Gabby. He reached out, the back of his fingers smoothing over the injured cheek. "Who the fuck did this?"

CHAPTER FOURTEEN

GABRIELA FLINCHED.

She wasn't sure what she expected when she walked into Salazar's. Certainly not her uncle and Ryder speaking amicably. Her fear of walking into a war zone had her rushing to be a mediator. Not that her uncle didn't deserve a beat down from Ryder, especially following the bruised cheek he had given her earlier.

It wasn't the first time she had angered Raúl to the point he had abused her verbally, just as she knew it wouldn't be the last. Over the years, Gabby had learned not to infuriate her uncle. His temper knew no bounds. And although she knew beyond a shadow of a doubt he loved her and wouldn't kill anyone who dared to lay a hand on her, there were a few times he had unleashed that fury on her with his words, though never striking her before.

In her haste, and her concern for Ryder, she had momentarily forgotten the large purpling bruise on her cheek, or what Ryder might think when he saw Raúl's handiwork. Ryder's greeting told her exactly what he thought of someone laying a hand on her.

With a large, work-callused hand, Ryder gently gripped her chin, causing a shiver to pass over her shoulders, reminding her all-too-well how it felt having those same hands brushing against her bare skin. He turned her head to the side, giving him a better view of the damage.

"If Sergio did this, I swear to all that is holy I'll chop off his nuts if your uncle doesn't get to him first."

She'd live, but by the looks on his ruggedly handsome face, her uncle might not. "It wasn't Sergio, Ryder. My uncle would kill him if he laid a hand on me."

"Then whoever it is will be lucky if Raúl gets to him before I do."

"I'll be fine, really."

"Gabby…" His tone brooked no argument. Ryder wasn't about to let her sideswipe the truth.

"You have to promise, Ryder, that you won't take action. He may have bruised my cheek, but he wouldn't think twice about killing you."

"Who?" His pupils damn near swallowed the whites of his eyes in his fury. Surely, it was the dim lighting that caused the unnatural effect. His voice thickened. "Tell me who the fuck hit you?"

She stepped back from his touch, clasped her hands in front of her and looked at the floor. "My uncle."

"Raúl?" His response nearly shook the windows. "Because of what we did?"

Gabby looked at Ryder, holding his furious gaze. "Yes. Somehow, he knows we had sex… He said he could smell it."

Ryder growled. "That bastard. I'll fucking take him apart limb from limb."

"You'll do no such thing." Gabriela closed the space between them and placed her hand on his forearm, reveling in the taut muscles. "My uncle has too many men in his employ. Surely, you know that. He'll have you killed before you ever get near him."

Something shifted in Ryder's gaze. Gabby couldn't mistake the care she saw there ... and possibly something more, though she couldn't be sure. They may have had sex, but they still barely knew each other. Ryder's heated gaze dropped to her lips. Gabby thought he might want to kiss her. Lord, she practically begged him to as she leaned forward. Closing the distance, he slanted his lips over hers.

Not waiting for an invite, he slipped his tongue past her lips and took possession. Her breath caught in her throat and her blood pounded in her ears. Slipping a powerful arm around her back, he pulled her flush against his taut body. She felt the hard evidence between them that spoke of his want to have her again. She reveled in the fact he hadn't used her only to slake his urge earlier, but that he was far from done with her. He kissed like he fucked, deep and penetrating. Every fiber of her body took notice, especially her libido. Had he reached beneath her skirt now, he'd not only find her sans panties but wet with desire.

Gabriela slipped her palms up his chest and circled his neck, linking her fingers at his nape. Kissing him, she gave as good as she got. Her desire to have him slide hot and heavy inside her had not diminished in the least. On the contrary, had she not needed to open Salazar's for business, due to her uncle's parting demand, she'd be suggesting one of the restaurant tables for something other than what they were designed for.

Lord, this man made her no better than the *puta* her uncle had accused her of being. She'd never tire of this man, this drifter who'd come into town. He'd likely break her heart when he packed up and moved on. And he would. Ryder Kelley was an American. His home was north of the border. He didn't belong in La Paz. If nothing else, the lighter color of his skin against hers was a stark reminder.

Ryder stepped back, leaving her shivering from the loss. He palmed her face, his eyes darker than natural. It had to be the low lighting causing the black-like mirrored effect.

"I have some business that needs attending." He kissed her forehead, then gently, her bruised cheek. "Leave your door unlocked, *ángel*. Tell the guards to expect me."

A smile curved his lips. She couldn't help but wonder the cause of his sudden humor. "What?"

"Tell Raúl to expect me for breakfast. Let the motherfucker suffer for what he did." He kissed her lips with the promise of what was to come. "Tonight ... I'm taking my time with you. Don't expect to get much sleep."

Heat traveled through her like molten lava, searing her flesh as if his hands had touched her rather than his promise. Gabby had it bad. She wasn't sure what this was between them, if he cared for her more than "friends with benefits," or if "love at first sight" was actually a thing, but this man made her believe in the possibility of it.

Kaleb sat on one of the sofas at the clubhouse, arms outstretched and resting along the back as he waited for Kane's arrival. Life had been so damn busy of late, giving him little time to hang out with his brothers. Fuck, he missed that ... a lot. The clubhouse was eerily quiet with Grigore down south and Alexander looking for a new place for him and his mate to live. Once he'd found out India was carrying his child, Alexander had wasted little time looking for a new home, reasoning that the clubhouse was no place to raise a kid.

Kaleb couldn't agree more.

He had moved his own family for that exact reason.

Hell, truth be told, he was missing out on so much more. Suzi had put in her two-weeks' notice so they could start on kid number two. She had certainly called his bluff, he thought with a chuckle. Not that he was opposed to expanding his family. But two kids underfoot and a mate he needed to spend more time with? Something needed to give.

They were also in the middle of opening the new K&K Motorcycle shop in Washington. Kaleb's second love, building choppers, he was damn good at it. He'd love nothing more than to start spending more time working on bikes.

Standing, Kaleb paced the floor, thinking about why he wanted to speak to Kane. He sure in the hell hoped his brother understood his position. The last thing he wanted was to heap more work onto his twin's plate. Kaleb wasn't about dumping his workload on someone else, always willing to fill in where needed. He'd just like to lighten it a bit so he could get back to the things he used to enjoy, starting with rebuilding his own fucking chopper that Bird had torched.

The door opened and Kane strode in, looking freshly showered. He certainly didn't appear as though he had ridden straight through from Washington.

"How's the Sons up north?"

"Hello to you as well." Kane chuckled. "Let's break out the whiskey first, then we'll talk."

Kane stepped to the bar area and pulled a new bottle of Gentleman Jack from the cupboard. After screwing off the cap, he poured a couple of fingers of the amber liquid into highball glasses, handing one to Kaleb.

"We're back in business." He held up his glass, clinking his against Kaleb's, then tossed it back in one swallow. "You approved Gunner's roster changes. Thank you. Gunner as club P and Smoke as VP, I like both men and choices. They're go-getters and loyal to a fault. I think they'll do fine. You hear from Wolf or Ryder?"

"Wolf is supposed to be calling today with a rundown of what's happening. Seems they did find Raúl right under their noses."

"Great news, Hawk. Where's the little fuck?"

"For now, he's staying at his main house in La Paz."

"Can Ryder manage to keep an eye on him, make sure Raúl doesn't move out of the area until we get there?"

"I don't think that's going to be a problem."

Kane's gaze darkened. "Care to elaborate?"

"Apparently, Ryder got caught fucking Gabriela. Raúl didn't actually see them in the act, but he knew Ryder was there, had scented as much."

"Then he knows Ryder's a vampire."

Kaleb shrugged. "Only a matter of time before that happened anyway, Viper."

"What's Ryder's plan? We heading out before sunset?"

"If Wolf thinks he'll stay put for a few days, then it's likely. We need to get down there before the slippery fuck takes off for who knows where."

Kane's smile stretched across his face. "I'm so ready to ash that bastard. His time has been coming for too long. I doubt anyone will mourn his sorry excuse for a life. The world will be better without him in it."

"I can't agree more." Kaleb leaned forward, his glass between his palms. "There's something else I wanted to speak to you about."

"Everything okay?" Kane's gaze darkened with worry. "Suzi and Stefan alright?'

"Yeah, we're good. Look, there's something I want to ask you, bro ... and feel free to tell me to go to hell."

"What's up, Hawk? Spit it out."

"I want to step down as club P."

Kane straightened his spine, his gaze narrowing. "And let Gypsy step up? Not that I don't love the man, but this is our club, Hawk."

"That's not who I was thinking of."

"Then who?"

"You."

Kane's gaze was skeptical, surely not fully trusting Kaleb's motives for giving up the head of the table. "I never thought I'd see the day you'd want to step down, bro. You sure about this?"

He nodded. "You should've never lost your position. I know you went against club rules. And maybe I allowed my own ego to get in the way, too, not going to bat for you when you tossed in your patch. But, Viper, *you're* club P. You still should be. I plan to take it to the rest of the Sons when we get back from La Paz. Put it to a vote, if it's alright with you."

"What about you?" Kane asked.

Kaleb shrugged. "I was hoping to go back to VP if Gypsy and the rest of the Sons will allow it. I don't want to step away completely. But if not, maybe I'll step into Past P."

"No way, Hawk. The only way I'll step into the pres's shoes is with you as my VP. We'll make it happen. I doubt Gypsy will give two fucks."

"Gypsy was sergeant at arms before he became VP. That's Wolf's position now, maybe he can revert to treasurer. I doubt Rocker will care since Wolf sponsored him. Rogue will remain secretary and Xander will stay as road captain. Let's get things back to the way they used to be."

"And how exactly will this be helping you?"

"I'm tired of making all the decisions. I know you've always been there for me, but I want to have more free time, raise my family, build more bikes."

"And you don't think I want a family?"

Kaleb laughed. "You'll have to convince your workaholic mate on that front, dude. But even so, you've never had trouble juggling your personal life with club business. You were born to lead this group. I just gave you a little time off."

"You know I'll do right by you." Kane smiled again. "And if you want to step down, I'll gladly step up to the helm, providing the rest on our brothers agree."

"All or nothing, Viper."

"All or nothing," he agreed. "Now, back to this fucking piece of shit down south. What's the plan?"

As if on cue, the phone rang. Kaleb picked it up and hit the green TALK button, putting the call on speaker. "Give me the deets, Wolf. You're on speaker with Viper and me."

"I hope Ryder knows what he's doing," Grigore growled.

"What's up, dude?" Kaleb asked. "Give it to me straight."

"Ryder just left. He's heading back to Raúl's estate later tonight. Apparently, the mofo thinks spending the night in the kingpin's niece's bed is the best course of action."

"Foolhardy is what this is. This shit could blow up in his face." Kaleb tapped the bar. "You agree with his decision? Give him the go-ahead?"

"Not at all," Grigore said. "On the contrary. I told him I was against it. He could keep an eye on Raúl from a distance. I think he's letting his dick do the talking."

Kane ran a hand down his whiskered jaw. "Not that we all haven't been guilty of that."

"Don't include me. You two are the mated ones. Me? Ain't happening. I went down that path once, thought I knew what love was."

"What happened, Wolf?" Kane asked.

"I walked away, that's what."

Kaleb shook his head and chuckled. "No regrets?"

"None. She didn't need me holding her back."

"You've never talked about a woman from your past before," Kane said. "We know her?"

"No, and you aren't about to either. When I walked away, I shut that door, locked it, and threw away the key. I doubt she'd even remember my ass. That four-letter word isn't in my DNA. I'll leave that to you fuckers."

"What's Ryder's plan if he isn't listening to you?" Kaleb steered the conversation back to the mission and bringing down Raúl.

"Not sure he has one, other than spending the night there."

"In Gabriela's room?"

"No, in *Raúl's* fucking bed, Hawk."

Kane laughed so earnestly it was hard for Kaleb to even retort. Kaleb slapped him on back of the head, but it only made Kane laugh more, which in turn had them all chuckling.

Finally, Kaleb said, "I certainly hope Ryder knows what he's doing. At best, it's a thirty-four-hour drive straight south for us. The last thing we need is him pissing off Raúl and having him either retaliate and take Ryder out, or have him splitting."

"My bet is on the first," Kane said. "If it was my niece, no way in hell would I be leaving her there with this new guy to fend for herself."

"Then we need to get our asses down there ASAP."

"When are you leaving, Hawk?"

"As soon as we can wrap things up here, Wolf. Expect Viper and me down there day after tomorrow. We'll be in touch."

Kaleb clicked the END button, then slid the phone away from him on the bar. "Well Pres? What's the plan?"

Kane laughed. "I'm still past P until a vote's been taken."

"In my eyes, you already have the job. So what's on the agenda?"

"You head home, square things with Suzi. I'll do the same with Cara. Let's meet back here around nine tonight. We'll head for the Blood 'n' Rave first, tap a couple of arteries, and then head south. I don't plan on stopping, except for gas, until we get there."

"Sounds like a plan, Viper. I'll meet you back here by nightfall."

Kaleb watched his brother leave the clubhouse a little straighter than when he'd walked in. President looked good on the man. He shrugged on the vest, then looked down at the President patch resting over his heart. A few more days and that patch would be back to its rightful owner. Kaleb was about to set things back to right and he felt damn good about it.

It was about fucking time.

CHAPTER FIFTEEN

Ryder ascended the stairs to Gabriela's suite. Stopping on the red-tiled veranda, he took a slow sweep of the estate. He wanted to make sure Raúl and his crew knew he was here. If Raúl had anything to say about it, Ryder was more than ready to confront the bastard. He'd gladly take the first swing. Breaking the motherfucker's face would give him great pleasure.

Hitting a woman was uncalled for.

Abusing his own flesh and blood?

Yeah, Ryder wanted to take Raúl's head clean off his shoulders, make sure he'd never manhandle another woman. Too bad he had to await the Tepes brothers' arrival and their own need for revenge, or he'd end this tonight. The son of a bitch didn't deserve to live, let alone the deserve house he lived in, or the beautiful niece who shared his space.

He spotted a gunman on one of the top balconies overlooking the pool, watching him. Ryder saluted the man, made sure the fuck would report back to his boss. Cocky? Maybe. But he didn't give two shits what they thought. They'd need an army to take him down and her uncle didn't keep that many men underfoot. Raúl's soldiers were extremely loyal.

He could count on them announcing his arrival. Exactly what he was hoping for.

Ryder was sporting for a fight.

He might not be able to take out the vampire per the mission, but he'd put a world of hurt on him if he so much as sneezed in Gabby or his direction. He'd make sure he got his point across.

Touch Gabby again and you're a dead man, Tepes brothers be damned.

Stepping up to the French double doors, he was about to knock when Gabby swung the doors inward. Her large smile washed over him, making him completely forget about his need to fuck up Raúl. Christ, he could get lost in her deep brown gaze. Her happiness to see him was like a kick to his gut, though. Once she found out about his duplicity, forgiveness would be hard-won. Getting her to believe he actually liked her and that he wasn't fucking her to get to Raúl, yeah ... that wasn't happening either. Ryder was pretty sure Gabriela Trevino Caballero would despise him, never want to see his sorry ass again.

Not that he could blame her.

In a few short days, he'd be heading north anyway. No matter what his heart or libido had to say on the matter, this woman was not his and never would be. They came from two different worlds. When the Tepes brothers were finished, this would all be hers. Not the business side of things, but the estate and fortune the man had amassed. This was her home. Hell, he lived in a tiny bedroom in the Sons of Sangue clubhouse, for crying out loud. No way he could ever hope to compete. But he'd damn well make sure she'd never forget him.

"Glad you could make it."

Her smile warmed the part of his heart that had frozen over, making him shelve his negative thoughts. He could put them away for a night, show her what it was like to be cherished.

And cherish her he did.

Ryder ran a knuckle down her bruised cheek, keeping his darkness at bay, not wanting Gabby to see the other side of him. But it was there. Just waiting to pay back Raúl.

"I always keep my promises." His smile turned feral. "And my promise that you won't get much sleep tonight? Still holds true."

A small shiver passed over her shoulders, easily visible with her strapless, ankle-length dress. The red color accented her warm skin tone while the silk hugged her curves. Her light brown, highlighted hair cascaded freely down her back, brushing her shoulders. His fingers itched to sift through the sleek strands. Ryder advanced a step, noting a hint of jasmine and vanilla, the scent of her desire a pleasant undertone.

"Can I get you something to drink? Iced coffee? Tea? A beer?"

Her nerves were quite apparent. Each step he advanced, she retreated. And although they had already done the vertical bump, he found her shyness endearing.

"Nothing for me. Thank you."

What Ryder thirsted for he had no intention of quenching. An undercurrent to the delicate scent of her perfume was the sweet and spicy bouquet of her blood. The tang of it burned within his memory. Shaking his temptation for another sip would be arduous at best. Taking sustenance from her, though, was not going to happen. Crossing the line and sleeping with her had been careless enough, though he'd be damned if he regretted a second of it. Partaking of her life's blood and having to erase her memory of it would be extremely callous.

Gabby picked up a glass of what appeared to be iced coffee, and took a sip. Her full lips closed around the straw and his mind went straight to those ruby-red lips encircling his erection. His cock went instantly hard at the thought of Gabby, in her ridiculously sexy dress, on her knees in front of him. Fuck, that was one fantasy he hoped would come to life before the night was over.

"Does your uncle know I'm here?"

She grimaced. "If he didn't hear the arrival of your motorcycle, I'm sure one of his men has informed him."

"You have no worries, *ángel*. I won't let him touch you again. I promise you that."

Ryder closed the gap between them, stopping just inches away from the shell of her ear. He whispered, "He'll have the opportunity to confront me at breakfast."

Gabby laughed, a sound he had grown quite fond of. "I wasn't aware you were invited."

"I wasn't. But I did promise to keep you up all night, meaning I'll likely be famished come morning."

And he would, but not for what Raúl or his staff might be serving. His gaze dropped to the pulse of her neck. Denying himself was going to take some serious fucking willpower.

He quirked a brow. "Are we not of the same mind?"

Her pink tongue traced her lower lip. "Same mind?"

Ryder chuckled. "I didn't exactly come by for a gab session. But if that's what you're wanting, *ángel*, I'll sit right here by your side until the sun comes up. We won't do anything you aren't comfortable with."

He wanted to make sure he wasn't overstepping her boundaries. "What will it be, *ángel*? A night of watching the stars over the ocean, or white-hot fireworks from your bed?"

Gabby laughed again, shaking her head. "You're pretty sure of your abilities."

"I think I've already proven my abilities." His gaze went back to her bruise, his fingertips smoothing over the downy skin. "If you want the truth? I'm spending the night so your uncle doesn't think he can hurt you again because I dared another visit. You're not his personal punching bag. If he so much as tries, he'll answer to me."

"Ryder, his men—"

He shushed her with a finger against her lips. "You let me worry about your uncle and his men. I can take care of myself, *ángel*. I've been doing it for a good long time."

"I wish I could believe you, but I've seen what my uncle is capable of."

One side of Ryder's lips curled up. "But you haven't seen what I'm capable of."

Snaking one hand around her waist, he pulled her flush against him. There would be no mistaking his hard desire. "How about we drop all of this talk about your uncle? I can think of more pleasant things to converse with you about. That is, if you wish to talk."

She slid her palms up his cotton T-shirt and threaded her fingers through the overlong hair at his nape. "Talking is overrated."

Slanting his lips over hers, Ryder wasted no time taking possession. He slipped his tongue past her lips and tasted her, deepening the kiss. Her silky tongue entangling with his left him wanting ... wanting the kiss to go on forever, and yet wanting so much more. He tightened his hold while his free hand smoothed up the satiny side of her dress, past her hip and the curve of her waist, stopping just beneath the swell of her breasts.

The last time they had come together had been fast and furious. Hell, he hadn't even taken time to worship her properly let alone get a gander at her ample tits. Tonight, he'd make no such faux pas. Tonight, he planned on getting up close and personal with every inch of her. Ryder had every intention of taking his fill. His memories would have to last him a lifetime. And being a vampire, lasting a lifetime took on a whole new meaning.

Once the Tepes twins arrived, he'd be giving up Gabby forever.

Her moan fueled his desire. Gliding his hand over her silk-covered breast, he felt her nipple pebble beneath his palm. He teased the taut bud with the pad his thump through the thin material. Arching her back, she pressed against his hand, giving him the go-ahead. Ryder wasted little time, pulling down the bodice of the strapless gown, finding she wore no bra.

Breaking the kiss, he glanced downward, seeing her dusky rose-colored nipples for the first time. *Perfection*. His eyes heated, and his gums ached. Ryder knew he could go no further without hypnotizing her. His vampire DNA was quickly taking over. He palmed her cheeks and brought her heavy-lidded gaze to his eyes.

"Gabby." She nodded slowly, misunderstanding his need for her attention. "Hear me now. You'll not remember what you see. You'll feel me, know me, but my face will remain a shadow. Nod if you understand."

Gabby did as he instructed, her eyes more glazed than before. Fuck, he hated hypnotizing her. He wanted her to remember, wanted her to know who he really was, what he became. A part of him wanted her to love all of him, not just the man but the monster hidden within.

His fangs punched through his gum, filling his mouth, aching with the need to sink into her carotid. Not happening. Instead, he ran his tongue along the soft flesh of her neck from her ear to the hollow of her throat. Her hands fisted his hair as he continued south. Palming the undersides of both breasts, Ryder used his tongue to circle one of the nipples, teasing the taut bud before drawing it between his teeth and tugging gently.

So fucking tempting.

Her blood rushed just beneath the surface, calling to him. Never had he been so motivated to take something not given. He could almost taste the sweetness as the scent tickled his senses. Ignoring the calling, he released her nipple to lavish the other. After all, he was all about equal opportunity.

Fuck, she had a nice set of tits.

Definitely, more than a mouthful.

Ryder could spend all day paying homage to what God had given her. They were a perfect fit for his large hands, and the thought of someone else touching them put him in a murderous state of mind.

If only things were different.

There was no way on God's green Earth, though, that Gabriela would forgive him once she discovered the truth, his real reason for coming to La Paz. The good guy in him warred for a change of plans. Talk to her, watch the sunrise together. Don't make things worse.

The bad guy placed an arm beneath her silk-covered knees and easily lifted her off the floor. No way in hell the vampire was listening. That good guy? He was long gone for the night. He'd give her one hell of a reason to remember him, regardless of how pissed she'd be once the Tepes brothers left their carnage, altering her life forever.

Laying her on the king-sized bed and its white with blue-trimmed duvet, the red of her dress stood out in stark contrast, reminding him of his favorite beverage. Funny, but after his turning, he didn't think he'd have the stomach for blood, cringed at the very thought of drinking it. Now, he fucking craved it.

Gabby did her best to wiggle up the mattress, making little progress as her legs tangled in the crimson-colored fabric. Grabbing the collar of his T-shirt from between his shoulder blades, he pulled the cotton over his head. Her eyes dipped to his chest, spending little time on the ugly scar marring his flesh before continuing down his abs, to the bulge in the front of his jeans. She licked her lips again, reminding him of what he had wanted her to do with those brightly painted lips.

Ryder slowly lowered his zipper, careful not to pinch his skin. He hadn't worn boxer briefs, preferring to go commando. Reaching inside the taut pants, he withdrew his cock, smoothing his hand over the stone-like flesh as he held her fevered gaze. Christ, what a fucking turn-on, seeing her hunger rise as she watched him.

Mind-blowing.

Widening his stance, and anchoring his jeans on his hips, he stroked his cock from root to tip and back. A small droplet of pre-come beaded at the surface. Before he had a chance to spread the natural lubricant, Gabby scooted to the edge of the mattress, replacing his hand with hers.

He hissed as she fully encircled his cock and mimicked his earlier ministrations. After dropping from the bed to her knees, she worked his erection like a pro. He bristled at the thought of any other man having enjoyed her touch before him.

Jealous? He never got jealous.

Ryder growled, wanting proprietorship, knowing he had no right to it.

Her gaze went to his. Gabby leaned forward, her tongue capturing the small bead of fluid resting on his tip.

His balls tightened, and his need to be inside her increased ten-fold, but before he could pull her from her knees and spread her beneath him on the bed, her lips closed around his erection. She licked the underside of his shaft before fully sucking him into her mouth. Much more and he'd not be a gentleman. Ryder fisted her head, meaning to stop her, but her hands went to his jeans-clad ass and held tight.

It was the only approval he needed. He thrust deep into her mouth, the soft flesh surrounding his cock … so damn good. His ass muscles tightened. He gritted his teeth, holding his climax at bay. Gabby continued to work him. The vision he had of her on her knees earlier now come to life, driving him to a state of frenzy. His gaze held fixed on her red-painted lips tending to his cock. Her free hand now caressed his balls. Ryder couldn't hold out. When she gave him another squeeze, he was a goner.

"Fuck!" he roared as his climax reverberated through him.

Gabby took him deep, drawing from him until he had nothing left to give. With a final lick of her lips and an impish smile, she rose to her feet and shimmied out of the thin red fabric, wearing nothing but a pair of red strappy heels. Apparently, Gabby hadn't felt the need to wear undergarments either.

Mind-blown for the second time in the span of an hour.

She sat on the bed and scooted toward the headboard, crooking her finger. "I do believe you promised me an all-nighter."

Ryder laughed, quickly shucking his jeans. "Gabriela Trevino Caballero, you are my fantasy come to life. I'm pretty fucking sure one night won't nearly be enough."

"I hope not. I'm afraid I might be growing quite fond of you."

Red flag.

At least it should have been. The last thing he wanted to steal was Gabby's heart. He could ill afford their emotions getting tangled up in the mess their lives were about to become.

She quirked a brow. "Do you need a bit of time?"

His hand indicated his already heavy cock. "Does it look like I need time to recuperate?"

Her humor greeted him as he knelt on the mattress, dipping beneath his added weight. Placing a hand on each side of her legs, he smoothed his palms up her shins to her knees.

"*Ángel*, you're going to be my downfall."

Gabby bit her lower lip, her teeth stark white against the red lipstick. Ryder smoothed his hands up her thighs, opening her legs to him. Her sex glistened; her pheromones called to him like a beacon. Lord, if he wasn't careful, his useless heart was going to open up. He had tried love once and that hadn't ended so well. Ryder had no intention of doing so ever again.

His nostrils flared at her alluring scent, drawing him forward. He slipped his tongue along her folds, tasting her. "So fucking good."

The only thing that could trump the sweet sampling was the piquancy of her blood pulsing through her veins. The thundering of her heart had the warm, vital fluid pulsing close to the surface. It would be so easy to sink his fangs into her thigh, to partake of the smallest fraction of her blood. But to do so, even the tiniest of samplings, would fuck any willpower he had left.

Ignoring the craving, he slipped two fingers into her heat while using his tongue to encircle the tight knot of nerves. Gabby arched her back, gripping the duvet at her sides. Fuck, she was the most beautiful woman he had ever had the chance to pleasure. Why the hell she was giving his ugly, scarred ass the time of day, he didn't know.

Gabriela was the epitome of grace and class, putting her completely out of his league. And yet, as she lay before him in the throes of the oncoming orgasm, he was exactly what she needed.

It didn't take class, style, or money to please a woman.

Using his hands to ease her legs farther apart, he dipped his tongue into her hot core. Fuck, her sweetness came in a close second only to the taste of her blood. Her femoral artery pulsed near his ear. With his enhanced hearing, the sound thundered through his brain, making it hard to concentrate on anything other than how easily it would be to sink his fangs into the soft flesh of her inner thigh.

Not that she wouldn't enjoy it.

Had he bowed to the temptation, her oncoming orgasm would be immediate and far more intense ... not that she'd ever know because he couldn't allow it to happen.

Her thighs trembled; her knuckles whitened as she squeezed the cotton spread. Holding her fast to the bed, he slid his fingers back into her core, using his thumb on her clit for added pressure.

Ryder lightly dragged the sharp points of his fangs over her smooth flesh, careful not to break the skin. Gabby sucked in air, his name tumbling from her lips as her climax washed over her.

Smiling, Ryder sat up and wiped a palm down his beard. Hell, she was so fucking sweet he'd been tempted to go another round. His erection wasn't about to be denied, though. He was hard enough he could damn near drive through a cement block wall. This time, though, he planned to take his good ol' time, show her what it was like to be cherished by a man and not just used for his gain.

Ryder's conscience warred with him, smacked him right upside the head.

Wasn't that what he was doing? Using her?

Hell. To. The. No.

He was using her to get to her uncle, that much was true. But this? No, this was all him, the Tepes brothers and their need for revenge had nothing to do with his present actions.

He hadn't needed to sleep with Gabby to complete his mission. He'd already found Raúl. Making love to her wasn't a part of that equation.

Crawling up the mattress, seeing her lying there languid with a moony smile that he had put there, Ryder knew exactly what it felt like to have the walls he erected around his heart kicked down, brick by brick. Christ, he was in danger of falling, even if he had thought it wasn't in his DNA to love again.

Pretty fucking stupid, Ryder.

When Gabby kicked him to the curb, which she no doubt would, he'd be leaving a piece of himself right here in La Paz. Ryder shook his head; now was not the time for making any death-bed declarations. Hell, he still needed to come out of this sordid affair with his head intact.

Ryder settled himself between her thighs, carefully displacing his weight as he braced his arms on each side of her head. "Ready for round two?"

Lacing her fingers at the base of his skull, Gabby brought him down, meeting his lips with hers. It was the only answer he needed. He returned her kiss with the passion and desperation of a starving man. His hunger for her bordered on out-of-fucking-control. He fit perfectly between her thighs, like the ying to her yang.

Gabby wrapped her legs around his waist, crossing her ankles at the base of his spine and trapping his erection between their bodies. She slid deliciously along the naked length, one hell of a turn-on. Damn, but he needed to be inside her heat, feel her fitting him like a tightly worn glove.

Breaking the kiss, Ryder growled, the sound more animal than human. He guided the tip of his cock to her center. Their gazes held as he pushed forward, slowly sliding into her heat. Her mouth opened; her breath caught.

Her dark eyes were like windows to her soul.

She held nothing back.

Somehow, this connection became far more than just a romp in the sack. Ryder could feel it in the way she gave herself to him, in the way she opened herself. And if he was being fucking truthful, it was already too late for him as well. He could easily see himself spending the rest of his days with her, making his miserable life worth living. Too bad she had no idea she was fucking an immortal, a vampire ... one who was bent on destroying the only life she knew.

Ryder slowly thrust into her, not wanting to rush the moment, and yet the animal part of him wanted to quicken the pace, to fuck so hard she'd never be able to forget him, regardless of how much she might hate him in the end.

Gabby traced her fingers along the scar tissue, the ugly reminder of how cruel life could be. Shivers danced along his flesh at the delicate touch. But when she brought her head from the pillow and placed a tender kiss where her fingers had been, the last brick fell and his heart opened up.

It was then he knew it was too late. He was already a goner.

His thrusts increased; his muscles contracted. Her head tilted into the pillow as she cried his name, music to his ears, reaching her own culmination.

"Fuck!" he roared, just before his climax took possession and ripped through him.

It was then he knew that he loved her.

CHAPTER SIXTEEN

Gabriela stretched her aching muscles and smiled, feeling as if she had been put through a vigorous workout. And she had, a sinfully delicious one. Ryder had certainly held true to his promise, allowing her very little sleep over the course of the night. Not that she was complaining. No way, not after being on the receiving end of what could only be described as award-winning sex. Gabby rolled to her side, cushioning her head with her hands, as she looked at Ryder sleeping peacefully beside her. Just seeing him and remembering the night they'd shared had her desiring another round ... or two.

Sun streamed through the glass French doors, warming her naked flesh. They'd slept half the morning away. A quick glance at the clock confirmed as much. Not wanting Ryder to have to deal with her uncle this early in the day, or maybe never, she swung her legs to the side of the bed and stood. She pulled a sports bra over her head, tugging it into place, before donning a tank. Stepping into her lounge pants, she drew them up over her hips, then padded to the door.

A quick glance at the bed told her she hadn't disturbed Ryder. She tiptoed into the hallway, then closed the door with barely a click. Gabby planned to return with a tray laden with treats and a pot of Jamaican Blue Mountain coffee, her personal favorite. Tomas, her uncle's personal chef, would already have a pot waiting for her as he did every other morning.

Gabby couldn't help smiling. Although she knew there was a strong possibility Ryder was only passing through and had been in search of temporary work, she wasn't about to pass up a good thing no matter how short his stay. Maybe she'd be able to convince him to hang around a while longer. After what they had shared last night, she was pretty certain he cared for her more than just a casual romp.

Her heart agonized at the thought of him leaving. No matter how foolhardy it was, her heart had opened and gotten tangled up, even though she knew better. It had been Ryder's response to Raúl's cruel actions that had done her in. No one had ever offered to protect her from her uncle or his men. Most men were afraid of the cartel and the power they wielded in Mexico, and rightly so.

As endearing as Ryder's offer to champion her was, she couldn't allow that to happen. To do so would be suicidal. No one crossed Raúl and lived to tell about it. Gabby would have to plead her case to her uncle, beg him to leave Ryder to her should he overstep his bounds. Unfortunately, she wasn't all that certain he'd listen. Men could be so stubborn and pigheaded.

Conversation from down the hall caught her attention. She immediately recognized her uncle's voice. Good. The sooner she had this discussion with Uncle Raúl, the better. It was time to put him in his place. Gabriela was a grown woman and the matters of the heart were her own. No exceptions.

Her uncle's chef was absent upon her arrival in the kitchen, but he had left dozens of pastries from which to choose. Her pot of coffee sat on the warmer, ready to be poured into a waiting stainless steel carafe. Uncle Raúl stood on the other side of the large center island, his back resting against the counter with his arms crossed over his chest as if he had been waiting for her. Two of his men, heavily armed and wearing bulletproof vests, stood on either side of him. Their conversation ended the moment she walked through the large archway.

Had she been the topic of their conversation?

Gabby wasn't alarmed by the presence of the guards, as they often entered the kitchen for a bite to eat. What caused her anxiety was the look on her uncle's face. It wasn't like him to be up this early either. Most times, she sat in the kitchen, eating Tomas's creations, conversing with the chef before she readied herself for work. She had never been an early riser, so her uncle and she were rarely home at the same time, which Gabby preferred.

Raúl was not a nice man, other than to her on most occasions. Of course, providing she hadn't upset him in one way or the other. By the look on his face, she had certainly displeased him again, no doubt Ryder being the cause.

Gabby pulled out a stool on the opposite side of the island and took a seat. This might take a while. When Raúl lectured, she could be held up for a good deal of time. Hopefully, if Ryder awakened, he'd wait for her return and not go looking for her. Approaching Raúl on a good day was foolhardy enough. Doing so on a bad day? Ryder would be lucky if these two goons didn't become his firing squad.

After grabbing a pastry, she took a bite of the sugary delight, stifling the moan. Although she wasn't about to show weakness in the face of her uncle's temperament, she wasn't so foolish as to goad him either. She'd wait for him to initiate whatever the hell was on his mind. If he didn't start soon, she'd head back to her room and hurry Ryder out the door, leaving her to deal with her uncle's mean spirit on her own. Ryder's safety came first and foremost.

"I think your new toy likes to see just how far he can push me, little princess. I'm not sure I approve of his behavior."

Gabriela dusted off her hands, then poured herself a large mug of coffee. "Why's that?" she asked before taking a sip.

"He spent the night in your room, no?"

"And if he did?"

Raúl placed his hands on the white marble and leaned forward. "Call me old-fashioned. I don't like it. This is my home. Him rutting like an animal with my niece isn't very considerate. I shouldn't have to be subjected to your *puta* like behavior. *¿Lo entiendes?*"

"I'm no whore, regardless of what you think of my actions. This is my home, too. Or have you forgotten?"

Her uncle bared his teeth and she swore his canines appeared elongated, yet not quite long enough to be considered fangs. Surely the kitchen lighting was playing tricks on her vision.

"Princess, this is your home as long as you mind my rules. Never forget that. You may be my flesh and blood, but you come from my brother's loins, not mine. You're living here out of respect for him."

Gabby jerked as if he had physically slapped her. "Then I shall pack my bags—"

Before she got the words out, Raúl leaped over the island as if it were no larger than a small barrier. For a man of his short stature, it was quite a feat and simply impossible in her eyes. *What in the world?* He landed with a light thud beside her, barely audible. He should have made enough noise to wake the dead.

She gaped at him. Gabby couldn't have formed a sentence if she'd tried. Her gaze went to the two men standing opposite the island, who acted as if what her uncle had just accomplished was an everyday occurrence.

Looking back at her uncle, she asked, "Joining the circus anytime soon? That's quite the acrobatics."

Raúl grabbed her one-handed by the throat and lifted her off the stool as if she weighed no more than a fly.

"You'll not get smart-mouthed with me, princess. I'm beginning to think my earlier assessment of this *Americano* may have been a bit hasty. I thought he might be good for you, keep a close eye on you for me, but instead, it seems he might be more of a bad influence. Maybe, this new problem needs to be eliminated."

Gabby gasped. "You wouldn't dare."

"He means no more to me than a gnat. When gnats become pesky, we swat them."

He looked back at his two goons, who chuckled at his poor attempt at humor. Bastards. When her uncle returned his gaze, his eyes were damn near black as coal, the unnatural darkness swallowing most of the whites. Gabriela had little time to dwell on the strangeness of what she was seeing as his fingers squeezed her windpipe with considerable strength, making it impossible to draw breath, her toes barely touching the marble tiled flooring.

"Don't ever question me, princess. While you live under my roof," he growled, sending shivers of fear sluicing down her spine, "you'll do as I say. You want to see this man, then I suggest you take your dalliances elsewhere. I shouldn't be subjected to hearing the two of you fuck."

She would have drawn in a breath at his odd statement had she been able to. Unless he had camped outside her door there was no way he could have heard them. Even so, the doors were thick...

"How?" she managed to squeak.

Raúl loosened his hold, and somehow she managed to stay upright. "I heard your man arrive. When I meant to be the hospitable host, I came by your suite. Needless to say, I wasn't pleased to hear your guest offend me."

Gabby's hand covered her throat as she attempted to speak. It was a wonder her uncle hadn't done permanent damage to her windpipe. She racked her brain, trying to remember what had been said.

"What ... did Ryder ... say?" she wheezed.

"That you weren't my personal punching bag. That if I hit you, I'd answer to him." He chuckled, waving a hand in dismissal. "I own all of this, little princess. And as long as you live here, I own you as well. Which means if you want that boy to live, you'll encourage him to go home."

"And if I don't?"

"Then I'll take care of him personally. Mark my words, he no longer has a job with me. The only way I won't take his head is if you convince him to go north of the border. He's no longer welcome in Mexico."

"Then she goes with me."

All eyes turned to Ryder. Raúl didn't look the least bit surprised at seeing the man now standing in his kitchen. It was as if he had expected him.

"I was wondering how long you would hide in the hall like the *cobarde* you are."

Ryder raised a brow as he came to stand between Gabriela and her uncle. "Coward? You're the one who hides behind your army. Even now they stand at your ready. Should you mistreat your princess, as you call her, they would do nothing to help her. You are the worst of cowards."

Raúl's complexion darkened. "You have five minutes to vacate my property or I'll have your head."

"Careful of that temper, Raúl. Unless you want your niece to see your true nature."

It was a strange warning, and yet, Gabriela watched as her uncle considered Ryder's advice, taking several deep breaths. Even the oddity of his black gaze returned to normal.

"If you leave now," Raúl continued, "then I'll allow my men to give you safe passage."

"Your word means nothing to me." Ryder chuckled. "Once I'm far enough from Gabby's watchful gaze, you'll have me killed, telling her I left the country. How far off am I?"

"Uncle Raúl! You wouldn't."

Raúl leveled a gaze of pure hatred on Ryder and hissed. This man wasn't the uncle she loved, but the one she feared. "Mind your tongue or I'll have my men cut it out."

Again, Ryder's brow arched in challenge. "You and I both know they wouldn't stand a chance with me."

"Ryder..."

He glanced briefly at Gabby, a look of warning on his face, which she heeded. He returned his attention to Raúl. "I'll leave, but she goes with me."

"She stays. Gabriela belongs to me, you *idiota*."

Ryder gripped the front of Raúl's shirt and shoved him so hard against the far wall, dishes on the shelves rattled and crashed to the tiles. One look from Raúl to his men and they rounded the island, taking Gabriela within their collective grasps, one holding a handgun to her temple.

"Your move." Raúl smiled menacingly. "One word from me and she dies."

"You'd kill your own niece?"

"Try me, *gilipollas*."

Ryder quickly dropped his hold and stepped back from her uncle, his jaw tightening as he looked from one man to the other. Gabby's heart pained at the thought of never seeing him again. If she left with him, her uncle would hunt them down and Ryder would die at his hand. Her only hope of saving his life was to send him away without her.

"Go," she whispered, hoping he saw the plea in her eyes. Moisture gathered and tears slipped down her cheeks.

Ryder walked over to her, his eyes black and unyielding. Much the same as her uncle's had been moments ago. "Hear me now. Close your eyes, *ángel*, and don't open them until I say so. Do not question me on this."

Oddly, she did as instructed. Gabriela couldn't open her eyes. It was as if her lids had grown too heavy. A crash resonated beside her, and the cold steel against her temple was no longer there. A man screamed in horror, then his voice cut short with what sounded like the crunching of bones. The other hand holding her fell away just as quickly. She heard a grunt, then another scream, and more crunching. A man dropped to the floor at her feet.

Gabby gasped, not knowing who without the sense of sight.

A roar came from the other side of the room, sounding much like her uncle. Suddenly, the air became charged with electricity, standing her hair on end. She could feel the movement in the way of a breeze fluttering across her flesh as things crashed around her. A heavy thud hit the wall. Wood splintered, and pots and pans clattered to the ground.

Try as she might, she couldn't open her eyes. Her breath caught and her heart hammered against her sternum. Her stomach crawled up her throat, churning and making her nauseous. The smell of blood filled the room. She feared for her uncle, the man who had taken her in, and yet she feared more so for Ryder, the man she barely knew.

"Ryder?" she whispered.

A final thump sounded, then all grew still. Strong arms picked her up and carried her down the hall faster than what she deemed humanly possible. Without the benefit of sight, Gabby had no way of knowing. What the hell had happened to her? Ryder's fresh-outdoors-and-musk scent enveloped her, telling her whose arms she was in. What had happened to her uncle?

Before she had time to ask, Ryder deposited her on the bed, brushed his knuckles against her cheek and said, "Open your eyes, *ángel*."

And she did. A quick look around her room proved they were alone ... for now. She glanced at Ryder and gasped at the blood that stained his skin and clothes.

"Are you hurt?"

He shook his head.

"My uncle?"

"He's alive. I can't say the same for his goons." He knelt in front of her. "Pack your bags, Gabby. You're no longer safe here. When your uncle comes to, he'll be looking for me and he'll use you to find me. I can't let that happen, not as long as I draw breath. If he'd try to harm you because of me again? I won't allow him to live. Do you understand?"

She nodded, acknowledging the truth of his statement. Ryder had easily killed her uncle's men and could've taken Raúl's life but didn't out of reverence for her. Hadn't he warned her? Gabby suddenly worried if she weren't jumping from the frying pan into the fire. What if Ryder was worse than her uncle and she had misjudged him? Gabby drew her lower lip between her teeth.

"*Ángel*, we're running out of time. It's only a matter of minutes before your uncle's other men find the carnage in the kitchen with Raúl passed out among the chaos." He framed her face with his palms. "Pack a few things, only enough to carry on my motorcycle, and let's get the fuck out of here."

She wet her lips, drawing his gaze down. Ryder bent, slanting his lips over hers, and took a brief but nonetheless deep possessive kiss. Releasing her, he asked, "Ready?"

Gabby stood, ran to her bureau and tossed some clothes into a backpack, followed by makeup. Picking up her cell, she faced Ryder. "I'm ready."

And the truth of it was, she had never been more so.

Ryder took the phone from her and tossed it to the floor, smashing it beneath his booted heel. "You won't be needing that. He can trace us through it."

After throwing open the double doors, he led her down the steps and helped her onto the back of his motorcycle. He placed his helmet on her head and snapped it into place, tightening the strap, then stepped over the seat in front of her. Gabby shrugged her backpack across her shoulders, then wrapped her arms around his middle.

He looked back at her. "Hang on tight."

With one last look at her uncle's estate, Gabby did as she was told. Ryder started the engine, turned the bike, and headed down the driveway. Not being able to help herself, she took one last look back and saw her uncle standing in the doorway, a murderous look on his face.

She shook her head and gripped Ryder tighter. Fear had caused her to hallucinate. Had she not known better, she'd swear that, when her uncle let out a mighty roar, a pair of vampire-like fangs flashed in the sunlight.

CHAPTER SEVENTEEN

F*UCK!*
    Well, that had gone incredibly wrong, Ryder thought, pulling his motorcycle to a stop on the side of a dirt road in the middle of nowhere. Only brush, palm trees, and sand could be seen for miles. Truthfully, he had no fucking clue where they were, other than near the ocean. The smell of salt water told him as much. Over an hour ago, he had made a left out of the drive from Raúl's estate, heading straight south down Highway 1 to 19. Somewhere along the way, he had veered off the main road and headed in the direction of the shore near San Pedrito Beach. If the earlier signs were any indication, they were only about a mile down the dirt path.

Thankfully, Raúl hadn't alerted his soldiers to take immediate chase. They were given a clean getaway, but by now Raúl had surely sent out the masses. Ryder's hope lay in Raúl thinking they had gone north for the States. But even so, they couldn't afford to stay in one place overlong. Raúl's men were everywhere and Ryder was positive word would spread like wildfire throughout the country. Ryder might not be highly recognizable, but Gabriela would be.

He needed to call Grigore and give him the rundown. Grigore would be pissed. And rightly so. Ryder'd had one job, to keep an eye on Raúl's whereabouts. *Fuck!* Now, he might've blown the whole mission, putting Raúl on the move because Ryder couldn't keep his dick in his pants.

Kicking down the stand to the bike, he cut the engine. The sound of lapping waves rolling up on the shore confirmed their location. Gabby stepped off the bike first and unsnapped the skull cap, shaking out her damp, long hair. A sheen of sweat glistened along her skin. Nevertheless, she hadn't complained once. The day was already warm, with a promise of getting only hotter. She hadn't taken the time to change out of her lightweight gray lounge tank and pants, making it a bit more bearable.

Ryder stripped off his black T-shirt and wiped the sweat from his face. Luckily, anticipating spending the night at Raúl's estate, he had packed a change of clothes. His black shirt drew the sun's heat, roasting him.

Gabriela's gaze took a slow path from his chest to his abs before landing back on his face, further warming him. Ryder smiled at her appreciation. She could drink her fill any day. At the moment, though, there wasn't time to act on the rising desire he scented from her.

Not only had he fucked up his mission, but Gabby's life. Even though it was a heady thought that she wanted him, even in the face of danger, it pained him to know she could never go home. Not as long as her uncle lived. Hell; Gabby still had no clue that she had been a pawn, helping him in his assignment. He needed to get that call in to Grigore ASAP, with hopes the Tepes brothers could still catch up to Raúl and end the piece of shit's life. Maybe then Gabriela could be set free.

Yeah, Ryder was pretty sure this thing between them would end badly.

"You're a long way from home." Gabby placed the helmet on the leather seat. "I thought we'd be heading to the United States."

"I'm counting on your uncle and his goons thinking the same." Ryder pulled his cell from his jeans pocket and checked the signal strength, thankful for small favors. "Give me a sec, Gabby. I have to make a call. When I'm done, we're heading to Cabo San Lucas, where I hope we can get lost among the tourists."

"Then what? We can't run forever. At least not in Mexico. Uncle Raúl has men everywhere." Her lips turned down. "They'll recognize me, Ryder, and you'll be killed outright."

He placed a thumb under her chin and raised it. "You let me worry about me, *ángel*. But rest assured, I won't let anything happen to you."

"Uncle Raúl won't have me killed."

"Maybe not, but he's not going to be too thrilled you left with me. He hit you once, he'll do so again." Ryder turned her head to the side, happy to see the bruise already starting to fade a bit. He held up his cell. "I'll be back in a second."

Ryder pulled her close and gently kissed her forehead. Lord, he cherished this strong woman, marveled at the fact she chose to go against her uncle and leave with him. Turning away, he strode far enough from the bike as to not be overheard. Soon enough, she'd know his duplicity.

Scrolling through the burner phone's contacts, he tapped on Grigore's number then placed the phone against his ear.

"Talk to me," Grigore answered. "Tell me Raúl is still in the house."

"There's a problem. Raúl and I had a falling out."

"Is he still alive?"

"I left him that way, yes. But I can't say the same for the two soldiers he tried to unsuccessfully use against me."

Grigore all but growled. "Want to tell me what the fuck happened?"

"I messed up. I was worried about Gabby. I wanted to show that fuck if he tried to hurt her again, he'd have to answer to me."

"He hurt Gabby? I can't say I'm surprised. I'm sure it wasn't the first time."

"Raúl struck her across the face. I had to do something, man."

"Of course, you did," Grigore said, then grumbled something Ryder couldn't quite make out, but he was pretty sure Grigore was calling him some sort of a dumbass. Instead, he said, "Only fucking cowards hit women. Where are you?"

"Gabby and I hightailed it south, down the coast. I figure they'll think I headed north. I'll keep Gabby safe. She's my number one priority. I'll leave Raúl for you and the twins. Unless, of course ... he finds us. Then all bets are off. I'll take his fucking head myself. He's no match for my strength. I already proved that back at his estate. We're heading for Cabo San Lucas to lay low and hide among the tourists. How far out are Viper and Hawk?"

"About a day. They should be here sometime tomorrow. For now, I'll hold tight and try to keep an eye on Raúl's fortress. If he leaves, I'll follow him. Maybe, with any luck, he'll send his fucking goons after you and he'll stay put."

"One can hope, Wolf."

"Look, bro, stay alive."

"That's the plan."

"I have no doubt you will. With your primordial strength, I pity anyone getting in your path." Grigore chuckled. "As soon as Viper and Hawk get here, I'll be in touch. We won't waste time. We find Raúl, the fucker dies. I hope you can explain that to your little *señorita*."

"When this is over, Wolf, she'll want nothing to do with me." He ran a hand through his hair and looked back at Gabby. "But hey, my fault, right? I signed up for this. Besides, she'll be rolling in money, what would she need me for?"

"Yeah." Grigore laughed again. "Who'd want your ugly ass anyway."

The call went dead and he pocketed his cell.

"Is everything okay?" Gabby asked as he returned to her side.

Ryder ran a knuckle down her soft cheek. "I just uprooted your life and you ask me if everything is okay with *me*? Fuck, I wish…"

He trailed off, not wanting to finish the thought in his head, not wanting to complicate things further. Hell, he had already fucked up her life enough. The last thing she needed was to hear confessions of his heart.

"You wish what, Ryder?"

Her gaze was so innocent. When all was said and done, he was going to take that from her. Fuck, he hated himself for it. Where Raúl was evil and corrupt, Gabriela was the opposite. Sure, she knew what her uncle did for a living, the kind of man he was, and yet she had managed to keep a semblance of innocence along the way.

"I wish things could be different for you. I wish for you another life, one without death, corruption, the fucked-up shit your uncle brings to the table."

"I know what my uncle is like, what he's done. I hate him for that." She frowned. "And yet I love him because he's my uncle and he took me in. What was I to do?"

He brushed the pad of his thumb across her lower lip. "You could've left, should've left when you were of age."

"How? He wouldn't have let me go. And even if he did, his enemies wouldn't have hesitated to use me against him. I'd be a pawn for their gain."

Ryder dropped his touch as anxiety raced through his heart and shortened his breath. Once she found out, he was toast. She'd never look upon him the same. His gut clenched at the thought of her glaring at him with the same contempt he saw in her now. And yet it was unavoidable.

"You have a point, *ángel*. Anyone using you for their gain is unconscionable. You were meant to be loved, not used."

No truer words were ever spoken. He only wished he were free to love her. After she found out about his hypocrisy, his chance to do so would be off the table. Gabby wouldn't be able to get beyond her antipathy for him. Nothing he didn't deserve. Fuck, Ryder should've kept his hands to himself and his dick in his pants.

Filled with self-loathing, Ryder picked up the helmet and handed it to her. "We need to get back on the road. I think I saw a sign back there for a seaside diner. Let's get you something to eat."

He took a white T-shirt from his saddlebag and pulled it over his head. Much more time and he'd be in serious need of sustenance himself. Hopefully, this nightmare would be over and he'd be on the road to home by then. The thought of leaving Gabriela behind was a kick to his gut. Losing his girlfriend and unborn baby to the cartel had been the single hardest thing he had ever had to live through. But losing Gabby because of his and the Tepes brothers' fucked-up need for revenge against them? That would kill him.

KANE FOLLOWED HIS TWIN through the door of the small rustic cabin Grigore had secured for his stay in Mexico. Constantine and a few of the Sons of Sangue members from Washington lounged on the rustic furniture. The sofa had moth-eaten holes in it, and if Kane's sense of smell was any indication, the place was also infested with rats and mice. It appeared as if the cabin had been long-ago forgotten, which meant it was off the cartel's radar. Grigore had chosen wisely, though that didn't come as a surprise. The man never did anything without thoroughly thinking things through from every angle.

Grigore wasn't only a man of action, but one with a plan.

He had been the best man for the job of keeping an eye on the mission. If things went south, it wouldn't be Grigore's doing. Ryder had managed to do that all on his own, from what Kane had been hearing.

He took a deep breath, already counting the hours he needed to be here before making his way back to Oregon. Tracking down the kingpin had been a long time coming. Kane needed to finish his revenge and move on. Raúl Trevino Caballero was about to have his fucking head displaced and Kane would finally be able to put to rest his only son, Ion. He thought about that, had for the past few days. It seemed fitting, once Ion was at peace, then it would be time for Kane to start his new family with Cara. Gone was his ex-mate, Rosalee, thanks to Vlad, and soon it would be Raúl's turn to go.

Once they returned to Oregon, and he took back the presidency from Kaleb, all would be right in Kane's world. His heart swelled. Fuck, it felt damn good to have his axis righted again. He'd never have asked for Kaleb to step down from the presidency. His brother had been doing a damn good job of heading the club when Kane's head hadn't been exactly in the right place. He had never been prouder of his twin.

Now, though, the timing seemed perfect to take back the reins, and he had his brother to thank for that. Kaleb hadn't allowed his ego to dictate his actions, preferring to step down, spend more time with his family and build his custom bikes.

His brother was a good man and father. Watching Kaleb play with Stefan had made Kane more than ready to be a dad again. And once he returned home, he planned on telling Cara, hoping to hell she would be on board.

Grigore walked over to the brothers, shaking both their hands, followed by a bump of shoulders. "Fucking great to see you two."

"Got here as soon as we could." Kaleb brushed the dirt from his chaps. "I think there are more fucking dirt roads down here than asphalt. Times like this I wished I had a full face shield on my helmet. I think I ate enough dirt to make a sandcastle."

Kane laughed, slapping his brother on the back. "Maybe you shouldn't have talked so much, bro."

Grigore opened the fridge and handed them each a bottle of water. "This should help."

"What's the plan, Wolf? Ryder have any fucking clue if Raúl is still in his fortress?"

The big guy scratched behind his ear, looking even more wolfish. "I'm not entirely sure, Viper. As I told you on the phone, Ryder had to make tracks."

"Don't tell me we lost Raúl," Kane all but growled. "Ryder had one fucking job—"

"Gabriela complicated matters."

"Give us the lowdown, Wolf," Kaleb said before taking a swig from the water.

Grigore filled them in on the events leading up to the moment they'd walked through the door. "So, Ryder and Gabriela are likely in Cobo San Lucas by now and laying low. He had no clue if Raúl took chase himself or sent his goons. I'm betting the latter because Raúl isn't going to want to go traipsing all over Mexico looking for them. I'm thinking he's waiting for word."

"Anyone keeping an eye on the estate?" Kane asked.

"I've had someone watching the grounds twenty-four-seven. Rocker's there now. We believe Raúl is still in residence, but we haven't had eyes on him yet."

"Good," Kane said. "I'm ready to get this shit over with and get on with life. Raúl doesn't deserve any more of my time."

"We got this, Viper." Kaleb set his empty plastic bottle on the old Formica kitchen table. "That fuck doesn't stand a chance. I'm ready whenever you say the word."

"I'd rather not make this messy." Kane's eyes heated with his simmering ire. "No need to bring the entire cartel down on our heads. Once we have confirmation he's at his estate, we take a head count. If the numbers are low, we go in. If there are a lot of his soldiers, then we wait until he leaves the grounds and follow him. Either way, he's a dead man, along with the crew who stupidly chooses to stay and fight with him."

"That's one way of putting it," Constantine put in his two cents from his seated position. "If you ask me, though, none of those fucks deserve to breathe air. They fucking make money off distributing drugs. They don't give a rat's ass who dies from their product. They're now lacing the shit with fentanyl, hoping to keep their clients addicted and coming back for more. Except these addicts are dropping like flies. If you ask me, I say we go in and kill every fucking one of them."

"Can't say I disagree with you, Lightning, but the main goal is Raúl." Kane jabbed the table with his forefinger. "I don't want to lose any one of you because we decided to play cops and robbers. There are far too many of them. They're like moles. The minute we go in, they'll go underground. We leave the rest of those fucks to the Federales."

"I agree with Viper," Kaleb said. "Let's stake out the estate, find out how many men we are looking at, and make our plans. Once Raúl is dead, we get the fuck out of there. Anyone resists, then we take them out as well. Those we don't take out, we make sure they don't remember vampires or the fact their boss was a bloodsucker. We make sure they have no idea the Sons of Sangue was behind this. We don't need the rest of these fucks hunting us down. Revenge ends here."

"Any questions?"

"Not that I can think of, Viper," Grigore said. "Let's rock 'n' roll."

CHAPTER EIGHTEEN

RYDER TOSSED THE KEYS TO HIS BIKE ONTO THE DESK IN THE hotel room. The thud echoed off the walls and caused Gabby to jump. He had paid for the room with cash, not wanting to leave a trail for Raúl or his men to follow. His gaze traveled to Gabby who skirted the bed, most likely making sure it was safe to sit, a telltale sign that they came from two very different worlds. While the hotel room was nice by most standards, it wasn't what Gabriela Trevino Caballero was used to. Soon enough she'd be on her way back to the life she was born to and Ryder would be on the road headed north.

So why the hell did it feel like such a kick to his gut?

Yesterday, after securing her a bite to eat at the little diner by the beach, Ryder had wasted no time heading for Cabo San Lucas. They had stopped at a small bed and breakfast on the outskirts of town for the night before heading into Cabo this morning. The short, plump *señorita* running the B&B had recommended this hotel. Far enough away from the hubbub, to be affordable but close enough to fit in as tourists. If they stayed overlong, his dinero would run out, leaving him little choice but to use one of his cards to transfer them more cash. Hopefully, Kane and Kaleb will have found Raúl by then.

Ryder ran a hand through the hair at the top of his head.

What a fucked-up situation.

Using the story that the two of them had just arrived in Cabo San Lucas on their honeymoon, he'd been pleased when the hotel clerk upgraded them to one of the nicer, more spacious rooms. It was the best Ryder could do for Gabby under the circumstances. As it was, she had grown increasingly quieter the farther away they got from La Paz, worrying him.

None of this could be easy on her.

She could have refused his demand that she go with him and yet here she stood. Ryder reminded himself, no matter what the bastard had done, Raúl was still her flesh and blood and had saved her from a life of poverty. Surely, she loved the man.

Gabby tossed her backpack onto the bed and began digging through it. She pulled out a floral sundress and a pair of panties. "I'm going to take a shower."

Without waiting for his response, not that he had one, she padded across the floor and entered the bathroom. He heard the lock snick into place, effectively shutting him out. Ryder couldn't help but wonder what she was thinking as he had done nothing more than defend her against her uncle's goons. Yes, he had killed them, but they had given him little choice. Her uncle, on the other hand, deserved more than Ryder had given him. At least knocking his sorry ass out had bought them some time.

Ryder hadn't harmed Raúl, no matter how strong the desire to do so.

Hearing the shower start, he pulled his cell from his pocket and called Grigore. He needed to know if the Tepes twins had made it to La Paz.

"Where the fuck are you?" Grigore answered.

"Hell of a greeting." Ryder steeled his jaw, reminding himself that he had caused this mess. "I'm in Cabo San Lucas with Gabby. We're safe for now. Viper and Hawk make it?"

"A few hours ago."

"What's the plan?"

Grigore grumbled. "Finishing what you started."

Kane's voice came on the line. "Ignore Wolf, Ryder. We got this. You just keep Gabriela safe."

"Do you know if Raúl is still at his estate?"

"We've had men casing the place," Kane said. "We haven't had eyes on Raúl yet, but I'm betting he's still in residence. The soldiers walking the grounds are far too alert for him not to be there. I think you've made the man nervous. We're going to lay low today, keep an eye on the place and go in tomorrow. With any luck, the world will be wiped clean of this son of a bitch by this time tomorrow."

"Good luck and stay safe. Cara will have my ass if you don't make it back."

Kane chuckled. "No doubt in that. Gabriela know what's going on?"

Ryder sucked in a deep breath and released it. "No. She only knows that I took out two of her uncle's men because they tried to harm her."

"She know you're a vampire?"

"Fuck, no. I hypnotized her."

"Good," Kane replied. "Lay low and keep her away from the public eye. We don't need Raúl's men recognizing her and complicating matters. We'll take care of things here. We'll be in touch when it's finished."

"Great. I can't wait to get the fuck back to Oregon."

"You're leaving?" Gabriela exited the bathroom. *Just fucking perfect.* "Oregon? I thought you were from California?"

Ryder stifled a groan. It figured she'd be the one woman on the planet who could take a quick shower.

"Got to run. I'll chat with you soon."

Ryder hit END on his phone and glanced at Gabby. Without makeup, hair wrapped in a towel, she looked young and innocent. Fuck if his dick didn't harden at the sight. Wanting her wasn't a problem. Honesty, though? Ryder shook his head and crossed the room, gripping her bare shoulders. The stellar sundress she'd donned hugged her every curve, barely covering her ass. Damn, but she was stunning, even with her hair in the towel. So much so, she robbed him of his breath.

Moisture gathered in her eyes. "You lied to me?"

"I am from California, *ángel*, or at least I was. I was a Devil, part of their MC, for a big part of the last decade." Ryder opted for as much of the truth as he could. "Those fucks wanted me killed for being a snitch, only I didn't die. So, I moved north to Oregon and joined a rival MC. That was before I came here looking for work."

"You said you couldn't wait to get back to Oregon. Is that true? Are you leaving me in Cabo San Lucas?"

He shook his head. "No, *ángel*. I wouldn't leave you to fend off your uncle and his men on your own. I won't head home until I know you're safe."

"But you're still leaving." It was an accusation, not a question.

He nodded, feeling like the biggest asshole. "I doubt your uncle will roll out a welcome mat for me now. I killed two of his men. You realize that, right? Your uncle will have me killed, Gabby. I can't stay."

She lifted her chin. "Then I'll go with you."

Ryder stepped away from her. "You belong here. Your uncle would never stop looking for you. Besides, we come from two very different worlds. I sleep in a small room at my MC's clubhouse. I have no place I call home. We don't have a pool unless you count the bathtub. And a view of the ocean? You can't even hear the waves lapping the shore."

A tear slipped past her lashes. "I don't care about all of that, Ryder. It's just stuff."

"You say that now. But if I let you come with me, how long before you start missing your designer clothes and shoes? How long before you start to resent me for not being able to afford you any of that? Your uncle is the only family you have. Mexico is your home."

His chest pained him, right in the area of his heart, to know that he and the Sons were taking the only family she had from her.

"I don't need him."

"You say that now. Tell me, Gabby, why have you been so fucking quiet on the way here?"

She drew her lower lip between her teeth and looked at the floor. He brought up her gaze by tipping her chin, refusing to let her hide the emotion in her eyes. Ryder wanted to see the truth, already knew what she'd say.

"Because I was worried about him."

"Your uncle?"

Ryder dropped his hold and she nodded, clasping her small hands in front of her, casting down her gaze again. Fuck! Just as he thought, she was never going to forgive him once tomorrow was over and the Sons headed back north. She'd be one rich woman, but her uncle would have gone the way of her father.

"He was alive when I left him, Gabby. I swear that to you."

"I believe you. It's just, I know he has to be worried about me and I have no way of letting him know I'm okay."

"He has to know I'd never hurt you."

"I'm sure, but it's not the same as hearing it from me." She looked at Ryder. "Can I use your phone, let him know he doesn't need to worry? I want him to know I came of my own free will, Ryder. It might help should his men find us."

"You're worried he'll kill me?"

Gabby stepped closer, placing her palm on his face. More tears slipped down her cheeks. "I *know* he will."

Just hearing that she worried about him spiked his need for her. Now was not the time and yet he couldn't help the desire sluicing through him. Ryder drew her closer so there was no mistaking the hard evidence of his hunger trapped between them. He pulled the terrycloth white towel from her head. Soft brown curls tumbled about her shoulders. Never had she looked more beautiful. And never had he wanted her more.

Slanting his lips over hers, he took possession, sliding his tongue into her mouth. The feel of her tongue against his spurred his craving. She tasted of fresh mint. Gabby threaded her fingers through his hair at the base of his skull, giving of herself. And although he knew he should stop, practice a little self-control for once since starting this fucking mission, he didn't have it in him.

Breaking the kiss, he quickly used the words to shadow his vampiric features that were swiftly emerging. Once her eyes glazed over, he picked her up and carried her to the waiting bed. In his haste, he shoved the dress up her waist and pull down her panties. Ryder wasted no time tugging his shirt over his head and then releasing his cock. His jeans stayed low on his hips. He crawled between her legs and entered her in one quick thrust.

Fuck, she felt like home.

Covering her mouth with his, he made love to her, showing her with his body what his words could not. Telling her that he had fallen in love with her would only complicate matters. He'd not further violate her that way. Better for her to think he was an ass and took what he needed to get his job done than to know he loved her and had followed through with his mission anyway.

"You can't keep me for-fucking-ever!" Mircea roared when Vlad entered the room. "I swear I've lost my damn patience with you. If I get out of here, I'll fucking destroy everything you hold dear."

"Such language coming from you." Vlad chuckled. "And that, dear brother, is the reason I cannot allow you to leave. Not until your mindset changes where my relatives are concerned."

"You're a smug bastard. I'll give you that." Mircea narrowed his gaze. "But mark my words, Vlad, you son of a bitch ... I will get out of here."

Vlad sat on the sofa, crossing a bare foot over his knee. He rested his hands on his thighs and smiled. "You know, we could get beyond all of this silliness if you would just call a truce."

"A truce?" His brother's voice went up an octave. "You're fucking kidding, right? You kidnap me and hold me against my will and you want a truce? Un-fucking-believable."

"I also gave you luxurious accommodations while you continue to drink through my collection of the finest wines, not to mention enough blood to sustain you. You have music, television, and books. What more could you possibly want?"

"To get laid, for one thing."

Vlad chuckled again. "How long has it been?"

"A couple of days."

His laughter cut short. "What do you mean only a few days? You've been here—"

It was Mircea's turn to laugh. "Thank you for the use of your servants. The petite one with the gorgeous red hair, is particularly good at giving head. Fuck, she looked fantastic on her knees while working my cock."

"My servants are not yours to toy with," Vlad roared. He created a monster.

"I'm a vampire, for crying out loud. Surely, you realize I wasn't meant to go without, and yet you don't provide me with that." Mircea shrugged. "So, I helped myself."

Vlad supposed Mircea had a point. The last thing he needed was a sexually frustrated bastard on his hands, taking his needs out on his non-consensual staff.

"I can't have you forcing yourself on the women. That's not what I pay them for."

Mircea rolled his eyes. "Tell me that you haven't used them for your own sexual favors."

"They come to my bed willingly, you ass. I would never force a woman to do anything she wasn't comfortable with. I have no need to force anyone. You on the other hand—"

"You have a fucking harem." Mircea ignored his jibe altogether, knowing full well Vlad was the better looking of the two. "I would think you could spare a few."

"A harem? There are only a few here who grace my bed."

"Then loan me the redhead."

His ire heated at the thought of the tiny slip of a woman being harmed by his brother. Hell, Vlad had never used her, afraid that someone of his size might unintentionally hurt her. "The redhead you speak of, did you force her?"

Mircea smiled and spread his arms wide. "No worries, dear brother. I hypnotized the entire event from her memory. She has no recollections of the fantastic blowjob she gave me."

And somehow, that seemed worse. Dear Lord, Mircea was an idiot. "You may use my staff only if they are like-minded. I'll not have you forcing them to meet your needs, then hypnotizing the entire event from their minds. Am I clear? If not, I won't allow my women staff members to come anywhere near your quarters."

Again, a roll of his eyes. Vlad was really beginning to think there was no saving this one.

"Agreed?" he said with a little more force.

"Yes, yes. Overdramatic as always." Mircea sat in the chair flanking the sofa. "If it makes you feel better, the redhead has taken a liking to me. I didn't have to force myself on her."

"Then why hypnotize her?"

"To keep you from getting so fucking bent out of shape when she started gossiping about our dalliances. Besides, it was much more fun telling you myself and watching your theatrics."

"I should've allowed Kane to kill you when he had the chance."

Mircea yawned and stretched. "So you've said. Now, I tire of this conversation. Don't you have something better to do?"

Vlad shook his head and blew out a stream of air. "There is so much more I could be doing than babysitting your ass."

"Then. Let. Me. Go."

"Nice try, Mircea. But at this rate?" Vlad smiled. "Looks like you'll be my permanent guest on the island."

Vlad stood and headed for the door. A vase crashed against the wall, just shy of hitting him. Glass tinkled to the marble floor. He sighed heavily before turning.

"That was an expensive vase, you son of a bitch."

"Then let me out of here or you'll need a fucking remodel of this entire room."

He raised a brow. "Need I put you in a room with nothing but four walls? Don't tempt me, I'll do it. I'm trying to make your stay comfortable, but for the life of me, I don't know why."

"I'll make sure you live to regret this, brother."

Vlad stuck the key into the door and unlocked it. "I'm sure you will," he grumbled as the self-locking door slammed behind him.

He really needed to come to a decision on what the hell to do with his brother. Mircea was starting to wear on his last fucking nerve.

CHAPTER NINETEEN

How the hell did she keep doing that? With Ryder's hearing, she shouldn't have been able to move without him detecting it. And yet this was the second time he had awakened to her giving him the slip. The slight click of the door closing brought him from his slumber. Fuck. He wiped a hand down his face. He must've been sleeping like the dead. Granted, he was in serious need of feeding. It wouldn't be long before his skin tone took on a translucent look. His body already ached with the stirrings of the death chill.

It had been four days since his last feeding. Much more and Gabriela might be questioning his appearance. Sitting up, he glanced around the room. The contents of her bag had been haphazardly scattered across the dresser. She must have been looking for something to wear. Ryder hadn't given her a lot of time to pack, so he doubted she had much to choose from.

After swinging his legs off the bed, he stood naked and padded to the bathroom, where he washed his face. A quick look in the mirror confirmed his need for blood. Hell, one look at him and Gabby might think he had come down with a bug.

Glancing at the watch he wore on his left wrist, he saw it was half-past ten. After making love through most of the night, they had managed a few hours of sleep. Maybe Gabby had run out to pick up breakfast, sustenance that would do little for him. His wallet lay open next to her backpack. Thankfully, she had the foresight to use cash. He'd need to make his own excuses soon, take a leave and find a housekeeper, clerk, or hotel guest. At this point, any artery would do.

If Ryder went too long without blood, the hunger would weaken him. He couldn't allow his guard down with Raúl's goons combing the country for them. Scrubbing a hand over his bearded jaw, he growled. Gabby should've awakened him, sending him for the food. He was obviously the less recognizable of the two.

He needed to get dressed and go look for her.

Ryder slipped on the jeans he had discarded the night before. After pulling his T-shirt over his head, he stepped into his boots before making tracks for the door. Just as he opened it, Gabriela squealed, joggling the paper cups in her hand.

"You scared me."

He frowned. "Where did you go?"

"I just went looking for coffee, Captain Clueless." She smiled, holding up the two cups.

Ryder gripped her biceps and pulled her into the room. He did a quick sweep of the hallway, seeing she hadn't been followed, before closing the door with his foot.

"You should've sent me, Gabby. We can't take any chances. You're too recognizable."

"You worry too much, Ryder. I didn't even leave the hotel. I found a quaint little shop in the lobby and no one paid me any mind." She handed him a cup of the brew. He could scent the rich flavor. "I thought you might need a little caffeine following last night. Speaking of, you're looking a little ashen. Are you feeling okay?"

Ryder set the cup on the desk and ran a knuckle down her cheek. He had never seen anyone more gorgeous, even someone fresh out of bed.

Don't get too fucking used to it. She's not yours to keep.

"I'm fine. Just a lack of sleep, thanks to you."

Gabby's grin turned naughty. "I know a way we can pass the time today, if you're up for it."

"Cards? Movies?" He laughed. Just the thought of playing with her had him semi-hard. "Not that I don't want to take you up on your offer and toss you on that mattress, but I need to go out. I'll bring you back breakfast. Any requests?"

"A yogurt and some fresh fruit maybe? We know we could call room service, if you'd like?"

"I need to take a look around, Gabby."

"Where?"

"I need to do a quick check of the hotel and surrounding grounds, maybe circle a few blocks. I have to make sure your uncle's men aren't snooping about. If so, you could've been seen. Besides, the sun might do me some good, help my pastiness." He winked. "While I'm gone, lock the door and throw the deadbolt. Don't answer for anyone. Not even housekeeping. Am I clear?"

She nodded, her lips turning down. "We can't live like this, Ryder. I can't run from my uncle forever. Maybe I should call him. Explain things."

Ryder pulled her into his embrace and kissed her forehead. "As much as I'd like to think that would work, I can't let you do that, Gabby. He'd kill me on sight and punish you for disobeying him. You and I both know Raúl is not a man of honor. We can't trust him, not even where you're concerned now."

She pressed her cheek against his chest and wrapped her arms around his waist. "Then what will we do? Uncle Raúl won't stop looking for me."

"I don't have the answers yet. But no, *ángel*, he won't." Ryder disentangled himself from Gabby, grabbed his cell and pocketed it. Opening the door, he glanced back. "Lock up. No one comes in."

When she nodded, he stepped into the hall, wasting little time. He moved along the shadows in stealth until he hit the stairs, where he descended with a speed unknown to man. Riding an elevator would have taken far too much time, being they were on the fourth floor. Reaching the ground level mere seconds later, Ryder slowed his pace, his gaze taking in the tourists and locals. No one paid attention to him. He slipped down first-floor hallway, spotting a housekeeping cart next to an opened door. If the housekeeper was alone, she was brunch.

Ryder slipped down the empty hall and ducked into the room without notice.

The woman smiled warmly as he entered, no doubt mistaking him for the room's occupant.

"*Hola, señor. ¿Qué puedo hacer por usted?*"

Ryder wasn't sure she understood English, which would mess up his plans to hypnotize her.

"Do you speak English?"

"*Sí.*" She nodded. "I will be done in a few. Is there anything I can do for you?"

"Actually..." Ryder smiled as he approached.

Moments later, he wiped the remaining blood from his lips and left the woman to go about her business none the wiser but with a lot less energy. Warmth spread through him, heating what was moments ago cold. Looking at his hands, he was pleased to see the healthy glow of his skin return.

Now, to do a quick look around the resort, find Gabby some breakfast, and head back to the room. Her idea of passing the time brought a smile to his face. Ryder wasn't about to pass up the chance to squander the day in bed with her.

Later, he hoped to hear from his MC brothers that Raúl had met the Grim Reaper. No way in hell was the son of a bitch seeing the pearly gates. He deserved nothing more than hell and damnation.

GABBY HEARD A KEYCARD slide through the slot on the outside of the door. With a smile and anxious to see Ryder again, she nearly skipped to the entrance and drew back the deadbolt. The door swung inward, stopping her breath. Some of Ryder's parting words tumbled through her addled brain.

"Don't answer for anyone..."

The hand that covered her mouth stopped the scream bubbling up her throat. They'd had a keycard to her room. How?

"Where the fuck is he?" Sergio growled.

Luis slammed the door behind him. The ugly smile on the portly man's face didn't reach his baleful eyes. He pulled back the curtains, opened one of the sliding doors, and looked across the terrace to the marina. A cool, salt-scented breeze filled the room. She doubted he was enjoying the view. Were more of her uncle's men outside or had these two come alone? Her heart sank to the pit of her stomach. Gabriela had fucked up. She shouldn't have gone with Ryder and insisted he leave on his own. It was obvious now that her uncle would never let her go. Her delusion in thinking otherwise would get the man she had grown to love killed.

Gabby squirmed in Sergio's grasp, but his grip proved too strong. He spun her in his arms so that her back rested against his chest, one arm acting as a band of steel holding her arms flush against her sides. Moisture gathered in her eyes. Sergio kept his hand clasped over her mouth, clamped so tight she couldn't sink her teeth into the flesh.

Luis turned, his smile gone. "Where the fuck is Ryder, Gabby? I'm going to ask Sergio to kindly remove his hand so you can talk. If you scream, I'll make you wish you hadn't."

Sergio removed his hand but kept her tight within his hold. She needed to think of a plan, one that would get them out of there long before Ryder returned. It would be her only way to save him.

"Now, I repeat, where is Ryder?"

Tears slipped down her face unheeded. Her gaze dropped to the gun Luis pointed in her direction.

"I don't know," she whispered.

How quickly could she get them on their way back to La Paz?

"Wrong answer, sweetheart." Luis stepped forward and slapped her. Her head jerked to the side, her cheek stinging and her ears ringing. "Where. The. Fuck. Is. He?"

"He's not coming back."

Luis struck her a second time. More tears sprang to her eyes. His nod indicated the motorcycle keys on the desk.

"Don't fucking lie to me, Gabriela. I'm not here to play games. I'll ask you one more time."

"Just take me," she replied. "Ryder is of no use to my uncle. I'll go peacefully if you'll let him go. It's me my uncle wants anyway."

Sergio laughed, his hot breath rustling her hair. Gabriela knew he had a mean streak, though he rarely showed it to her. Revulsion sent tremors through her. She'd not show them fear. Tightening her jaw and squaring her shoulders, she glared at Luis.

"You *estúpido coño*." Sergio hissed the last word, reminding her of a snake. How fitting. "You really think your uncle wants your fuck toy left alive?"

"Let me call my uncle. Explain to him. Surely he won't kill Ryder if he knows how much he means to me."

"How much he means to you?" Sergio slipped his free hand down the front of her sundress and between her thighs, sickening her. "This was to be mine, puta. Not some *Americano's*. And yet you spread your legs so easily to him."

"Get your hand off me." If she'd had Luis's gun, she'd shoot Sergio right between the thighs. "I never belonged to you. I never will."

"You're not good enough." Sergio spat at her feet. "Had your uncle not wanted you back alive, I'd make you fish bait along with your friend. But now, I must convince Raúl to let me marry a *puta*. It was never you I wanted anyway. You were a means to an end."

"I'll never agree." A sense of loathing washed over her, and she was no longer able to curb her mouth. "You disgust me."

"It really doesn't matter what you think, Gabriela. Your uncle won't give you a choice. After your little stunt, he'll need me to keep an eye on you."

Gabby choked back a sob. She'd die first. For now, though, she'd act as if she'd go along with his insanity. She needed to save Ryder. The thought of losing him damn near crippled her.

"You let Ryder go and I'll marry you. I won't even fight you unless you try to come to my bed."

"I'll need an heir, *puta*. Something to solidify my place in your family."

A shiver passed down her spine. Her hope lay in talking her uncle out of Sergio's crazy plan. The man was certifiable. To invite himself into their home, her bed? The thought had the bile churning in her stomach.

Her gaze went to Luis, his gun now aimed at Sergio's head, his finger still on the trigger. Luis's face damn near purpled in his mounting rage. Sergio had likely never voiced his designs on Gabriela, using her to better his position with her uncle. Had he done so, Raúl's captain no doubt would have taken him out long before reaching his goal. Gabriela would bet her life that no one had aspired to take over Luis's position and lived to tell about it.

Luis's gaze narrowed. "So, you think you can take *my* job? Take my place in the family?"

Sergio tightened his hold on Gabby, ducking behind her and using her as a shield. The man was a complete coward. "You were never going to step down, Luis. I had to look out for myself. What better way than to marry Raúl's niece? And the money will be all mine once I take out Raúl. *Everything* will be mine."

Luis's smile turned savage. If the shorter man could get off a shot, Sergio would be a dead man, but he'd not risk shooting Gabriela. Where Sergio wasn't loyal to her uncle, Luis was a company man. He had been with her uncle a good long time. She was pretty sure her uncle considered him like family. Luis would never think to cross Raúl.

He continued pointing his gun at both of them. "*Pinche idiota*! You won't get out of here alive."

Sergio took a few steps in Luis's direction, Gabriela still firm within his grip. "I'll take her with me."

Luis's gun arm wavered. "And where will you go? Raúl will have you killed once your deception is discovered. That is, if I don't kill you *first*."

Sergio laughed, the sound demonic, pure evil. "You won't get the chance to tell Raúl."

"And why's that, *cabron*? I'm the one holding the gun. Do you really want to chance that you can get to your pistol before I can pull the trigger?"

Without warning, Sergio shoved Gabby into the nearest wall, hard enough to crack her head. She slid to the floor a heap, her vision briefly splitting in two. Sergio charged Luis and the gun went off, the bullet missing the man. Sergio being the stronger of the two, grabbed Luis by the collar and shoved him through the opening in the sliding glass doors. Luis hit the patio table, the wood breaking beneath his weight, sending them both to the floor. The two men wrestled for the gun.

Blood ran down Gabby's face from the cut she'd received to her head. After stumbling to her feet, she placed a hand over the wound and floundered toward the ruckus on the terrace. Using their scuffle as her means of escape wasn't an option. She could barely stand on her two feet. Blackness edged her vision, threatening to claim her.

Gabriela lost her balance, nearly tumbling over the barrel chair facing the terrace. She prayed Ryder would stay gone, fearing for his life. Luis's scream rang in her ears just as she stumbled to the terrace. In horror, she watched Luis flip backward over the railing. She heard the sickening thud on the cement walkway four stories down.

Sergio turned, his crazed gaze finding her. After pulling a gun from his boot, he pointed it at Gabby. *Like he needed the gun.* What was she going to do in her present condition? Hell, she could barely stand.

He bared his teeth. "Too bad you're worth more alive to me than dead, my little *puta*. I could say that Luis had shot you and I'd tried defending you by pushing him over the railing, but that would gain me nothing. So, we will wait right here for your friend. Once I kill him, we'll blame Luis's death on *him*."

"I'll never agree to that story, you fool."

"Then I'll kill you both. Either way, with Luis dead, I'll step into his position and bide my time. I'll be the son your uncle never had. With you out of the way, I'll inherit it all once I get rid of Raúl."

His savage grin caused her stomach to further churn. Gabby wrapped her arms around her middle and tried to calm the nausea. Her stomach cramped and she bent at the waist. Vomit hit the floor near Sergio's feet, splashing onto his boots. Just as he raised his gun to backhand her with it, an animal-like roar had them both gaping at the terrace.

Ryder stood on the railing, arms stretched to the sides as if he had leapt four stories to the balcony. Great, now she was hallucinating. No way he could have jumped. And the last time she'd checked, Ryder didn't have big white fangs.

Gabby plopped into the chair. She placed a palm on her head wound and groaned. A fairly large lump protruded from her skull and hurt like hell. Thankfully, the blood flow had slowed. She might live. Or at least, that was her hope.

Sergio screamed like a little bitch. Ryder picked him up as if he weighed no more than a toothpick and hurled him against the adjacent wall. The room shook. Paintings rattled against the wall as he crashed to the floor.

Blinking to clear her vision, she watched Ryder advance on Sergio, who had somehow still managed to hold onto his gun. He aimed it at Ryder, and to Gabby's horror, fired. The bullet hit Ryder in the chest, just above the heart, and he stumbled back.

She screamed.

But before she could get to her feet and run to him, he squared his shoulders. Righting himself, He let out an ear-piercing roar and advanced on Sergio with inhuman speed. Gabby blinked again, shaking her head.

Ryder growled, white fangs glistening in the sunlight streaming through the sliding glass doors. Grabbing Sergio's head, he gave a twist. Bones cracked and the man's neck snapped like a twig. He dropped to the floor, his head hanging at an odd angle.

Gabriela sucked in a sob. Her gaze flew up to the hole in Ryder's chest. While blood still flowed from the cut to her head, his wound no longer bled. How in the world? Her gaze traveled to his face. She barely recognized the man before her, his cheeks hollow, his brow more prominent. His eyes had become mirror-like pools of black ink. But nothing compared to the long razor-sharp fangs still visible beneath his upper lip. Ryder closed the distance between them in the time it took her to blink.

"*Ángel*," was the last thing Gabby heard before blackness consumed her vision. His strong arms caught her before she tumbled out of the chair and lost consciousness.

CHAPTER TWENTY

On the opposite side of the pebbled drive from Grigore, Kane and Kaleb hunched down by the massive iron gates leading into Raúl's fortress. Peter had called an hour ago, informing them that he had finally spotted the resident's owner, the slippery little rat. Raúl was indeed within the walls of the estate. Grigore wasted little time relaying the message to the twins and the rest of their crew who now surrounded the place.

Constantine had used his computer skills to temporarily rewind the live feed to the cameras, giving them about an hour to get in and out without being discovered. Grigore hoped it took less time. The mission was simple, get in, kill anyone who resists and hypnotize those who don't, take out Raúl, and get out. Leave the carnage to the authorities, but ash Raúl's remains. They couldn't chance leaving his vampire DNA to an autopsy.

Grigore tipped his nose to the sky and sniffed. He wasn't able to detect another vampire in the area other than those on his team, which meant Raúl wouldn't be able to detect them either. Once they moved beyond the thick cement walls encircling the estate, that might all change, depending on the thickness of the structure and how much Raúl's vampire DNA had progressed. Being newer, his skills would be lacking compared to theirs. Even so, once in, they needed to act fast. Leave nothing to chance.

Kaleb touched the speaking device in his right ear. "Is everyone in position? We go in five."

Grigore heard the affirmations in his earpiece.

"When any of you have eyes on Raúl, tell Kane and me. No questions asked. He is not yours to take out. Copy that?"

Grigore's gaze landed on Kane, knowing the man was about to serve long-overdue justice after years of anguish from losing his only son to the bastard.

An eye for an eye.

It had to feel damn good.

"No one goes in that hasn't tapped into their vampire. Take no chances. These men are deadly and I'm sure Raúl has told them how to take out vampires. We don't know for sure how many men are with him, but I'm betting it's a skeleton crew. He no doubt has his best men combing Mexico, looking for his niece and Ryder. I want every damn one of us walking out of there today. No casualties on our side. You run into trouble, don't play hero. Ask for help. Are we clear?"

Excitement coursed through Grigore. Man, he lived for this shit. Some days, Oregon was just too damn quiet for his liking, what with the Devils crippled losing their leaders and the Knights becoming Sons. Hell, even Vlad had Mircea under control. Where was the fun in that?

He glanced at Kaleb, waiting for his direction to storm the place. He had no idea how many soldiers were inside, but anticipation channeled through him, ready to start taking down these fucks. Time to dismember the cartel, one miserable fuck at a time.

He rubbed his hands together. "Let's fucking rock!"

Kaleb smiled, his fangs protruding past his lower lip as he gave a thumbs-up. Kane's lips turned down, his obsidian, marble-like gaze trained on the upper balcony where Peter had last seen Raúl. When Viper and Kane's inner vampire came out, they were scary motherfuckers, leaving no doubt they came from the loins of Vlad.

Showtime!

Grigore called forth his vampire. A growl bubbled up his throat. He was so pumped, every muscle in him ached with the need to cause some serious fucking damage. His hot gaze landed on Kaleb, who held up his hand and started ticking off his fingers one-by-one.

When his pinky touched his palm, Kaleb barked into the intercom, "Let's rock!"

Grigore moved to the thick iron gates. A keypad was positioned to the right. He wouldn't be needing the code. Gripping the bars in his fists, Grigore's muscles bunched as he pulled them apart. Metal screeched and bars popped from the frame, though not separating the opening and triggering alarms. The same reason they had decided not to leap the gates. Kane and Kaleb slipped through the opening he had created. Grigore followed along the wall behind them as they stayed out of the line of sight and headed for the mansion. Hell, he didn't think he had ever been inside an estate this elaborate. Raúl had good taste, Grigore would give him that much.

Skirting the swimming pool and the spa, Kane and Kaleb arrived at the first-floor entrance without being seen, most likely due to their speed and agility. Grigore had a hell of a time keeping up. Raúl had a complex alarm system, one Constantine hadn't been able to disarm. Once they opened a door or entered through a window, chaos would in all probability ensue. They were about to take the house by storm.

"Everyone in position?" Kaleb whispered into the mic.

Once all affirmations arrived, Kaleb looked at his brother. Kane's smile was scary as fuck, making Grigore glad he wasn't going to be on the receiving end of Kane's unleashed temper. "You ready to put an end to this, bro?"

"More than ready," Kane replied, his tone thick due to the massive fangs filling his mouth. "Let's get that motherfucker."

Grigore had the best men for the job by his side. It was time to take out some of Mexico's lowlifes. "Let's roll."

The first alarm sounded as one of their men entered the estate from a different side. Kaleb looked at Kane, then smashed his fist through the window of the door, setting off another wail. Getting a grip on the window frame, Kane and Kaleb yanked the steel door from its hinges. Metal scraped metal and alarms grew in volume as their men entered from all sides.

Stepping into the hall, Grigore heard booted feet running above them. He could tell by his surroundings that they had entered through the servants' quarters. As Kane and Kaleb headed for the stairs, Grigore manned the front of the house, his gaze taking in the area, seeing no one about.

Where the fuck was everyone?

He tipped his nose to the ceiling, smelling the first of human blood being spilled. Screams sounded over the sirens. Grigore skirted the interior hall, keeping an eye on the rooms, making sure he left no one alive behind. His nose picked up the scent of a human ahead. Quickly casing the rooms as he moved down the hall, he then entered a massive pristine kitchen. A robust man in chef's garb cowered in the far corner near the ovens.

Grigore growled, earning a scream from the man. "You want to stay and fight, or you do want to walk out alive, *amigo*?"

"Alive, *señ* ... *señor*."

The scent of urine and the wet spot on the man's trousers told Grigore he wasn't a threat. He framed the man's cheeks with his palms, quickly hypnotizing him, sending him running out the door and likely off the estate. Grigore canvassed the rest of the rooms, finding no other humans, then took the steps to the first floor where most of the activity could be heard. And to his dismay, was already starting to die down. His brothers had a handle on this area of the estate. Damn, he was missing all the action.

Grigore took the stairs four at a time to the top floor to check on the twins. The real action would be with the kingpin. Raúl's best men would be guarding him, though Grigore seriously doubted they would've been a match for the Tepes brothers. Clearing the stairwell, he rounded the corner and was hit square in the face by the butt of a gun, snapping back his head and breaking his nose.

"Motherfucker!"

Grigore grabbed the guy by his bulletproof vest and threw him down the stairwell. Judging by the angle of the guy's neck, it wasn't necessary to go after him. Grigore pinched the bridge of his nose and jerked it into place, hearing the tiny bones and cartilage snap. The healing would be swift, but it still hurt like a son of a bitch.

Grigore headed for the room at the end of the wide hall. Neither seeing nor hearing anyone else alive in his path, he followed the sound of Kane and Kaleb's voices. Someone screamed like a little bitch, Grigore betting on that being Raúl since he could now scent the bastard. As he passed several open doors, he spotted dead soldiers along the way, no doubt the work of the twins.

Grigore stopped just shy of entering what looked to be a massive master suite. After taking a quick look down the empty hallway, noting he hadn't been followed, he ducked into the room. This motherfucker had spent a small fortune on lavish decorations. Grigore bet he could feed an entire community on the cost of the ornate items in this room alone.

Raúl screamed again, bringing Grigore's focus to the en-suite beyond the sitting area. He jogged to the opened door. Kane held Raúl high off the marble floor, his throat firmly in his grasp. The kingpin's face mottled purple. At present, Raúl didn't look like a man responsible for the deaths of thousands. Instead, he looked like a sniveling coward, vampire or no. His obsidian eyes damn near popped out of his head. Blood ran from already healing cuts, proof of the beating Kane had likely already given him.

And Kane? He appeared ready to snap the motherfucker's neck. Maybe Raúl should've thought of that when he'd ordered Kane's only son to be murdered, even if it was in payment for Rosalee killing his brother. Raúl's mistake was making Ion pay for the sins of his mother.

It's well past the time to put this shit to rest.

Kaleb stood to the side, hip cocked against the nearby counter, arms folded across his chest, smiling, clearly enjoying the show. The rest of the house grew quiet as the alarms cut short, no doubt one of the Sons, likely Constantine, having had enough of the ear-piercing screech.

"Today you die," Kane growled, baring his fangs.

"I'll give you money … anything! Just ask," Raúl sniveled, his arms and legs flailing.

Kane's answering laugh echoed through the massive bathroom. "You have nothing of value I'd want. You already took the one thing from me of any worth. For that, I'm giving you a one-way ticket to hell, motherfucker."

"Son of a fucking bitch," came across their collective earpieces.

Kaleb's smile left his face and Kane's arm wavered, Raúl jostling in his grip. Kaleb touched the mic on the earpiece. "What is it?"

"It's Lightning, man," came Peter's shaken voice.

"What about him, Rocker?" Grigore growled, not having a good feeling about what might have happened to Constantine.

"Motherfucker! His head's blown clean off."

Grigore roared. Anguish gripped his chest and damn near stopped his breathing. "Where the fuck are you?"

"Level two, man."

"And the fuck responsible?"

"Dead. I already took him out." Agony laced Peter's tone. The two men had been like brothers since they had prospected together. "Looks like Lightning got caught with his back unprotected when he silenced the alarms."

"Bring his body," Kaleb said.

"On my way." The intercom cut short.

Grigore looked at Kaleb. "What do we do with him?"

"As much as I hate to say it, we'll have to ash him with this fuck."

Grigore hardened his jaw. "Lightning deserves *better*. I'll personally carry his body back to Oregon."

"Be realistic, Wolf. We can't take his body with us. How the hell would you get him across the border? We need to finish this and get the fuck out. We all agreed, in and out."

Grigore knew Kaleb was correct, but that didn't make swallowing the bitter pill any easier. They couldn't be seen with Constantine's headless body. The fucking police in Mexico worked for Raúl. They'd have a heyday with the Sons.

The longer they spent here, the better the chances of getting caught in the melee.

"Then finish this and let's get the fuck out of here," Grigore growled.

Kane's lips thinned. Without another word, he twisted Raúl's head from his body with his bare hands. Blood splattered and Raúl's scream cut short. Kane strode to the four-person spa tub and dropped the head next to the body with a thud. Peter came skidding to a halt and gently laid Constantine's body and head onto Raúl's. Tears streamed down his comrade's face.

Motherfucker!

Grigore grabbed the can of gas one of his Washington brothers had brought. They all circled the tub, distress and heartbreak in their gazes.

"I'll drink to you when we get home, Lightning! You didn't deserve this, brother."

Grigore poured the gas over the bodies and tossed in a match. The accelerant caught and flames climbed toward the ceiling, the heat nearly unbearable. Grigore was the last to back away. If the son of a bitch who took out Constantine wasn't already dead, he would've made the fuck suffer a good long time. His death had been too fucking easy.

"Let's get on the road before we have more of these moles to deal with." Kaleb placed a hand on Kane's shoulder. "We good?"

Kane's black gaze looked at each one of the men. "Lightning is on me. I failed him in my need for revenge."

"Fuck, Viper," Grigore said. "This ain't on you, brother. You know as well as I do nothing is guaranteed in any mission. Let's get the hell out of here, bro, and back on the road. I, for one, am ready to get back to Oregon."

With one last look at the conflagration crawling up the curtains and wall, the crew walked to the patio, jumped the four stories to the grass, and hit the ground running.

GABRIELA SAT UP, UNSURE OF her surroundings. It wasn't the same hotel room she had shared with Ryder. As a matter of fact, it wasn't a hotel at all. Judging by the salt-scented breeze fluttering through the curtains on the open window, she guessed it to be a small cottage by the ocean. Swinging her legs to the side of the full-sized bed, her head swam with memories.

What the hell?

Fangs?

Bending forward, she gulped in large amounts of air, hoping to stave off rising nausea. Images of Luis flipping backward over the railing, Sergio's head hanging at an odd angle, blood on her hands from the cut on her forehead, Ryder standing on the balcony rail as if had just leaped four stories, all came back in stark HD reality. Maybe the knock on her head had been worse than she thought, causing her to hallucinate.

Surely, the fangs are the product of my dreams.

Right?

Vampires weren't real.

Gabby righted herself as nausea began to subside. She glanced around the room. The bedroom bore a bed, nightstand, and small dresser. The only door led to what looked like a small sitting room. Standing slowly, making sure she wouldn't pass out again, Gabby made her way to the door. The living area connected with a kitchenette. A bathroom stood adjacent to the bedroom, its door also open, proving she was alone.

Where was Ryder?

Leaving the bedroom, she was drawn forward by a breeze from the cabin's open door fluttering her dress. Sunlight streamed through the screen facing the ocean. Gabby stopped short of going onto the deck, spotting Ryder with a cell phone to his ear, pacing the white sand of the beach. He turned as if sensing her, concern visible in his gaze. He quickly pocketed the phone and headed for the cabin.

No fangs. No black marbles for eyes. His face was as handsome as ever. The wallop to her head must have knocked her senseless. And yet, the fangs? The memory of them was almost too real to dismiss.

"You're up." Ryder looked at her, something in his gaze amiss. "I was worried about you."

"Who were you talking to?"

"No one. I didn't get an answer."

Gabriela opened the screen and stepped onto the small front porch, the breeze shifting through her hair. She tucked the stray strands behind her ear. "Where are we?"

"An hour up the coast, about a mile outside of Todos Santos. With Sergio and Luis dead, I couldn't take the chance of your uncle's men finding us again."

"So that really happened?"

He nodded but added nothing, eyeing her with caution.

Moisture gathered in her eyes. "Uncle Raúl won't stop. Maybe you should take me home."

"Is that what you want?"

She bit the inside of her lip, trying her damnedest to hold the tears at bay. Of course, she didn't want to go home. She wanted to stay with Ryder. Well, at least she thought she did until the fangs came to mind again. Gabby shook her head, telling herself it had to have been part of a dream. But if Sergio and Luis's deaths had been real? With Ryder confirming as much, maybe it hadn't been a hallucination after all. Gabby wasn't sure what she wanted, nor did she know any longer what was real or a figment of her imagination.

"What I don't want is you dead, Ryder. If Luis and Sergio had come looking for me, it's only a matter of time before my uncle sends more soldiers. He'll be furious his top two men were killed. Not to mention the two you killed earlier. He'll stop at nothing."

He nodded but again stayed strangely quiet.

"Can I ask you a question?"

"What is it, *ángel*?"

"Are vampires real?"

Ryder stared at her for so long, that for a moment, she didn't think he'd answer. Maybe he thought her certifiable.

Hell, the idea of vampires being real was certainly insane in her book.

"What do you remember, Gabby?"

"I remember Sergio and Luis fighting and Luis falling to his death. I remember Sergio plotting to kill you and blaming you for Luis's death." She paused, looking at the wooden decking, toying with a knot in the wood with her big toe. "I remember seeing you on the balcony railing, and being unsure of how you got there."

She glanced up. "I remember you looking different, and yet you were still you. But mostly? I remember your fangs. Tell me I'm crazy, Ryder."

Ryder peered down the beach to several other cottages squatting along the coast. Families milled about, playing in the surf, kids making sandcastles. He grimaced, then looked back at her.

"You aren't crazy, *ángel*."

She sucked in oxygen. "You're a vampire? Then you're dead? And that's why the bullet to your chest didn't kill you."

He smiled, though it wasn't the smile she had grown accustomed to. This one seemed tinged with sadness, as if he knew they had no future. And maybe they didn't. Maybe she needed to do what was best for both of them and go home. So why did her heart hurt so damn bad?

"I'm not dead, nor do I sparkle in the sunlight. I don't have rotting flesh and I don't sleep in coffins during the day. Sunlight"—his hands indicated the daylight—"doesn't turn me ash, though I may burn easier than most, and garlic does nothing for me. That's all part of the fictional vampire you've read about."

"You drink blood?"

He nodded. "It's what keeps me alive."

Gabby rubbed the side of her neck. "Have you...?"

One of his brows shot up. "I assure you, I haven't taken any of yours. I would have asked your permission first, Gabby."

"We made love."

"We did." His smile grew a bit naughty. "As I recall, you did give your permission for that and you quite enjoyed yourself."

She couldn't argue. "Then where do you get your blood?"

"For the most part, we have donors. Women who belong to a society that gladly offers us sustenance."

"You don't kill them ... do you?"

"There is no need to drain them. We take only what we need. Trust me, it doesn't hurt them in the least. As a matter of fact, it can be quite pleasurable."

"Do you eat regular food?"

He shrugged. "I can and even enjoy it, but it does nothing for me. I have to drink blood if I'm to stay alive."

She nodded again, not sure she fully understood. There was just too much to process and her head was already spinning. "Are there others?"

"Yes. From where I come from."

"Does anyone else know about you?"

He rubbed a hand down his jaw. She could tell he wasn't comfortable with her questions even if he answered them. "No one other than the donors who are sworn to secrecy. If others knew, we would be hunted down and killed. Think about it, Gabby. Even now you look at me differently. You fear me and you have to know that I would never harm you."

Gabby thought about it. Ryder was still the same man she had fallen in love with. The only difference was the whole vampirism thing. Well, to be honest, that was a pretty *big* thing.

"Where do we go from here?"

"That's up to you, *ángel*. You can either go home once it's safe ... or you can come with me to Oregon. Either way, I'm not safe here. You said yourself that Raúl will stop at nothing to see me dead."

She tugged her lower lip between her teeth, torn with doing what was right and what she wanted. While her heart chose Ryder, her head knew he'd never be safe with her. They would always need to be one step ahead of her uncle. It would never end.

"I should probably go home."

His face darkened and his lips turned down. Surely her admission hadn't wounded him, had it? Was it possible he loved her, too?

"As you wish. I'll see that you get home safely."

"What do you want, Ryder?"

He tilted his head toward the sandy deck beneath his feet, hiding his expression. "What I want is to keep you safe. That's all that really matters to me."

"Do you want me to go with you?"

He glanced up and crossed the distance between them. She could see in the way he looked at her that he cared. But did that mean love?

"If I knew I could keep you safe from your uncle ... fuck, Gabby, I'd never let you go. But at this moment, I can't promise you that. I can promise, though, that I'd die trying."

"See? And that's why I can't go with you. Like it or not, Ryder, and as crazy as it all seems with this whole vampire thing, I've fallen in love with you. I can't go with you and allow my uncle or his men to harm you. Maybe, once I talk to Uncle Raúl..."

"You have to know, *ángel*, he won't change his mind about me, not for you or anyone."

She nodded, knowing Ryder was correct. Her only way to protect him was to leave him. "Then I need to go home. But before I find a way back to La Paz, tell me ... do you love me?"

Ryder looked at her as if he meant to deny her. But instead, he gripped the back of her head and slanted his lips over hers, kissing her in what felt like desperation. And yet, it still wasn't an admission. Gabby clung to his arms, hating with every fiber of her being that she may never see him again. She kissed him with passion and need. Vampire or not, she still loved this man.

When he set her away, tears streamed down her face. Gabby wished things could be different, wished her guardian was anyone but the man who had raised her.

Instead of making a fool of herself and begging Ryder to go on the run with her, she asked, "Can I borrow your cell? I'll make arrangements for someone to come pick me up in town."

He paused, tightening his jaw, but reached into his jean pocket, pulling out the phone and handing it to her. "Who are you going to call?"

"Adriana will come to get me. At the moment, I trust her the most. She won't let anyone know where she's going. That will give you time to go to America, get a head start."

The cell vibrated in her hand. She glanced down.

Raúl is dead. Your mission is done.

Gabby gasped. Another text came across the screen.

Secure the little princess a trip home and get the hell out of Mexico.

She gaped at Ryder. He grabbed for the phone, but she jerked it from his reach. A third text came through.

It was better that you got her out of there so we had a clean shot at Raúl.

"My uncle is dead?" Gabby had trouble catching her breath. "I was a part of a mission to you, so you and your friends could kill my uncle?"

Lightning took a fall. Hawk wants you back in Oregon in 2 days so we can give him a proper send off.

She looked up at him, feeling more shocked by this news than the unbelievable truth of what he was. This other realization hurt more than she could bear. "You never loved me, did you? That's why you wouldn't answer me. I was just part of your assignment."

Watch your back, dude, stay safe. See you back at the clubhouse.

Ryder grabbed the phone from her now slack grip and read through the texts. His face paled. Glancing up, he reached for her arm. Gabby stumbled backward, away from him, snatching his phone in the process. She quickly punched in Adriana's cell number and waited for her to pick up.

"It's me, Adriana."

"Gabs? Are you okay? I don't recognize this phone number."

"I'm fine. I need you to come pick me up."

Gabriela looked at Ryder, who rattled off how to get to town from the cottage and the name of a small eatery she could meet Adriana. She repeated the directions to Adriana, asking her friend to come alone and to tell no one, that she would explain everything once she got there, then ended the call.

"Gabby, listen—"

"No, *you* listen. I don't ever want to see you again. Adriana is coming. I'm no longer your problem ... your *mission*. But you need to leave Mexico."

"Christ, you may have started off as a mission to me, but—"

"But what, Ryder?"

Her anger hit a high note. She had never been so furious. Ryder had used her. The exact reason she didn't do relationships. And now? She was responsible for the death of her uncle.

He managed to get a grip on her wrist and pulled her to him. She slammed against his solid chest. Struggling in his grasp, her efforts proved futile.

"Damn it, Gabby, I'm trying to tell you that I love you."

She laughed hysterically. "Now you suddenly find the words. That's just great. Well, guess what? They're insincere and you have rotten-fucking-timing. Let go of me."

Ryder did as she asked, his gaze filled with sorrow. Lord, she wouldn't do this ... couldn't do this. She wouldn't be played for a fool a second time.

"Ryder Kelley, you're dead to me."

A muscle in his jaw ticked. "I can't allow you to leave here knowing about vampires, what I am."

Gabby shook her head and repeated, "Dead. To. Me. Your secret is safe. That is, unless you feel the need to kill or have me killed, too."

He placed his hands on his hips, drawing her gaze down his shirtless torso, then back to his face. She should've known no one like him would ever be interested in someone like her. Where he had the body of a Greek god, she had curves he couldn't possibly appreciate. Gabriela looked away, feeling ashamed. How had she been so stupid?

"They're not just words, *ángel*."

"Then prove it to me."

Ryder's brow furrowed. "How?"

"By letting me go. I promise I won't tell anyone what you are. Your secret is safe." Gabby licked her lips. "If you really love me, then let me go."

Ryder took a step back, turned, and headed for the ocean. Sobs tore through her as she watched his retreating back. Gabriela ran into the cabin, gathered her things, then slung her backpack over her shoulder.

She returned to the deck. Ryder stood by the ocean, overlooking the horizon. Gabby wiped the wetness from her cheeks, circled the little cottage, and headed for town.

CHAPTER TWENTY-ONE

"WHERE THE FUCK IS HE?"

Vlad's mighty roar shook a nearby vase on a pedestal, sending it crashing to the floor. Tiny shards of porcelain tinkled about the marble. Ignoring the mess, Vlad stomped off in the direction of the kitchen. Most of his servants would be gathered there sharing a morning meal, knowing that he was rarely up at this hour.

When he entered the room, all talk ceased as everyone turned to look at him. He could see it in their fretful gazes that the thunderous look on his face caused trepidation among his people.

He took a deep breath, hoping to calm this rage. *Anger will get you nothing ... anger will get you nothing.* He didn't care how many times he repeated that line in his thick skull, it wasn't going to help. Not today, not with Mircea missing.

"Please tell me my brother has gone for a stroll on the beach and is not missing altogether. Can anyone explain to me why the locked room I last left him in is now empty?"

It was obvious by the way they all turned and looked at each other that none of them knew Mircea had even flown the coop. Wait ... the little redhead, Nina, was missing from the fray. He knew she had taken a liking to his brother, Mircea having said as much. If the gossip he had been hearing in his bed from his own dalliances were true, then Nina had been spending a considerable amount of time the last couple of days with his brother.

He doubted that both gone missing was a fucking coincidence. Christ, he had been made a fool. Vlad would bet if he searched the entire island, they would both be long gone, along with one of his prized yachts.

"Where is Nina?" He looked at the young blond who had been friends with her since their coming to the island. "I don't see her this morning."

She wrung her hands in her lap. "She wasn't in our quarters when I woke this morning."

"And you didn't think to tell me this?"

"I thought she was with your brother. After all, she was quite taken with him."

"I'm sure she was." He looked around the room no one moving and rolled his eyes. "Seriously? Do I need to fucking ask you to get looking for the pair? I want him found!"

The servants jumped up and scurried from the kitchen. Vlad didn't bother, knowing full well Mircea would be long gone. Unfortunately, Mircea was damn good at hiding when he didn't want to be found and Vlad would likely have to wait until he popped up from going underground, so to speak.

Vlad would need to make immediate plans to head for Oregon and let his grandsons know that Mircea was out, likely gunning for them. Kane and Kaleb would need to be prepared. And this time? They had his fucking blessing to take Mircea's fucking head should he try anything.

GABBY SAT WITH HER FACE in her hands, sobbing in the front seat of Adriana's car as they headed north toward La Paz. Her uncle was dead, along with a good share of men left at the estate. Adriana relayed everything Gabby had told her to Mateo, who had gone to Raúl's and found the carnage. He couldn't positively identify Raúl's remains, but it looked as if he had been torched in the en-suite bathroom.

Set on fire, for crying out loud!

No one deserved that.

Mateo had warned Adriana to take Gabriela to her apartment and not allow her to go home. "It's a fucking mess," had been his exact words. And Gabby had been the one to blame. Her uncle and his men were dead because she had fallen for Ryder, who had used her to destroy the last of her family.

Thankfully, Mateo had been with Adriana at the time and not with Raúl or Gabby would've been consoling her best friend over her fiancé's death as well. No way could she have faced Adriana, knowing his death had been on her shoulders.

Anguish crushed her.

Gabriela knew what her uncle was and what he was responsible for. Something like this could have happened at any given time knowing the enemies he had made in business. But the death strike coming from someone she loved? How could she have been such a fool?

And yet, not only did her heart ache for her uncle and all the men who lost their lives, it ached for Ryder, already missing him. When she had fallen in love with him, she had fallen hard. Nothing had changed that fact. It certainly was possible to hate and love someone simultaneously.

Adriana patted Gabby's knee before taking her hand and lacing fingers with her. Gabriela looked out across the passing scenery, not really seeing it. She could think of only Ryder's devastated expression as she'd told him to let her go if he truly loved her. He had walked away without another word.

Wasn't that what she'd asked for?

"If you really love me, then let me go."

And he had done it without question. My God, he had loved her. More tears streamed down her face as she hiccoughed. After taking back her hand and grabbing a tissue, she blew her already sore nose. The sound filled the silent car. Adriana was giving her time to mourn, to let her express herself, when what she really wanted was someone to tell her everything would be all right.

"What am I going to do, Adri? I feel so lost."

"You love him." Of course, she did. "And he loves you?"

She nodded. "I believe so."

"It sucks what he did, Gabby. I would never pretend to justify it. But your uncle probably had it coming. You must know that. Did you even bother to ask Ryder why?"

Gabby shook her head. "I was so mad, so damn disappointed in him. I told him I never wanted to see him again."

"And yet, you really don't want that. That's why this"—she patted the center of her chest, over her heart—"hurts so much."

"What am I going to do?"

Adriana glanced at her briefly before turning back to the road. "If your uncle had died at the hands of anyone else, would you be so distraught?"

"Yes and no." Anger itched up her spine. She welcomed it, anything but the grief threatening to consume her. "I knew who Uncle Raúl was. I know he was responsible for the death of so many. I truly despised that man. But yes, I would be sad because despite who he was, I loved him. He was all I had. He gave me a home and cared for me after my father was killed."

"Raúl wasn't a nice man. Hell, let's be honest. He was evil."

Gabby hung her head. As long as she could remember, she'd lived in fear of someone using her against Raúl. Or worse, being kidnapped, tortured, and killed because of his enemies. He had caused so much grief in so many lives. Yet, it was as if he'd owned Mexico. Even the police were afraid of him.

"He was a bastard of the worst kind," Gabby whispered.

Adriana didn't reply, allowing Gabriela to process it. Ryder may have been responsible for what had happened, used her so the men who had taken her uncle's life had easy access to him while making sure she was far away from the carnage.

Leaning her head against the seat rest, she groaned. He had even protected her from Sergio, who had turned out to be downright certifiable, killing Luis and wanting to pass the blame to Ryder. Had she not gone along with framing Ryder, Sergio would have killed her as well.

She sighed and repeated, "What am I going to do, Adri?"

Her best friend gave her hand a squeeze. "Nothing right now, sweetie. We're going back to my apartment and we're going to rest. Nothing needs to be decided. Soon enough, you'll need to plan your uncle's funeral. I'll make sure when the police are through, your house is scrubbed clean before you return. You can either sell it or keep it. It's really up to you. With Raúl dead, it all belongs to you. Where you go from here is also up to you."

Gabriela leaned back again, returning her gaze to the horizon. Her head swam, no closer to answers than she had been when Adriana had picked her up in Todos Santos. The one thing she knew, though, was her heart ached for Ryder. Being used by him didn't change that fact. And she'd bet he felt the loss as well. The question wasn't what she was going to do about her uncle's funeral and his estate, but rather what was she going to do about her damn heart?

No longer bound by her uncle, Gabriela could go anywhere in the world. She thought about Adriana and Mateo, wishing she could take her friend with her, as far away from her fiancé as she could. But then, that was Adriana's choice. She'd have to make her own choices in life. Ryder, however, and what to do with him was Gabriela's decision to make. No one could make that choice for her.

She longed for the right answers.

Her head filled with thoughts of Ryder and the way he had used her, but mostly the way he had loved her, Gabby closed her eyes and drifted off to sleep, exhaustion claiming her.

THE CLUBHOUSE WAS STRANGELY dormant. Not that Grigore was complaining, but it wasn't the norm. He wasn't sure where everyone had run off to, though most were likely catching up with their mates. Alexander and India were settling into their new home, leaving him and Ryder the clubhouse's exclusive residents at the moment. With Constantine gone, he couldn't help but wonder if Peter might want to move into Alexander's old room. The house they shared would be a hurtful reminder of the friend Peter had lost, the friend they all had lost.

Grigore leaned back and took in the peace and quiet. He wasn't in any big hurry to offer up the space and further take away what privacy he had. Too many times the clubhouse was splitting at the seams with members and their families, more so than he liked. There was a time to party, and then there was a time to go the fuck home so he could enjoy his seclusion once again.

Why the hell did I move into the clubhouse?

He knew the answers. Because he needed chaos in his life to quiet the memories, to help him move beyond his troubled past and forget who he had left behind. Sometimes you just had to let go.

Ryder was due back shortly. Even though Grigore was enjoying the silence, he'd be glad to see his brother. He wondered how well he was handling the fallout from their mission. Ryder had texted and let them know he was on his way back … alone. Grigore's return message to him had gone ignored.

Stretching his legs and plopping his bare feet on the coffee table, Grigore crossed his arms behind his head. He knew all too well what Ryder was going through. Sometimes, regardless of how much you love someone, you had to do what was best for them. It didn't really matter how much you liked it.

And sometimes, it fucking sucked.

He was pretty sure Ryder was going to be of that frame of mind and Grigore would be there for him, whether Ryder felt like talking or not. He wouldn't push, he'd let Ryder do the speaking. Sometimes, you just needed someone to listen. Because sure as fuck, Grigore didn't have any answers.

His cell rang. After digging it out of his pocket, he looked at the unknown numbers stretching across the screen. He had half a mind to ignore it, to send the call to voicemail, but his past always kept him from ignoring them.

What if she needed him?

Of course, that would be a cold day in hell. Over fifteen years had gone by and none of the unknown callers had ever been her. Still ... he hit the green answer button and brought the phone to his ear.

"If you're selling something I ain't buying."

"Is this Grigore Lupie?"

He rolled his eyes, ready for the sales pitch sure to come. "Depends on who the fuck wants to know."

"Good." The caller seemed a bit nervous but jovial that he had found him.

"You have about two seconds to tell me what the fuck this is about, dude."

Something about this didn't sit well with him. Call it a sixth sense, but Grigore always listened to his gut intuitions. They proved right more times than not. He dropped his feet onto the wooden floor and sat forward, suddenly antsy. Pulling the phone away from his ear, he hit the SPEAKER button.

"Talk to me. Who the fuck are you and why should I care?"

"Does the name Caitlyn mean anything to you?"

Grigore went cold. It was as if his entire body temperature had dropped ten degrees. His ears rang and his throat constricted. He hadn't heard or mentioned her name in years. There had to be a damn good reason this caller had looked him up now.

"Cait Summers? What about her?"

"I should have introduced myself." The man cleared his throat. "My name is Ryan Baxter. I'm Caitlyn's manager. We're just about to go on tour, and well, we can't exactly cancel the dates. People are counting on her. Her shows have been sold out across North America for months."

"And why would you want to cancel?" He rubbed a hand down his beard. "What the fuck does this have to do with me?"

"She's received some death threats."

Rage dug its talons into him, prickling his skin. If anyone harmed her, they wouldn't live to tell about it. "From who?"

"That's just it, we don't have a clue. It all happened so quickly. She's never been threatened before. Everyone loves Caitlyn and her music."

"How exactly did she bring my name up?"

"She didn't. Caitlyn doesn't know I'm calling you."

Of course, she didn't. "So, who do I have to thank for this call?"

"Her mother. She told me the other day while I was waiting for Caitlyn to get out of the shower—"

"Are you fucking her?"

Why it mattered, Grigore refused to examine. Surely, she'd had many boyfriends over the past fifteen years. She wasn't his problem anymore, and he should tell her manager as much, but still...

"What? Fucking her? No!" Ryan grumbled something about an insecure ox. "Look, her mother liked you, said if there was anyone who could protect her little girl, it was you. That we should hire you to be her personal bodyguard."

"Why should I care?"

Ryan chuckled. "Pardon me for saying so, but I think you already established that you do, due to your earlier accusation. I'm her manager. I've hired bodyguards for her in the past, but most weren't worth the money we paid them. Her mother is staking Caitlyn's life on you. She says that if you agree to go on tour with her daughter, she won't insist the shows be canceled. I don't have to tell you, Grigore—"

"Wolf."

"Excuse me?"

"It's Wolf. No one calls me Grigore but my mother and Cait. My mom passed quite a few years ago."

"Okay, Wolf. We need to put this show on the road. Canceling the shows this late in the game would be detrimental to Caitlyn's career. We can't let that happen."

He raised a brow. "Wouldn't it be worse if this crackpot killed her?"

"Well, of course. But you won't let that happen."

"You're damn right I won't."

"So you're saying you'll do it?"

What? "No, I ... uh ... if I don't, is the tour still happening? Or will her mother put a stop to it?"

"Her mother quit calling the shots long ago. She'd like to think she could stop her daughter, but Caitlyn's determined to move forward."

Every curse word known to mankind ran through his head. "Stubborn damn woman. When does the tour start?"

"Next week."

"You don't give a man a lot of time, do you?"

"As I said, these death threats just came." His tone lightened. "When can we expect you?"

"When and where is the first show?"

"The Progressive Arena in Detroit, Michigan." Her hometown ... *their* hometown. Baxter rattled off the first date and showtime. "Check in backstage when you get there. I'll leave your name and be sure you're given VIP passes and clearance. I can't thank you enough."

"You might regret it once Cait finds out you hired me."

"You won't let her talk you out of helping, will you?"

"Hell, no. If someone wants to kill Cait, they're going to have to go through me."

Grigore didn't wait for a response, hitting the red END button. Well, ain't that just the shits. He stood, tossed his phone to the leather sofa and ran both hands through his shoulder-length hair, pushing it from his eyes and smiled. He couldn't wait to see Cait's reaction when she found out that Grigore Lupie was about to stick to her like fucking duct tape.

After walking to the bar sink, Grigore turned on the cold water and splashed his face with it, then grabbed a hand towel as the door to the clubhouse opened. He ran the cotton down his face, then dried his hands, seeing a dejected Ryder enter the room.

Ryder's lips turned down, his gaze haunted. He likely would've headed straight for his room and slammed the door if Grigore hadn't stopped him. Even though Ryder didn't seem to be in any mood for a conversation, Grigore wasn't about to let him off that easy.

"Welcome home." Grigore braced his hands on the counter. Ryder looked as if he were about to ignore him. No such luck. "How was the ride?"

"Not in the mood, Wolf."

"Want to talk about it?"

Ryder stopped, pinning him with a glare. "Do I look like I do?"

"Too fucking bad." He reached for the bottle of Jack and placed it on the counter between them. "Have a drink with me, then if you still don't feel like talking, go sulk in your room. I'm here to tell you it won't help."

Ryder grabbed the bottle of whiskey, unscrewed the cap and downed a fourth of the bottle. "There. Happy? I still don't feel like talking."

"It fucking sucks, dude. I get it."

One of Ryder's brows arched. "Do you?"

"I may not have been through the same thing as you, but letting her go, you did the right thing."

"How the fuck would you know?" Ryder took another healthy swig from the bottle.

"Because I left someone behind years ago. I wish I hadn't. But the best damn thing for her? I wasn't it."

Ryder took a deep breath, then sat on the bar stool. "How do you get past it, move on?"

"One day at a time, dude. I don't have a better answer than that."

"What happened to her?"

Grigore took the bottle, poured himself a couple of fingers into the tumbler, then handed it back. "She went on without me, made a name for herself."

"Would I know the name?"

"Cait Summers. Most know her as just Caitlyn."

"The pop star? Are you shitting me?"

Grigore shook his head and grinned. "I loved her. Fuck ... still do. But as long as I was around, she wasn't going anywhere. I was holding her back. She was too afraid to do anything that didn't include me, so I left."

"You did tell her goodbye, right? Why you were leaving?"

"Nope." He took a sip of the amber liquid. "I wouldn't have had the balls to walk out if she cried. So we made love, she fell asleep in my arms, then I left. I haven't talked to her since."

"That's fucking cold."

"Yeah, well, enough about me. You think Gabriela will come around?"

He leaned his chin on his palm, elbow braced on the bar. "She hates me, and rightly so. I used her to get to her uncle. That's inexcusable. I couldn't ask her to forgive me."

"So *you* just left?"

"No, she did." Ryder looked tired, as if he had been run through a ringer. "She said if I loved her, I'd let her go. So, I did, man. I turned my back and let her walk away."

Grigore took another sip of the Jack. "If she loves you, she'll come find you. Gabriela has to know the kind of man her uncle was. We did her a fucking favor. We gave her her freedom."

"She won't see it that way."

Grigore placed a hand on Ryder's shoulder. "Give her time, Ryder. I have a feeling she'll come looking for you."

His brow pinched. "Why didn't Caitlyn come looking for you?"

"Because I'm an asshole." Grigore shrugged. "Besides, she likely found some other jerk more worthy of her love."

"Maybe Gabby will find someone else."

Grigore held up his glass and clinked the bottle Ryder held. "Na ... you're one of the good ones, Ryder. Gabby will see that."

CHAPTER TWENTY-TWO

Two weeks had passed since his return home from Mexico. Two miserable fucking weeks. The Sons of Sangue had since paid their final respects in a memorial to Peter, sending him off in grand fashion. The party had gone well into the night. Peter would have approved. The following day, Grigore had mounted his motorcycle and made tracks for Detroit. He had no idea when he'd return, telling Ryder he'd keep in touch. Seemed the big guy had a heart beneath all that muscle, hair, and tattoos after all.

Ryder's heart, on the other hand, hurt like hell, missing Gabby so much it nearly crippled him. He seemed in a constant state of self-pity. In the past he had suffered loss, taking months to move forward. But this ... he was fucking miserable knowing Gabby was out there and there wasn't a damn thing he could do about winning her back. She'd never forgive his deception, not that he could blame her.

Scrubbing a hand down his razor-stubbled face, having recently shaven off the beard and cut his hair back to his normal shorter preference, he blew out a steady stream of air. Ryder deserved her contempt and more. Hell, he was responsible for the upheaval of her life. Gabby had been left without family.

He couldn't help wondering how she was faring, hoping she was doing okay, wishing he was there to comfort her, knowing she'd never allow it. Maybe one day, her hate for him would diminish.

Who was he kidding? From her standpoint, there was no explanation that would make what he did okay. Gabby's hatred for him would not likely subside.

Their parting was no doubt for the best. She didn't need him, likely never would have. Gabby was used to riches well beyond his grasp. And him? He didn't need a mate. There were plenty of women at the Blood 'n' Rave willing to share his bed. So why hadn't any of them appealed to him since his return?

Time heals all wounds.

Bullshit.

Whoever coined that phrase must have been an idiot, that or never loved someone more than life itself. Ryder doubted he'd ever get past losing Gabriela Trevino Caballero. If there was truly one special person out there for everyone, Gabby was it for him. He had known it from the moment he had first kissed her. She had knocked him flat on his ass and had stolen his heart from the get-go.

Not that he regretted it.

Loving her was the one thing he had done right.

Ryder took a few bottles of Jack from the cupboard, placing them on a large wooden serving tray, adding some cut-glass tumblers, and carried the tray into the meeting room. The clubhouse had been eerily quiet with Grigore gone and

Ryder the only resident the past couple of weeks. He figured everyone was likely avoiding his sulky ass.

Talk about a Debby Downer.

Today's church meeting was actually the bright spot in his day. He was getting tired of staring at the four walls since K&K Motorcycles was closed, being a Sunday. Lately, Ryder had poured himself into work at the shop, learning some custom work from Kaleb, coming home long enough to catch a few hours' sleep, then heading back. He found he liked the craft and enjoyed the camaraderie with the guys. He, Kaleb, and Grayson had worked long hours on the latest custom commissioned by an A-List actor. Word on the street was no one did better custom work, increasing their workload.

Ryder wasn't about to complain. He hated idle time. Even surfing didn't appeal to him at the moment, thus turning down offer to head out to Grayson's on the coast.

After setting down the tray, he took his seat at the table. A glance at the clock told him the men would be arriving soon. Ryder poured himself a glass of the whiskey and knocked it back, savoring the burn. If he repeated the statement that he didn't want a mate enough times, maybe he'd actually begin to believe it. In truth, if she walked through the clubhouse door at that moment, he'd get on his knees and beg her to forgive him, to take him for all of eternity.

A chuckle left his throat.

That would be a cold day in hell.

The outside door opened. Kaleb and Kane's boots thudded against the wood as they approached the meeting room.

Ryder's scenting ability had improved, laying truth to his primordial proficiency. He had actually scented the twins about a half mile down the road. Their laughter drifted into the room before they did, each slapping Ryder on the shoulder before taking their seats.

Kane oddly sat at the head of the table, while Kaleb stood behind. They each took a tumbler and poured themselves a glassful of the Gentleman Jack. It didn't take long for the table to fill with the remaining Sons. Conversation bubbled about the room, mostly centering on Raúl and his demise. The consensus seemed to be that everyone was glad to put the chapter behind and move forward, Kane in particular.

A large smile stretched his face. "Since you're all here, rather than having you gossiping like hens behind my back, I'm just going to put this out there. I'm happy to say Cara and I are officially ready to start a family."

Kaleb returned his grin. "About damn time, bro. Stefan needs a cousin or two to play with."

"From what I hear, Hawk, Suzi plans on you guys supplying the second part of the 'or two' part. Cara and I will start with one for now."

He laughed, not in the least bothered by Kane's statement. "Yeah, well … happy mate, happy life."

Grayson rolled his gaze. "You idiot, that doesn't even rhyme."

Ryder looked around the table at his brothers, glad to see most were happily mated, though he wasn't about to join that club. Without Gabby, not likely ever.

Kaleb whistled, gaining everyone's attention, and the room quieted. "Let's get this meeting started, shall we? I invited the women and children here for a little celebration, should the vote go the way I think it will."

"Just what are we voting on, Hawk?" Bobby asked.

Kaleb took a slow gander around the room, then placed his hands on Kane's shoulders. "I want to step down from being president, let Viper take back the reins."

"What about you?" Anton asked.

"I want to put it to a vote that we all resume our previous positions before I took over as president. That means I'll once again be VP ... if Gypsy's okay with that."

Discussion among the men began anew. Ryder didn't see an angry man among them. In fact, they all seemed pleased with the proposition.

Kane looked at Grayson. "You okay with that, Gypsy?"

"Hell, yeah." He nodded. "More time for me to surf and spend with my family. I'm just surprised. Never thought I'd see the day you give up the throne, though, Kaleb."

"I need to get back to building customs. It's what I love doing. Besides, we have a lot of work coming our way. We'll all need to get our hands dirty while Kane handles the business side of things." Stepping back from his twin, he continued, "I motion that Kane returns to the rightful head of the Sons of Sangue, I go back to being VP, and so on."

"I'll second the motion," Anton said.

Within seconds, all ayes were counted, and not a single "nay" was heard. The buzz of conversation grew again, with everyone seemingly happy with the outcome. Ryder tipped his nose upward, scenting the arrival of another vampire, one much more powerful than any other vampire in the room. Moments later, the double doors swung open and Vlad strode into the room as if he was expected.

"Boys, we have a problem." Vlad Tepes's presence damn near filled the room, silencing the men. Some gaped at his unexpected appearance. "Now that I have everyone's undivided attention, I'm here to say that my brother has given me the slip. And unfortunately, Mircea is gunning for my grandsons."

Kane lifted a skeptical dark brow, obviously still taking the sting personally that he had failed to take out Mircea when he had the chance. "If he shows his face? Do I need to call you?"

"You have my permission, Kane, to do whatever is necessary to stop him. Mircea knew what the consequences would be if he left my ... care."

Squaring his shoulders and hardening his square jaw, Vlad took his wrist to his mouth and ripped open a vein with his fangs. He held his arm out to Kane. "I am giving you and Kaleb my primordial blood. Should the son of a bitch come to Oregon snooping around, you both have my permission to end his miserable life. With primordial blood running through your veins, I'm ensuring that he won't have the upper hand ... not this time."

Kane stood and took Vlad's wrist in his hand. "Are you sure? Hawk and I already have your blood running through our veins, grandfather."

"Through birth, yes. But it isn't *primordial* blood. Drink and you will be equal to me, and one day be just as powerful."

Without hesitation, Kane took Vlad's wrist to his mouth, sinking his fangs and drafting from the vein, then licking the remains from his lips. Vlad offered the same to Kaleb.

Once finished, Kaleb asked, "Do you have any idea where he might be?"

"Not a clue. I haven't been able to get a lead. I have my men looking for him. He won't make it easy. He's taken my servant Nina with him, and, like a mole, has probably gone underground. Hard telling when he will surface."

"I'm sure he'll try to blindside us, but we'll be waiting," said Kane.

"He'll no doubt use his blood to turn the maid, meaning you'll also have a primordial bitch on your hands. He's a loose cannon. I had hoped I could change him. Unfortunately, I was wrong. Take them both out, boys ... unless I get to them first. If that's the case, there won't be anything left of either of them to find."

With that, Vlad breezed from the room. The man never stayed in one place overlong, probably out of self-preservation. Ryder almost pitied Vlad's brother. Mircea and Nina didn't stand a chance against the Tepes crew. Add in Ryder, Draven, and Brea all with primordial blood, not to mention the fact that the rest of the Sons of Sangue were looking to take him down, and it would be damn suicidal for Mircea to show his face here.

Excitement coursed through the room, everyone thrilled with the idea of taking out Vlad's ungrateful kin. Kane resumed order around the table, striking the mallet against the plate.

"Other than changing the patches on our vests, do we have any other business to discuss?"

When no one spoke, Kane continued. "Then this meeting is adjourned. Call the women and let's get this fucking party started."

This time the chatter thankfully centered around Mircea, instead of Raúl. Ryder wasn't in the mood to discuss Gabriela's uncle, or his demise. As a matter of fact, he wasn't up for partying at all.

Kane grabbed the remaining bottles of whiskey, leading the men from the meeting room and into the main living area of the clubhouse. Ryder remained seated, a tumbler in his hand. There really wasn't a way to avoid the festivities since he technically lived here. Maybe they wouldn't notice his absence in the main room.

Extending his legs, he crossed his feet at the ankles and leaned back in the chair. Quite frankly, he wasn't ready to be part of any celebrations including the mates and their sons. Christ, he was a selfish bastard, but it was a painful reminder of what he'd never have.

He took a sip of whiskey. Maybe he ought to go to the Rave and hang out for a spell. It certainly held more appeal than the goings-on here. He was just about to do so when another familiar scent caught his attention, one that awakened all of his senses,

No. Fucking. Way.

His imagination *had* to be playing tricks. Ryder stood, walked into the living area, and headed for the exit like a man possessed.

Before the knock even came, he opened the door, finding Gabriela standing on the stoop, hand raised.

Her gaze widened and she gasped.

Wetting her lips with her cute little tongue that he knew all too well, she squared her shoulders. "You didn't call."

Ryder's breath stuck in his throat. Had he suddenly become prone to hallucinations? If so, he didn't want to stop the fantasy. Seeing her standing in front of him was a dream come true.

He thought about sending her on her way, doing what was best for her, but then quickly squashed that logic. Ryder wasn't in any hurry to repeat the last two weeks. He needed to hear her out, see what had brought her two thousand miles north.

"Were you expecting me to call?" Ryder raised a brow. "After everything that went down? Christ, Gabby, had I thought you could've forgiven me, I wouldn't have left Mexico. As I recall, you asked me to let you go."

Heartache and misery stared back at him. If he knew she wouldn't push him away, he'd gather her into his arms and hold onto her forever. Noise from the living area reminded him of the celebration that had started. They weren't alone and the last thing Ryder wanted was an audience.

"Did I come at a bad time? I can come back."

Ryder gripped her by the wrist and pulled her into the clubhouse, shutting the door. He wasn't about to lose her a second time, not before he heard what she came all this way to say.

The room quieted as his brothers became aware of their guest. Ryder gave Kane a quick nod, telling him it was okay to approach. Kane held out his hand to Gabriela, which she took. Ryder's heart ached for their shared losses. Kane had been responsible for her uncle's death, the man who had killed his son. One day, Ryder would explain the entire sordid tale to her, when she was ready to hear it. That is, if she wanted to keep him in her life.

"Gabriela? Welcome. I'm Kane Tepes," Kane said. "I'm damn sorry about your uncle."

Gabby's expression gave nothing away. "Thank you."

"Look, we were just about to clear out." He turned to the Sons milling about. "Grab your shit, boys ... the party is moving to my farmhouse. Call your mates, have them meet us there instead."

It took little time for the men to file out as Kane had thankfully instructed, leaving Gabby and Ryder alone. There was much that needed to be said, to get out in the open so they could move beyond what had happened in Mexico. Ryder wanted her to know the truth, no more omissions.

Everything in good time.

First, he needed to know where he stood with her. Ryder led Gabby to one of the sofas, sitting next to her, but keeping enough distance so she would feel comfortable. He didn't want to push or scare her, and risk sending her running for south of the border.

"How did you find me?"

"Your friend Gunner."

"The one I buried."

"Yes." She pulled at the hem of her white tank, toying with the threads. "He had given Adriana his phone number the night at the club, just in case she wanted to see him should she leave her fiancé. Long story short, we thought maybe his death might have been staged if everything else had been a lie."

Ryder ran a knuckle down her cheek. She didn't shrink from his touch, giving him hope. "Not everything was a lie, *ángel*."

"If I thought that, I wouldn't be here." Gabby tucked a leg beneath her, still not closing the gap between her and Ryder. "Anyway, she tried the number and Gunner answered. It took some convincing, but he finally told her where I could find you."

"I'll need to give Gunner my thanks."

Her cheeks reddened. Glancing to her lap, she wrung her hands. Finally, she glanced up, moisture filling her chocolate gaze. "I can't stop thinking about you, about us. I know you were partly responsible for my uncle's death and that you used me. But I also know my uncle was a bad man. If it hadn't been you and your friends who came after him, it would have been someone else."

"I never wanted to hurt you, *ángel.* You have to believe that."

"I know that now." She took in a shaky breath. "You were trying to protect me from the inevitable."

Ryder had never lied about his feelings. "Do you believe me now? How much I fucking love you?"

She looked down again before he brought up her chin. Her lower lip trembled. "I told you that if you loved me you would let me go ... and that's what you did. You let me go."

"You gave me no choice."

"I didn't." A tear slipped from her lashes. "Please tell me I didn't come this far just to get rejected."

"Fuck, Gabby. I never thought you'd forgive me." He pulled her into his embrace, kissing the top of her head. She wrapped her arms around his waist, pressing her cheek against his hammering heart. "I love you so much it hurts."

She glanced up, the sadness in her eyes abating. "I realized, when I got over being mad at you, that I never gave you a chance to explain. We have a lot to work through. I won't pretend otherwise."

"We do," he agreed. Thank fuck she *wanted* to. "I'm not sure how to make that happen, though, since your life is in Mexico. I can't live there, Gabby. This is my home."

She glanced around. "It's cozy."

Ryder laughed. "Not even close to what you're accustomed to."

"I'm selling my uncle's estates, Ryder. I'm using the money from the sales and his accounts to start over."

He wasn't sure what he expected to hear, but certainly not that. "Where?"

"I was thinking Oregon has a nice coast. Maybe I'll find a nice little beach house overlooking the ocean. Nothing extravagant, of course. I kind of like cozy. You think Oregon has anything worth moving two thousand miles for?"

Ryder smiled. "There's this guy, who might be a bit of a vampire at times, but he would do just about anything to make that happen."

"Will you forgive me?"

His brow pinched. "For what? You didn't do anything wrong. Fuck, Gabby, there is so much I need *you* to forgive *me* for."

"As I said, I didn't give you a chance to explain. I hated you for what you did. But what I couldn't do was stop loving you and that's what hurt so damn bad." She placed a palm against his jaw. "Will you let me stay? Let me move to Oregon to be with you?"

"I'll do better than that. I'll take our box truck and drive you to Mexico. We'll pack up your things—"

"There's nothing in Mexico I want. Adriana is handling the sale and giving the things I didn't fit in my Escalade to those in need."

"And Adriana? What's she going to do without you?"

"She and Mateo broke up. Apparently, he thinks he can step in where my uncle left off, take over the business. She wasn't onboard with his plan. After everything sells, she's moving to Oregon as well."

"Moving in with you?"

Gabby shook her head. "She'll get her own place. I'll buy her a small cottage along the water, close to me, yet far enough away I'll have my privacy. What I was really hoping for…there is this vampire I've taken a shining to. I was kind of hoping he'd give cohabitation a shot."

Ryder tightened his hold. "You want me to live with you?"

"I do."

"I'm not the easiest person to get along with."

She laughed. "So you've proven. We'll work it out, Ryder. What I'm sure of, though, is that I can't keep mourning your loss. I lost my family. I can't lose you, too."

Ryder tilted his head, sealing his lips over hers and kissing her deeply. He'd prove to her that he wasn't going anywhere, that she'd never have to mourn his loss again. This woman had claimed his heart, offering him another chance not to fuck up. Once all of the ugliness of their past was behind them, he'd ask her to be his forever. For as sure as shit, he wasn't letting her go again.

Gabby needed to know more about vampirism and what it meant to be a mate. If she'd still have him, then he'd give her his blood and make that happen.

Breaking the kiss, he leaned his forehead against hers. "I love you, Gabriela, so damn much."

"Does that mean you'll move in with me?"

He laughed. "Have you already purchased a place?"

Gabby's smile warmed his heart. He'd make it his life's mission never to see her frown again. "No."

"Then you'll be moving in here ... with me. Because I'm not spending another night without you in my bed."

"Promise?"

He used his forefinger to make a cross over his heart. "And hope to die. How do you feel about makeup sex?"

Gabby swung her leg over his thighs and straddled him. "I happen to think it's pretty hot."

"Bedroom?"

She shook her head, situating herself more fully on his lap. There was no doubt she felt his reaction to makeup sex. She slid along his rigid length. "That would require us moving. I kind of like where I'm sitting."

"Christ, you'll be the death of me."

"Death? No way, Ryder Kelley. You and me? We're in this together ... for all of eternity. That's my promise to you. I'll never ask you to leave me again."

"Good," he growled. "Because I'm not fucking going anywhere. Now, about that makeup sex..."

ABOUT THE AUTHOR

A daydreamer at heart, Patricia A. Rasey, resides in her native town in Northwest Ohio with her husband, Mark, and her two lovable Cavalier King Charles Spaniels, Todd and Buckeye. A graduate of Long Ridge Writer's School, Patricia has seen publication of some her short stories in magazines as well as several of her novels.

When not behind her computer, you can find Patricia working, reading, watching movies or MMA. She also enjoys spending her free time at the river camping and boating with her husband and two sons. Ms. Rasey is currently a third degree Black Belt in American Freestyle Karate.

CPSIA information can be obtained
at www.ICGtesting.com
Printed in the USA
LVHW040507240622
722041LV00012B/62